the

SLEEPING

myth

SHADOW JOURNEY SERIES
BOOK THREE

the

SLEEPING

myth

SHADOW JOURNEY SERIES
BOOK THREE

JO ALLEN ASH

Potter Street Books
Zionsville PA
2023

DEDICATION

to all who believe in hope

Praise for the Shadow Journey Series

The Shadows We Make – Book One

"A beautifully crafted SF dystopia, boasting relatable characters and a skillful plot." *BookLife Reviews*

"…high stakes adventure…strong emotional themes." K.C. Finn – *Readers Favorite* – Five Stars

"Ash captivates the reader throughout…poetic… dramatic… suspenseful…" *BookTrib*

"Loved it…an amazing read." Sally Atlass – *ReedsyDiscovery*

The Thrice-Gifted Child – Book Two

"…imaginative…suspenseful…memorable…" *BookLife Reviews*

"…a page turner…intricate…gripping…doesn't allow your attention to waver for a single moment." Pikasho Deko – *Readers Favorite* – Five Stars

ACKNOWLEDGEMENTS

As always, I would like to thank my readers. Your enthusiasm, your heartfelt comments on social media, your supporting presence during book signings has made all the difference between thinking I am just shoving words out into the cosmos and the realization I am truly touching people's lives with this ongoing story.

I also wish to thank Pattie for her unbridled enthusiasm and her robust word-of-mouth campaigning. Also, to Bob, for one of the most amazing and impromptu affirmations as to the value of the series I have ever received.

Thanks to Let's Play Books, a local bookstore with one of the biggest hearts in the world. Also, to Natasha at Barnes and Noble, for putting up with me again and again.

Chapter One

War had spread across the provinces and we were being hunted down. This fact could not be denied. Yet, in the precise moment a projectile flew straight at me, my thoughts went from the vast array of dangers to something more imminent. Something which, despite my warrior's reflexes, I found myself unable to avoid.

"Ow!"

I glared at Ren and wiped icy, wet splatter from my cheek, rubbed the stinging tattooed flesh where the thing he dubbed a snowball had struck me. The midnight-blue warrior's mark provided a good target for him, a place easy to pick out through the spiraling white flakes, easy to hit with the rough sphere. He had lobbed one already at everyone else. Except Resa, of course. I knew he did not dare.

Before I could say anything to him another ball whizzed past my head, coming from behind me. It struck him square in the nose. He danced back, howling, his hands clapped to his face. After that,

Ren's pranks degenerated into an all-out battle among the boys and Hannah. Carina, Resa and I wisely stepped from harm's way.

Carina with her island heritage felt the wicked cold more than the rest of us. For the first time since meeting her, her nearly white flesh showed a little color, but not in a good way. Suffused with blood in a reaction to the frigid temperatures, any skin not covered seemed shaded in an odd purple like misted paint. Fortunately, not much remained exposed. The night before last we had cut up our blankets to wrap around our heads, our faces, our hands, to shove piecemeal inside our clothes and tuck around our feet inside our boots. We weren't going to use them again for sleeping. They did not provide enough warmth for that. Better to use them where they could do the most good.

Born and raised in the desert provinces, I ran a close second in reaction to the cold air and spinning snowflakes. Ren and Hannah were the only two who had ever seen this frozen precipitation, which made sense, given where they came from. Duncan, Mika and Resa were from Riley, the gambling moon, where, according to Duncan, only one season existed. I could not imagine such a thing. I liked the changing seasons, albeit changes far less drastic than what we had started experiencing here.

Duncan performed an odd little twirl over to my side, dodging a thrown snowball. He bent to squint at my cheek, lips compressed, jaw jutting forward. "All right there, Grace?"

"Yes," I said, and shoved him away before a flung ice ball could miss him and strike me instead.

"Are you really all right?" Carina asked.

I nodded. She had not been referring to the snowball, I knew.

Carina glanced at me again and away. "At some point, you're going to have to tell them." Beside her, Resa had taken a step forward, brows lowered, frowning at the packed ice hurtling through the air.

"I'm surprised Hannah hasn't already," I said.

"She doesn't have a full understanding, and I've explained nothing to her. It's your responsibility."

I sighed. "I know."

For the past three days, Skelly had been silent in the crystal to which I had consigned him, snug in the bag hanging from its silk cord around my neck. My hand almost went there, almost lifted to touch the place on my jacket behind which the bag lay. Clenching my fingers into a fist, I kept them by my side. My friends had every right to know what I carried because it endangered them as much as it did me. Skelly endangered everything. I needed to know why. I needed to know how. I needed to know what could be done to save him or to stop him.

Quite suddenly, Duncan's laughter cut to a pained cry. I looked his way in time to see all the snowballs the boys and Hannah had prepared, all those that had left their hands in flight or had been piled into arsenal mounds, spiraling now through the crystalline flakes like so many planets in swift orbit around a sun. The sun happened to be dark-haired Resa, who had slipped into the fray unnoticed. The players were taking quite a beating.

Mika, Ren, and Hannah raced away from the onslaught, arms over their heads. Only Duncan remained, ducking from side to side to avoid another direct hit and staring at his sister in disbelief.

I understood why. He recognized exactly what she was doing. As did I. Resa was playing.

Duncan hurried across the snow and scooped her up into his arms. All the snowballs succumbed once more to gravity and plummeted to the ground. He smiled at her in a wide grin, smiled so she would understand she'd angered no one, frightened no one, hurt no one. This time.

I wondered if what I had witnessed had been Resa's first real attempt at play. Twelve years old, and yet it was possible. The thrice-gifted child. I hated that title, given to her by those who would use her powers, a name dragged forward from legend. I supposedly had a place in that legend as well, and tiny, mystical Carina. The warrior, the witch, the thrice-gifted child. I would gladly dismiss the legend, the rumors outright, condemn them for nonsense, but so much pointed to an underlying truth. Even if it did not, there were those who believed the prophecy and who presented a danger to us all.

"We should get going," I said, following my thoughts to their natural conclusion. We had tarried here long enough over a midday meal. The season brought earlier nights, the elevation plummeting temperatures. We needed to find shelter before darkness fell.

All but Resa, who could not hear my voice,

turned their heads and looked at me in obvious disappointment. Frowned at me like a parent robbing them of a few minutes' enjoyment. I had not asked for the position. My place as leader had fallen to me through a natural selection. Grace, the warrior, Grace the ever-vigilant, Grace, the serious.

Grace who had never eaten birthday cake. The memory came to me in the most ridiculous moments. But they had been quite shocked, my fellow inmates, when I confessed to my lack back there in the juvenile facility on the Emerald. We had been celebrating Carina's fifteenth birth anniversary. I could almost taste the confection in recall. I had not liked it at all, although I had tried to muster some enjoyment. They all acted as though cake were a special treat. I had not wanted to hurt anyone's feelings.

Such small problems. Would we have been better off had we not escaped? Sometimes it seemed so. Up there we had been warm and clean and fed and no one tried to kill us. Well, not quite true. Warm and clean and fed, then. Yet, all sent there received unwarranted lifelong sentences. We would have remained imprisoned until we died. Our demise had been the intent either way.

Since our escape and return to Talia to rescue Resa from Stone Tiran our situation had only gotten worse. Out of the frying pan, into the fire, Duncan said, more often than necessary, but never more often than true. He had a fondness for quoting his grandmother. It could be annoying, sometimes, it really could, although deep down I found it amusing, endearing, a sign Duncan remained

Duncan.

I left Carina's side and strode over to where the *conjure* stood. He pivoted his huge head from side to side, shaking the snow from his thick fur, spattering the ground with clumped ice flecked with blood. He had only returned from feeding a short time ago. In the cold he apparently needed to eat more often, to build up fat around his muscles, to keep them cushioned, insulated, to give his body something to feed off if times got lean; which they undoubtedly would. The rest of us? We had no meat to spare on our bones. We had been too long in desperate straits.

"Chauncy," I said. He tapped his long, corkscrew horn against the nearest tree, brought down more snow around us. I sidestepped a large mass before it landed on my head and shoulders. Reaching out, I tugged more ice balls from his fur, tossed them to the ground. He had been taking turns carrying those of us with shorter legs, like Carina and Resa, occasionally Hannah, too. Hannah was not tiny like them, but she seemed to be tiring easily and as long as the *conjure* remained willing, I remained grateful. Breg, the Ogdonian cart driver with whom Chauncy once shared a relationship, would never have believed such a thing possible. He had been quite adamant about what a *conjure* would and would not tolerate, assuring me *conjures* accepted draft duties only. The fierce, ofttimes dangerous creature had no desire to perform as a beast of burden. I supposed it a measure of Chauncy's symbiosis with me, with my companions, that he did so now.

With a jerking movement, Chauncy suddenly lifted his head to the sky and bellowed. I stepped back, startled. The others turned and stared.

"What's wrong with him?" Duncan called.

I shook my head. "I don't know."

He did it again, and then one more time. An answering rumble came from deep among the stones and twisted trees in the snow-covered forest. Not one bellow, but many, in a strange chorus. I shivered beneath my snow-covered clothes. All my companions gathered at my side, peering past me toward the echoing sounds.

"Is that more of—" Mika nodded his head toward Chauncy. "—him?"

"Sounds like it," I said, disbelieving, unnerved. Worried.

"Is he calling them?"

I had no idea, but if the herd responded to Chauncy's call, we would be in a vulnerable position. I did not expect our presence to be tolerated by *conjures* in the wild. I remembered telling my companions how easily a *conjure* could rip a man's head off. Chauncy had not made any such threats, but I realized his behavior was likely not the norm. "Gather everything up. We'd better start moving and see what happens."

My statement did nothing to reassure them. Everyone hastily slung packs over shoulders for departure and we trudged on in the general direction we had been traveling from the beginning. We had no actual idea where we were going, only where we wanted to end up, and in order to find the Cavern of Sleeping Myth we had to follow the setting sun. Our inability to see the sun through the heavily falling snow had gone unremarked by any of us. Yet the sky ahead remained slightly lighter than the sky behind and, until darkness fell and we were safely encamped, we would have to rely on that.

Besides, the most important thing right now was to put as much distance between us and the City of All Dwellers as we could. Despite the recent frivolity, we all possessed the knowledge far worse than soldiers and warriors might be tracking us. Duncan, Mike, Carina and I understood all too well what Stone Tiran had brought down from the prison planet to help him fight his part in this war. Ren and Hannah had only witnessed the single creature Chauncy had killed, although they possessed a healthy fear based on what Duncan, Mika and I had told them. Carina had been quiet on the subject. I figured she fought to contain the remembered horrors as best she could in order to prevent Resa picking up on her emotions. Those two seemed connected now in ways never expected.

I feared the herd would come in response to the exchange with Chauncy. Because I felt uncertain as to his reaction if that should occur, it seemed best Carina and Resa stay on the ground rather than riding on his back despite the snow seven inches deep. Mika, Ren and Duncan tried their best to aid their travel, striding in front and sweeping hefty branches from side to side in an attempt to clear a path. Chauncy had stopped bellowing but kept looking over his massive shoulder. I started doing the same, gazing back along the clear trail we were leaving in our wake. I understood we could do nothing to prevent the obvious indication we had passed through the landscape, and yet it worried me greatly. A hope this snow would continue to cover our tracks also contained the threat we would reach a point we couldn't go on because of it.

Regardless, the day held only a few more hours of light. We would need to find a defendable spot in which to shelter very soon. We did not want to get caught out in the nightfall's chilling temperatures or to lose our direction toward the westering sun. Because this was all we had. Both Hannah and Ren had been raised on stories about the Cavern of Sleeping Myth, including that the way to reach it was to head into the setting sun. Except for its reputed ties to Carina, Resa and me, I would not have considered attempting to find the cavern in the vast mountain range. But since we three so clearly fit into the legends and the recent prophecy, I had to trust there would be some truth to this, too, as well as the answers I had failed to receive in the city. If nothing else, at least we might succeed in distancing ourselves from the forces now amassing in the City of All Dwellers.

Duncan and Mika came to an abrupt halt. Ren, not noticing, continued for several paces before turning with a question in his eyes.

"I think Resa and Carina need to get back up on Chauncy," Duncan said. "We're moving too slowly."

"Agreed," I admitted reluctantly.

I pulled off the remaining ice clinging to the *conjure's* dense hide. Steam rose into the air from his body's heat. Sensing what I wanted, he crouched down and permitted Carina and Resa to be placed atop his back. "Hannah, you too," I said, and she climbed up behind them.

With only four remaining on the ground, we increased our pace. I kept a lookout for the *conjures* and for anything else approaching. Thus far, we had seen no ships in the sky, but their absence did not mean nothing tracked us on foot. We had traveled for some time, though, before the snow began and had made certain to eradicate any trace which might otherwise have been left behind each time we stopped. Even so, I did not dare to be hopeful. Only vigilant.

"It's strange," Duncan said beside me, "not knowing where we're going. You always had some idea where we needed to be, which direction we needed to head. 'Straight into the sun' is a bit unnerving."

Duncan's thoughts, as usual, appeared to align themselves with mine. "I know," I said.

"It's okay," said Hannah from atop Chauncy's back. "This is the way. I feel it."

Duncan rolled his eyes, then immediately felt bad for having done so. I could see it in his face. "That's good," he said. "I hope you're right."

"I am," Hannah responded in a whisper, having caught the eyeroll, her feelings now hurt. Again. Hannah liked Duncan. I had tried to warn Duncan to be gentle with her, without giving away what I suspected. He seemed unable to grasp the meaning behind my hints. I supposed I should tell him outright, but I did not quite want to.

Hannah swiped her damp red hair from her

forehead and turned front again. The descending sun peeked for a moment through the clouds, glittering in the snow-filled air. Very possibly, Hannah did feel a pull from the place we were headed. Although much diluted over generations, she possessed enough mage blood, the blood of the gifted among my people, to have produced the free-floating flame-ball she displayed shortly after she and Ren and their companions—gone now to join their families—had come for us when we first entered The Wilds.

I glanced behind yet again, scanning the trees below. Shadows lay deep and dark beneath the snow laden branches. I spotted movement there.

"Duncan," I whispered. He followed my gaze, eyes widening.

"What the—"

Chauncy threw back his head and bellowed again, Carina and Resa dodging his sweeping horn. The creatures beneath the trees were not *conjure*. Indeed, I recognized nothing about them as they stalked out from the shadows into open, snowy field. Four-legged, not the creatures from Emerald either, but dangerous nevertheless. I understood by the sun's dying glint in their forward-facing eyes these were hunters, too.

"Ah, hell," Duncan growled, yanking the cutter he had stolen from the mine out from his belt. Ren and Mika did the same, moving to stand beside him. In the other hand they each clutched the glass daggers they had made before their escape from the doomed shaft. I grasped my *lathesa*, balanced anew with a bit of Duncan's crystal blade replacing the end the Lyoness had broken away. Chauncy stomped around to face the creatures below, his lengthy corkscrew horn shining in the fading light. Hannah and Carina slid once more to the ground, bringing Resa with them. If the *conjure* went on the attack, they would not only be a hindrance but at risk. They stood behind us, waiting, unarmed. I glanced back and found Carina digging around in the snow. For stones. The tiny island dancer had always been able to create worthwhile damage with those.

"Out of the fry—" Duncan began.

I poked him with my elbow. "Don't say it."

"Yeah," he said, "you're right. I've really got to find something new."

"Thank the gods," Mika muttered. We all laughed. Quietly. Nervously. Grimly. All except Resa, of course. She could not hear the exchange. I looked over my shoulder at her, found her gaze on the approaching creatures. I had no idea if she recognized the threat or even saw what we did. Her mind frequently took her to places so very far away. Real places. Places I could not even imagine. In part, this was the reason Stone Tiran and the Lyoness wanted her. Her ability to see those places, to 'hear' conversations there, could give them a clear advantage in war. The ability would not help us now, though. Nor would her other gift, to move objects through psychokinesis in frightening ways, as it did not come at our call. Only hers.

The animals below moved closer, nearly two dozen, like a pack with an obvious leader, outliers, main force. They possessed long, pronounced snouts and a great many teeth, filling the air with snapping, snarling noises as they came. Shaggy black coats did nothing to hide the broad shoulder structure, the narrow back end and short legs. Although they paced low to the ground, they appeared unhindered by the snow. I did not fool myself into believing their lack in height meant the creatures were slow. I had a feeling those legs could propel the front-heavy bodies forward with deadly speed and aim. If we had spears, real spears, we might manage to fend them off, but all our weapons required proximity for efficiency.

"This is where you usually start swearing, Grace," Ren said. "I'd feel a lot better if you would."

"Do you know these creatures?" I asked him.

"From lessons. I've never seen one in the wild." His voice had pitched a little and he cleared his throat. "I'd say run, but it would be pointless."

"That's what I was afraid of," Mika said. He reached back, took Carina's hand, pulled her closer.

Hannah appeared at my elbow. She held a stick in her hand. A hefty club. I nodded in approval.

"That flame thing of yours," Duncan said to her from my other side, "is it capable of damage?"

"It doesn't burn anything," she answered him. We knew as much. We had witnessed its lack of heat in the tunnels. A pretty show, a source of bright light, but little else.

"Can you make more than one?" he asked. "Throw them?"

"I...yeah," she said, straightening her spine, silver-blue eyes sparking. "Yes, I can."

"Keep your weapons handy," I said, "but start making more snow spheres. Maybe we can frighten them off."

Stone-throwing Carina had the best aim, and slapped snow around the rocks she had picked up. Before long, balls of hardened, packed ice and brilliant flame shot through the air, some falling short of their mark, but many, particularly Carina's, hitting targets. The creatures yelped, spun away, came back again and again, growling and determined. Chauncy charged forward a dozen feet or so, roaring skyward. The noise echoed off stone and tree and cliffside, causing the creatures to cringe but not retreat. Despite the bombardment, they moved relentlessly closer.

Resa pushed around her brother, stood before him, facing the animals below. She raised her hands. Carina darted forward, ready to shut her down. Without control we could all be destined for injury, not only the creatures marching up the hillside. I remembered, though, how Resa had saved Symick from the destruction in the city. I put a hand out, stopping Carina in her tracks. The air rumbled and the ground shook. I held my breath, worrying I had made a mistake delaying Carina's intervention. When a vast shadow swept in from our left, I let out a small cry, spying at the same moment Resa's hands dropping to her side.

Whatever came to us now was not her doing. I leaped forward, past them all, spinning my *lathesa* in my hands.

Chapter Two

Rock and soil vibrated beneath our feet. My knees shifted, throwing off my stance. I righted myself, whipping around to face the approaching mass of…things. They came through the snow with speed and great noise and with a confusing array of colors amidst the swirling, ice-filled gloom. They swept around us and past us and down the hill. The creatures stalking us scattered back into the tree line, baying like fiends.

I thought I heard Duncan's breath rush out. When he swore, I knew at least the voice was his. I could not mistake it. Not after all this time. I didn't say anything to him, though. I said nothing at all.

Instead, I watched in silence as the figures below wheeled around and charged back up the hillside. On *conjures*, every single one.

They circled around us, the beasts' chuffing breath smoking in the air. Each animal had been draped in brilliant cloth, each person atop it dressed likewise, in brightly dyed garments and long cloaks that draped over the *conjures'* backs. Tall, they were, these men and women, as tall as the tallest warriors among the tribes, among my people. For the most part they possessed, too, the same dark skin, but some also looked like me, a bronze with eyes that were not black or brown.

I gasped and bowed my head, my whole upper body. Seeing me do so, my friends followed suit. Upon straightening, I looked the nearest in the eye.

"You have our gratitude," I said formally. "We thank you."

He arched an eyebrow at me in a manner that seemed, and yet could not be, familiar. "You called us. We came."

Taken aback, I forgot myself, shook my head disrespectfully. "I did not—"

The warrior cocked his head toward Chauncy. "Your beast was heard."

"I beg your pardon," I said, "but he is not mine."

The man frowned, "Oh, but he is. Did you not know this? You and it are one."

"One what?" Duncan asked. "Sir," he amended.

"One with," the man said, with an amused look at Duncan, "not one what."

One *with* the *conjure*. As these warriors appeared to be. Clearly, he was mistaken.

Ren stepped forward. "Will they be back? Those animals?" He nodded toward the darkened woods sloped along the hillside below us.

"Undoubtedly. They are hungry. But we will be long gone before they reappear."

"And what will we do?" Ren demanded, unable to keep the ill-mannered tone from his voice, despite his obvious plea. He rarely could. Now that I knew his history, I understood why.

"You will be gone, as well," said the man. "You will come with us. We cannot in good faith permit you to wander these lands."

"Oh, here we go again," Duncan whispered at my ear. The warrior shot him another look, a little less amused. Again, I could not help but recognize a certain familiar trait in the glance. Of course, he looked like many I had known, people I missed greatly.

"Or you could die here or at any other point in your journey," he said. "The choice is ultimately yours."

He did not issue the words like a threat. His statement possessed no particular aggression nor even a warning, only an obvious factual expression. Danger existed. We could face it alone, or not.

"And if we go with you," I asked, "where will that be?"

"For now, to the nearest village, where you can get warm and rest and we can discuss what you are seeking here in these mountains."

"Where is the nearest village?" I had to question him, for all our sakes. The sun was nearly down, the last golden light vanishing in the falling snow far above our heads. The temperature had already dropped. We were ill-equipped to trek through the night.

"Here in these mountains, the distances are vast. You will all ride. It will make the going easier."

"I don't think we can all fit on Chauncy's back," I said.

The man's dark eyes, barely visible, narrowed at the corners. His lips turned up. "You have named him."

"Yes. It seemed…right."

"So, he is yours and you are his."

I said nothing.

"You do not believe me."

"I do not know what to believe anymore," I said. "But we will come with you."

I spoke once more to Chauncy, who dropped to his knees, allowing Resa, Carina and Hannah to climb up onto his back. I sent Mika up, too. If nothing else, he would add to the warmth with four bodies pressed close together. A warrior dismounted, came forward, handed up a blanket to wrap around them all. Chauncy returned to all fours, shaking snow from the fur around his eyes. He appeared unperturbed by so many others of his kind present and in proximity, or by the warriors. My shoulders relaxed a little.

"We will take you and the other two up behind us, if you feel you will burden…Chauncy, is it?"

I nodded. "Does the *conjure* you ride not have a name?"

"Of course, she does. It is Ellekea."

"A much better name than Chauncy," Duncan said to me as he passed, heading for one of two *conjures* brought closer by their riders for he and Ren to mount behind.

"Not necessarily," said the warrior, spokesman and therefore likely leader of those with whom he rode. "Ellekea translates to 'little star,' whereas, if I am not mistaken, Chauncy is a very old name meaning 'good fortune'."

I had not known that. I eyed Chauncy askance, marveling at how aptly, albeit unintentionally, he had been named. The warrior extended a hand to help me onto the beast he rode. Pretending I didn't see it, I danced forward, kicked off and sprang from the ground, swinging myself lightly onto the animal's back. The *conjure* made no protest.

"Showoff," Ren whispered. Duncan grumbled something at him. "Just saying," Ren added. "She could have climbed up like the rest of us."

"Sorry," I murmured in false apology. I had not been showing off. I wanted the warrior on this beast and those with him to know outnumbered as we were, my friends were not unprotected. I, too, was warrior. As lean, as disheveled, as unintimidating as I appeared, I still possessed strength and agility. I would not be dismissed.

"Well done," the warrior said.

I frowned and kept my gaze on the middle of his back. He raised his hand, signaling to the others. In an instant, we were moving forward. Fast. I had never realized a *conjure* could attain such speed.

The wind of our passage whipped through my hair, pushing back my hood, dipping down into my clothes, making me colder than I had been. I clutched my *lathesa* with one hand, the *conjure's* blanket to steady myself with the other. The pack on my back smacked against my spine with the animal's bounding steps. When I could, I glanced around for the others, to check how they fared. Mika's group was scarcely visible wrapped in a blanket to which the snow clung like ice petals. Duncan and Ren seemed to be coping about as well as I, hunkered down against the lashing wind and clinging tightly wherever they could to stay mounted.

At the mountain's peak, the cold became nearly unbearable, but when we plummeted down into the tree-filled hollows on the other side, I was able to straighten up again and peer around through eyes narrowed against the flying flakes. I couldn't really tell how far we rode or for how long. I knew I was grateful, though, not to be walking through the mounding snow, grateful for the promise of warmth, at least for this night. Grateful, too, for the kindness of these warriors and hoping I would not come to find such gratitude misplaced.

Exhausted, cold, having managed a rhythm with the *conjure's* pace and my fingers now firmly entrenched in the blanket's weave, I found my thoughts drifting, my eyelids closing with increased frequency against the blowing snow. I kept shaking my head, fighting to stay alert. I must have made some movement the warrior felt, because he turned his head and spoke.

"Almost there."

"Thank you," I said. He had not yet introduced himself or explained who they were and I decided to wait until more comfortable circumstances before I insisted. I looked around again at the others. Ren had fallen frankly asleep, his head bobbing about. I could not imagine how he managed to retain his seat. Duncan I found deep in conversation with the rider in front of him. I could not hear a word he said, and only knew by the woman's occasional turning that she did and answered him. I looked over my shoulder to Chauncy next, to the snow-covered hump on his back, the blanket draped over heads as well as bodies. The white circle around Chauncy's eye had become invisible in a face covered with ice. Breath swirled from his large nostrils like steam from a kettle.

A sudden noise pierced the night, a loud, single note. I leaned from side to side, trying to see around the warrior and finally spotted another, moving swiftly to the fore and holding a long instrument to his lips. He blew again. A responding signal came from somewhere ahead, beyond sight.

"We are welcomed," said the warrior riding with me, turning his head to make certain I heard him. A primitive communication, the blowing of horns, yet effective, and also in use among the desert tribes. I smiled, somehow comforted by the practice here, even though we faced the unknown.

I thought about Skelly, then, the biggest, most unimaginable unknown. Skelly, the entity he had become, tucked away and sulking in the crystal inside the bag around my neck.

I'm not sulking.

I snorted, a very Duncan-like noise. My riding companion glanced back at me at the sound. I rubbed my nose, feigning an itch or a sneeze or whatever he wished to believe. He turned away.

The *conjures* converged and plunged down a steep, white expanse between forest close at hand to either side. I would have expected them to slow, given the slippery surface beneath their cloven hooves, but they rushed on, heads lifted to keep corkscrew horns from spearing those before them. I held my breath and hung on.

When we neared the bottom of the incline, I spotted a settlement set at an elevation above a tumbling watercourse filled with icy formations over boulders and fallen trees. Lights burned in windows beyond a fortified wall made from timber and stone. A huge gate stood open and we rumbled through it, still mounted. Several men pushed the gate shut and barred it behind us. The *conjures* managed to halt rather abruptly before running anyone down. Ren lurched forward into the back of the warrior in front of him. I could hear him apologizing, somehow managing a tone both defiant and embarrassed.

Gripping my *lathesa*, I slid from the *conjure* and hurried over to Chauncy to assist Mika and the girls off his back. Duncan and Ren swiftly joined us and we stood, waiting, staring around at the others as they, too, dismounted. The clothing they wore beneath their dark cloaks was as bright as the woven cloth draping their *conjures*. We, on the other hand, were dressed in drab, natural hues. The residents in the fortified community seemed to be as plainly dressed as we, but with splashes of color here and there. It occurred to me the colors worn by the warriors who had come at Chauncy's call represented a uniform, perhaps a tribal delineation, or both. I watched them all with curiosity. They, in turn, observed me and my companions with equal interest. I had no idea what they might be thinking, nor did I care at that moment beyond the hope they planned only to help us, not hinder us in any way.

The man with whom I had been riding headed in my direction, his cloak flapping behind him, the villager he'd been speaking to following him with his eyes. He seemed wary, I thought, the other man, and yet they must have known these warriors were coming. They had opened their gates to them, to us.

I stopped the warrior before he spoke, breaking my own rule by preparing to give him my name. I bowed my head, lifting my eyes to him before straightening.

"I am Grace Irese," I said, "and these are my companions, Duncan, Mika, Hannah, Resa, Carina and Ren." I indicated each in turn where they stood. "And you are?"

His lips twitched, reminding me he had the advantage. "Well met, Grace Irese," he said. "And to your companions. I am Draig of the Ryder clan. We have been hunting for you for an entire day now."

Duncan groaned. I would have done the same, except I was not surprised nor entirely disturbed by the news. Deep down, I had possessed a feeling he already knew who we were. After all, would not the stories have traveled even here? Of course, they would have. And I did not believe he meant hunting with the same motivation as others who pursued us. Even so, I asked for clarification.

"Without ill intent?"

He nodded. "Without ill intent." Worn in multiple tiny braids, his long, dark hair swung forward at his head's movement. Small stone and glass beads woven throughout clacked together.

"I fear we are followed by more than those animals you chased away," I said, not naming the Lyoness and her warriors, or Tiran and his soldiers, or the dark, horrifying creatures Tiran had brought down from Emerald. Not yet. I did not want to inspire panic among the villagers standing nearby and I also wanted to learn more, first, about these warriors. Likely, Draig had some idea, anyway. "We did not mean to bring trouble here."

Draig was not the first to whom I had apologized for the conflict accompanying us. I'd had a similar, strained conversation with the Lyoness before she betrayed us, and later, in a more personal fashion, with Hannah. I longed for the day when all of this would cease and not, I could only hope, as the result of something worse than anything we had yet faced.

"Let us go inside by a fire and eat," Draig said, jerking his head toward a nearby building. From the noise within, it seemed occupied by more than a few. The smells wafting nearer made me salivate. Not far from me, true to form, Duncan's stomach growled. He was always hungry. I think the sustenance deficiency we had been dealing with was hardest on him.

Hearing it, Draig laughed, a surprisingly deep-bellied sound, nodded directly at Duncan and turned on his heel. Someone came forward to lead all the *conjures* away. I hurried after Draig, wanting to speak before we reached the tavern's doors.

"We have no credit," I said, "no coin or funds of any kind. We can work, though. Clean up after ourselves."

"We'll discuss that later," he said. "You and your companions eat first, thaw out your bones."

I thanked him and returned to Duncan and Ren, who had followed more swiftly than the others. Perhaps they worried I might require defense. They really had no need to, but I was quietly charmed by the thought.

I glanced back to where Resa strode at Carina's side, their hands loosely clasped. Mika hovered close to Carina's right and Hannah drew up the rear, her gaze roving everywhere. She appeared nervous, maybe even frightened. I would have gone back to her, but we had reached the doors. Draig thrust them open with both hands, ducking a bit beneath the lintel as he stepped in.

Steam rushed into the snow-filled air outside. We were struck with stronger food scents, too, and an odd yeasty smell. I thought it might be ale or mead. I had never really smelled either in such quantity. After our days alone in the forested mountains, the noise from conversation, crockery and cutlery seemed like a cacophony, like a battleground. I remembered the fateful dinner with the Lyoness and her people, where we were attacked, thrown into cells. The others must have been remembering likewise, because I saw their heads turning, hands moving discreetly toward the weapons at their belts.

"Grace," whispered Duncan near my ear.

"I think it's all right," I said.

Despite the worry among my friends, only a curious few seated around the large, smoky room turned their heads to look at us, as if the entering warrior crowd had been not only anticipated, but expected right at this very moment. Remembering the horn blasts passing back and forth, I supposed this to be true.

The further we strode inside, however, the more eyes I glimpsed sliding to steal a look at us, to size us up. Gazes followed us before moving on to the warriors who had brought us in. I held my *lathesa* upright at my side, the crystal points at either end glistening in the firelight. Eyes went there, too, wondering about the purpose, I supposed. Throughout the desert, weapons were left at the door when entering a public place. I didn't know about here. I would not have relinquished my *lathesa* anyway. Not one would have given up the bits and pieces of weaponry carried at our sides. We had learned better.

Following behind Draig, we made our way to

secluded tables grouped together at the room's far end. As we neared, the few occupants snatched up glasses, tankards, platters and relocated.

"Sit," said Draig. Most did, including the seven of us, but not all. Draig and several warriors made their way back to the main room. Those who were seated watched us in silence. We did not speak either, not to them, not to each other. Duncan bumped me with his elbow, trying to wordlessly reassure me. I reached under the table, grabbed his hand, gave his fingers a squeeze, taking care for their damaged state beneath the extra padding from the wrappings we all wore as protection against the frigid air. I worried about his hand. He had broken his fingers while still on Emerald, and had managed to rebreak them repeatedly since. Mika, with knowledge gleaned from his physician father, had been doing his best to take care of us. Circumstances contrived to thwart his efforts.

Head raised, I allowed myself to study each warrior seated with us. Three appeared curious, one disinterested, two stared back at me with hostile expressions. I addressed them, figuring they would, in aggression, be most inclined to speak. I might not like what they had to say, but it would probably be enlightening.

"Where are we?" I asked.

"I suppose you can't read," sneered the male about my youngest brother's age. Connor was older than me by several years. At the warrior's tone, Duncan leaned forward, opened his mouth. So did Ren, a boy always quick to flare. I shot them both a look and answered before either could do so in my stead.

"Meaning?"

"There's a sign outside."

"I saw it," I said. "We are in The Guardsman. Understood. I was questioning what lands we are in now. We have moved beyond The Wilds."

"Clearly," he said.

Duncan rumbled a word I did not catch. I had no need to understand the garbled expletive to conjure up any number of his favorites. I ignored him and merely nodded at the warrior.

"That's fine," I said. "I'll ask Draig when he returns."

My casual reference to their apparent leader served its purpose. The warrior exchanged a glance with the female who had been glowering at me from beside him. Their attitude reminded me of Ren and Hannah when first we met them, and yet those two were here with us now, steadfast and determined. The two warriors, however, seemed to be a different breed altogether. Even so, they both straightened on the long bench, unclamped their hands on the tabletop. The female wrinkled her nose a bit before speaking. At us? I believed we all still smelled too much like the frosty air to be offensive in that regard, so assumed her reaction to be habit rather than from any scent we carried. At least, I hoped so.

"Where are you all from?" she asked.

So, maybe I had been wrong about Draig knowing who we were. Or maybe he had kept the knowledge to himself. "I am from one of the desert provinces in Citadel," I said, not bothering to name it. They were numerous, tribal, and would probably mean nothing to anyone here. "Three of my companions are from Riley, one is from the Tansi Islands, and two joined us from The Wilds. And you?"

"All of us came from various settlements to serve. We now consider ourselves to be from wherever we are led."

On Ren's far side, sitting with his arm around Carina, Mika released a small hiss through his teeth. I could not blame him. I held no liking for what she had said either.

"Is it a nomadic life you lead now, then?" he asked. "Riding out to where you're needed?"

Like mercenaries, I thought, and began a discreet check around the table, counting numbers, assessing size, weight, position, glancing back toward the main area in the room to ascertain how far we had to travel to the door, if we could make our way through the gathered patrons to it unimpeded. How we would escape once we gained the village square. I had no idea where the villager had gone with the *conjures*. Without Chauncy, I feared for our survival in the snow-covered land.

All this passed through my mind in an instant. And in that same moment, Resa stood. Duncan saw, followed her upright, stretched his hand to her. Carina stood next, as did I. Ren's mouth dropped. Hannah and Mika stared, briefly frozen where they sat. Other than us and the two angry warriors who lifted their heads in surprise at our action, no one else at the table moved. They had no clue what was coming. I readied myself.

Chapter Three

To my surprise and relief, nothing happened.

More heads turned, staring at us where we stood braced and awkwardly waiting. Resa spun on her heel, though slowly, her eyes searching through the throng in the open room behind us. I pivoted in that direction as well, wondering what she looked for, what was coming. Carina drew close to her, placed a hand on her shoulder. Not to shut her down, I presumed, but to glean what she could from Resa's thoughts. Carina's eyes lifted straightaway to mine, then moved toward the crowd. I followed her gaze to the point where both hers and Resa's had been called. To the man named Draig, standing a head and shoulders above most of those present. He turned, too, head inclining until his eyes met Resa's.

His expression changed. I couldn't describe the alteration, yet it seemed to run a course from curiosity, to shock, to some form of resignation I didn't understand. He straightened, shook back his braided, beaded hair and continued in our direction with those others who had been with him, all carrying pitchers and mugs toward the table. Resa turned on her heel, following his movements until he arrived at the table's head, where I realized only then a place had been left open specifically for him.

The warriors who had accompanied him to the bar all waited for him to seat himself before they followed suit. If this was anything like tribe hierarchy when a battle group formed, he had his captains and counselors and it was they who sat by him now. I wondered if those who gathered around these long tables were only a small number from a greater whole, if they had parted from the rest in order to find us.

Although my unease had lessened, I still felt no comfort with the scenario. I did not like being hunted. I did not like being sought. I did not like being expected. Our lives were in turmoil—as were many—and all I really wanted for my friends, for me, were a few calm days, safe days, days to rest, to strategize, to be unafraid.

I also wanted, needed, answers. Maybe the only way to get them was destined to be through strife.

But I hoped not. I truly hoped not.

We sat down, too, my companions and I, gratefully received mugs filled with a liquid I sniffed at and analyzed with the tip of my tongue, even after I saw others drinking the same from the pitcher out of which ours had been poured. It had no alcoholic taste, resembling more a sweetened water. When I finally took a few tentative sips, my friends did the same.

"Food will arrive shortly," said Draig.

"We cannot thank you enough for your generosity," Duncan responded. Apparently, his eloquent gratitude startled Draig as much as it did me. His eyes flashed to Duncan before crinkling a bit in a smile that only just touched his mouth.

"You're very welcome," he said.

Resa could not take her eyes off him and he barely disguised his curiosity about her, although he didn't stare. Resa, the thrice-gifted child. I expected her story was the most well-known. Since this group had been looking for us, I supposed they, as well as Draig, knew part if not all the tales now circulating.

Still, my discomfort at his interest did not surprise me. Did he, too, have a desire to control and use Resa's power? I supposed any leader with knowledge of it could not help but want to utilize her gifts to gain the upper hand in this unfathomable war. What he could not know is that we would do our best to see that didn't happen. We were outnumbered, yes, but we had each other, we had unpredictable Resa, and—

You have me.

Skelly, please, not now, I thought back at him, deep in the crystal's confines at my throat.

What? You were annoyed with my so-called sulking. Isn't this better?

I closed my eyes, let out a small, slow breath, and refused to respond to him. He would not be let out again. I had done that once and not exactly under my own volition, back in the City of All Dwellers. The destruction had been tremendous.

Despite the fact it had enabled us to escape, I had nearly lost myself in that violent takeover. I hoped to find an answer to controlling him or safely setting him free, but no such answer had existed in the city. Now, we searched for the Cavern of Sleeping Myth, where legend indicated knowledge lay. Thus far, we traveled blind, knowing only that we had to head directly toward the setting sun. The exact location for this Cavern remained a mystery. Meeting Draig and his company might constitute a stumbling block, a salvation, or journey's end, and not in a promising way.

I drank again from the mug in my right hand, my left still holding the *lathesa* upright, the crystal point touching lightly on the crumb-littered, wooden floor. I experienced no ill effects from the beverage, but surreptitiously eyed my companions to make certain they fared the same. It seemed nothing suspect had been added to our cups as we satisfied our thirst, but I could not avoid recalling Resa being drugged by something she ate or drank before we were all set upon at the Lyoness' table. Duncan's thoughts ran in a similar vein, his gaze cutting toward his sister again and again.

Food arrived a short time later, huge platters piled high with steaming vegetables and meaty slabs. "Eat," said Draig. "You have nothing to fear from us."

"Where have we heard that before?" Duncan said under his breath to me. Draig caught his words and presented him a long, level look before raising a fork to spear food onto his own plate. As if the action operated as signal, his warriors began to load theirs. Always hungry, Duncan did not hesitate then, and transported food to his plate and to his sister's. Ren, Hannah, Mika, and Carina followed, as did I, a little more slowly, watching to make certain Draig and the others were eating the apparently random choices from the platters. I hated being so suspicious. I had good reason, though. We all did.

I waited a few minutes before speaking. "Draig…may I address you as such?"

He laughed. I could not imagine why I had amused him. "Of course," he said. "I introduced myself that way, after all."

I nodded. "What do you know about us, me and my friends?"

"Enough," he said.

My brows arched. "Then you have heard the stories."

"Yes."

His one-word replies felt less evasive than succinct, yet troubled me nevertheless. "Why were you looking for us?"

"Why?" he echoed.

To my left, Duncan released an impatient sigh, pausing with his fork halfway to his mouth.

"Yes," I said, "why."

"I was commanded to do so," Draig said.

"Why?" I asked again.

"I do not question my commands," he answered, somewhat surly now. Perhaps he only wanted to get on with his meal undisturbed. If he had any idea what we had been through, he would understand our need for information. I wondered if this might be precisely why he did not give it.

"Who commands you?" Carina asked. Mika's jaw dropped. Carina did not often speak out. Not that she wasn't brave. Sometimes I thought she was the bravest among us all, taking on and dealing with so many added burdens. "I ask this," she said, "because many have acted against us at another's command."

He stared at her for a long moment, watched her eye color change. Without flinching, which I found admirable. Others seated near enough to witness it exchanged glances as her iris went from a color unidentified in the dimness to a vivid red. Some even made signs with their fingers I assumed were meant to ward off enchantment. These were usually reserved for Resa. After a moment, Draig nodded, resumed his meal, but not before his gaze slid from Carina to Resa, and then to me.

"We will discuss this later," he said around a mouthful. "I suggest you eat and rest. There is a room for you all to share upstairs in the attic. It is likely cramped and uncomfortable, but it cannot be worse than what you have been used to. It is also warm and out of danger."

"And you?" I asked. "Where will all of you be housed?"

It seemed to me this tavern could not possibly possess enough space beneath its roof for them all. From the outside, it had not looked large enough to hold more than a few rooms on the second floor and only the one in its low-slung attic.

"We will take it in turns to sleep. Here," he added, with a nod at the table's scarred surface, "if necessary. We are used to laying our heads down in rougher places."

"And the ones who aren't flattening their faces on wood?" Duncan ventured.

Draig's lips lifted at one corner at Duncan's phrasing. In amusement, I hoped. Ren and Hannah watched with expressions schooled to caution. They had lived a long time in fear and aggression's shadow, especially Ren. Ren, who had faced a sentence that could only result in death at an order from one who should have nurtured him. All of them, all my companions, had led lives alien to me. I alone had been privileged to grow up in safety within my tribe and its influence.

"We will stand guard outside the walls," said Draig. "All of you, especially you, Grace Irese," he added, turning to me, "may ease up for tonight on your ceaseless watch."

I refused to acknowledge his words, but I did continue to eat. I tried not to worry, tried not to admit I hoped what he said might be true. When we were all well sated and could linger no more around the tables, we were shown to the designated room by a young girl in a brown dress holding a light in her hand. It wasn't like the lamps hanging from the ceiling below, but more like the light sticks Ren and his friends had possessed when we traversed the underground ways. We climbed two flights to the attic, where she pushed open a door and indicated we should enter. Before anyone could thank her, she'd hurried away and back down the stairs.

In our room, for which cramped was an understatement, Duncan and I paced in a tight circle at its center while the rest tried to get comfortable beneath the steep attic eaves, wrapping themselves in the blankets provided on cotton batting mattresses shoved in every conceivable space. It was indeed and thankfully warm, the hot air in the tavern below rising up through the chinks in the floorboards. It remained noisy, however, due to those same misalignments between the slats.

One window existed, facing the main gate. I knew when I finally settled down this would be my place, where I could see Draig's warriors passing in and out, their actions and reactions and, once the snow stopped, anything approaching. The white, frozen flakes continued to fall at a swift rate, mounding up on the cobblestones, the wall, the tree branches, the windowsill.

I spun to Ren. "Does this ever stop?" I demanded, jerking my thumb toward the swirling white outside the windowpanes.

He glanced toward the window, tossing his yellow hair from his eyes before he shrugged. "We're pretty high up in the mountains now. It could go on for days."

"Not what you wanted to hear, I'm sure," Duncan said to me, passing me once more as we circled.

Most definitely not what I wanted to hear, and yet I understood nature. Railing against it would do no one any good. We came around again, Duncan and I, drew near to each other in the room's center, and I whispered, "What did you make of your sister's reaction to Draig?" We continued to circle. He did not take the time to answer until we met once more.

"I don't know. Sizing him up?"

I paused. So did he. "Does she do that?" I asked.

He shrugged and shook his head. Much about Resa remained a mystery, even to him, her brother. The Sisterhood might have possessed a better understanding, but Tiran had seized her cruelly from their sanctuary in order to obtain Duncan's false testimony against me and with the desire to use her more frightening gifts in his continuing battle for domination. I sometimes wondered if allying himself with the Lyoness and any others unknown to us might be his biggest mistake. How could a person fight for supremacy alongside someone who wanted the same thing?

"Can you two stop the pacing?" I looked at Mika curled up in a semi-upright position against the low wall, his arm around Carina. He pointed at the floor. "Don't you think they can hear that downstairs? I'd be wondering what the heck we were up to."

Duncan gave him a curt nod and threw himself down onto an empty mattress near the window. With a grunt I followed suit, lowering my weary body cross-legged onto the mattress next to his. A chill draft drifted in around the loose glass, causing me to snatch up a blanket and wrap it around my shoulders despite the clear indications it had not been washed since prior usage. It didn't matter. Nothing like that really mattered anymore. I was grateful only to be warm. My muscles ached from shivering through the past long, cold days and my eyelids felt weighted. I wanted to sleep, to put my head down and really, truly sleep. Instead, I propped my arm on the sill and my chin on my arm, my face turned outward to the surreal, snow-filled scene beyond. I saw warriors, perhaps some even as young as we—I hadn't been able to tell—heading to the gate and slipping through to the outside.

"I'll take first watch," I said.

"No," Duncan countered quietly, "you won't. My turn now. You need to sleep."

He lifted his arms away from the blanket draped across his legs, held them out. My brows lowered in a frown. I knew what he wanted. He wanted me to relax against him, in his arms, and sleep there, like Carina with Mika. But Carina and Mika were a couple. Duncan and I were—I had no idea what we were, but not that. I loved him, I knew I did, blood and soul, but it was different than Mika and Carina…wasn't it? Of course, it was.

I continued to frown at him, watched his amber eyes fill with something resembling humor. He made a funny movement with his hands, like his fingers attempted to gather up grasses or wind. "You'll be safe here," he said. "I promise."

Capitulating, I wriggled closer to him with misgivings, turning my attention away from the outside world. I lay my head against his chest. His arms circled me in support. I felt so self-conscious I knew I would never fall asleep.

I was wrong.

*   *   *

I awoke with a start to slumbering respiration all around. No one was awake. Not even Duncan. Swearing, I lurched away from his sleep-slackened arms. Duncan snorted, but otherwise did not move. Shivering in the loss of his body's warmth and my blanket lying in a heap now on the floor, I leaned close to the window.

Snow lay everywhere, mounded in drifts like sand in the desert except for its whiteness, pure and shining in the light and as blue in the shadows as the tattoo on my cheek. Ice rimed the windowpanes. I scrubbed it away with my sleeve and peered toward the gate, the open land beyond, the trees, searching for signs Draig and his warriors continued to keep watch despite the weather so unusual to me, the desert-born. I wondered, briefly, if any of my tribe had ever seen snow. I spent a quick moment attempting to capture it in my brain in order to describe it when we reunited.

The possibility we never would wound its way through my mind, curling poisonous tendrils into and around my thoughts. I fully expected Skelly to speak to me. These were the moments he liked best, to taunt me at my weakest. But he remained silent.

I had no idea what the time might be. I only knew I heard nothing below, and nothing within this room except steady breathing and the occasional rustling fabric. Outside, delicate flakes hit the glass with a strange song unlike any I had ever known. The remaining world seemed steeped in silence.

I breathed in a way I had not in many days, instilling peace to match the hush, pushing back my troubling contemplation. I held my *lathesa* before me, unaware I had reached for it, clutching it upright in both hands, the knife-sharp crystals gracing the weapon at each end dim in the darkened room.

I spied movement, then, or thought I did, and pressed my face against the glass. The cold bit into my skin.

"What is it?" Duncan, whispering, so low I only just caught his question.

I shook my head. "I don't know yet," I answered as quietly.

He crept from beneath our shared blankets and rose beside me, where he pressed his face against the cleared glass, profile reflecting dully in the night. I raised my hand and pointed, tapping a dirty, broken nail against the pane.

"I don't—oh," he breathed. "Are those Draig's people?"

"I hope so."

Dark figures moved against the snow, nearly obliterated by the flakes swirling around them. I glanced again at the *lathesa's* crystal, the original, not the replacement, half-expecting to find it glowing blue in the gloom. When those shadow creatures on Emerald had been nearby, the crystals lit up like a beacon. I had no idea why they did so, but I suspected old magic. The orb from which the shards had come had always seemed to me to be imbued with it. For a brief time after we escaped the prison planet, I had set aside the fear I would find them glowing again, but now that Tiran had brought the beasts down to Talia for use in his war, we again had reason to worry.

I found Duncan's gaze had gone to the crystal as well, to the lightless, razor-edged shard. He raised his eyes to mine.

"Well, that's something at least," he said. "I wish you still had more of those. We could all carry them."

As far as Duncan knew, the crystal pieces had been lost in battle or flight. I still had the one around my neck, though, the one in which Skelly Shane's entity found itself locked away.

Carina knew what I carried, possibly Resa too in some fashion. Hannah had only witnessed the destruction in All Dwellers, had no idea the cause nor what I had loosed among them. For the time being, the truth remained secret. I released a long, shallow breath. I did not like keeping secrets from Duncan. He didn't like having them kept from him, either.

Together we watched the furtive movements outside the wall. More shadows moved toward the gate from inside. "Changing of the guard?" Duncan whispered.

I almost said yes and stopped. My breath caught in my lungs. I reached out, circled my fingers tightly around his forearm. He glanced down at them and then back up at me.

"Grace?"

Yes, Grace, said Skelly, *tell him what you think you see. He's a big boy. He can take it. Tell him about me while you're at it, that you won't let me out, even though I could put all of this behind you forever. Do you think he'll be happy you kept me secret for so long?*

I shook my head.

"Grace?" Duncan repeated. "What's wrong?"

"I don't know," I said. "Get dressed. Everyone needs to get dressed." I began yanking my discarded outer garments from the pile on the floor, followed by my boots. I had given up whispering and my companions started to grumble and waken.

Ignoring what I had said, Duncan darted back to the window, plastered his face against the pane with his hands to either side in order to see more clearly. Breath clouded glass. He wiped it away. And swore. There had once been a time when he did not swear quite so freely. I had been a bad influence on him.

"That sounds like fighting," he said.

I could hear the noises too, even where I sat hunkered down fastening my footgear. Everyone could hear. Everyone except Resa. She slept on, although Carina reached down to wake her up. The rest were standing, pushing through the cramped space to peer out the window beside Duncan, hurrying to add clothing to the bits and pieces they had not troubled to remove.

We had done nothing but fight or run for far too long, except during captivity. I hated the fear suddenly permeating the air; the rushed, panting breath; the look in my friends' eyes. They had been sleeping soundly for once. I had been sleeping soundly. My failure to remain alert had been negligence, a mistake I should not have made.

The door rumbled beneath a pounding fist. I raced over to it, followed by Duncan with his glass cutter drawn from his belt, one boot half on and dragging.

"It's Draig!" came the man's voice from the opposite side. "Open the door!"

Duncan looked at me, a question in his eyes. I nodded. He yanked the door toward him, stopping it with his foot, leaving only enough room for Draig to make his way inside. Duncan slammed the door behind him. He lowered the laser cutter, holding it along his thigh. He hadn't yet had to use a weapon against another person. He'd told me so, hoping, I knew, that he never would. I hoped so, too, but deep down I feared the time was coming.

Draig looked around the room, his head turning within inches of the sloped ceiling. "Gather your things. We must go."

"What's happening outside?" I asked as I scooped my pack from the corner and threw it over my back. "Is the village under attack?"

"Not yet. Scouts were intercepted. We have not permitted them to take word back."

I did not ask what he meant. I figured I understood what he would have ordered done to ensure such a thing. I glanced toward the window. "Whose scouts?"

"Unknown. They were seeking you, however. You, and the other females. They did not know about your male companions."

I swore, a swift, vivid, and somewhat colorful diatribe. Duncan laughed out loud. So did Ren. The look Duncan shot him contained far less hostility than it once had.

"We will leave, but you must stay to protect the village," I said to Draig.

His shoulders jerked, stiffened. I had spoken quickly, without thinking. I could imagine he had little experience being told what to do except by his superiors. I also expected he would not tolerate my impudence. He uttered his next words in confirmation.

"The village, its inhabitants, are as safe as they were before your arrival. As I told you, the scouts will not be sending back any news. I will leave a contingent here, but you will not be traveling alone."

I released a sharp breath through my nose. I could see we were being given no choice. I didn't *not* trust him, but I didn't feel confident in his motivation either. He had provided little information, it seemed purposely, about himself and his warriors, about where they came from, why they hunted for us in the mountain forests.

"May we take more food from the kitchens?" I asked. "These blankets?"

He nodded. "Of course."

"And where do we go from here?"

"Not to the Cavern of Sleeping Myth," he said, confirming he knew more about us than had been discussed. Apparently, he had decided for some reason of his own that we were not going there. I opened my mouth to protest, but he interrupted me. "You look surprised, but surely one among you knew that was not my intent."

His gaze shifted to Carina. She said nothing, her eyes narrowed and changing behind her white lashes. I was not at all sure she had known, had read it in his mind, yet if she had I wondered why she'd kept the knowledge to herself.

"If you are aware of our journey's destination then you must know we need to complete it," I said.

"Not yet," Draig went on. "Not in this weather. We go to another place, a safer one than this, where many of your questions shall be answered. We go to Gabrilon."

Mika muttered something unintelligible, drew Carina to his side. Duncan reached out and took his sister's hand. Resa stared at Draig, her expression unreadable. The Wildron two, Ren and Hannah, stayed silent as well, but took a single step closer to each other, adjusting the packs on their backs, blankets already folded across their arms. I stood alone, feeling oddly separate from them all. I tried to shake off the sense of isolation, grabbed the remaining blankets from the floor before facing Draig once more.

"We follow you, Grace," Duncan said from behind me, "wherever you lead us," and at once the disquiet, the loneliness, evaporated. Draig turned and strode out the door. We trooped after him down the darkened stairwell.

Duncan

Chapter Four

I'd known Grace long enough to figure out when she was hiding something she didn't want me to know. I wished, I really wished, she'd just come out with it. She'd started with the haunted look a while ago and it had only gotten worse. I couldn't ask her right this minute, though, because she was a bit preoccupied with seeing us all safely out the tavern's back door. That should have been Draig's job but Grace wouldn't let it be. She'd taken on the protector role and couldn't give it up. Even when she needed to. It would be her undoing. Anyone else would already have broken. And we couldn't afford to lose Grace. *I* couldn't afford to lose Grace.

It would kill me. I had no doubt it would, after all we'd been through, all we still had to face, all she'd shown me, offered me, forgiven me for, thanked me for.

I shot a sleep-muddied breath past my lips, grimaced at the taste of it. Resa tugged at my hand. It was harder to carry her now, my undersized sister, because she had her own pack to shoulder, as I had mine. I assumed we'd all be riding again once we made it to wherever the *conjure* had been stashed. Heck, we had to be. The snow outside the back door mounded nearly as high as my knees and still came down, hissing through the night sky. We wouldn't make it far on foot. I had my doubts we'd even make it to the *conjures*. I found myself longing for the warmth of those smelly beasts as I pulled Resa along behind me, pushing the snow aside with my legs. If not for the waterproofing, my trousers would have been soaked through.

Beyond the wall the clashing and shouting continued. I wondered if something more than scouts had come. I witnessed the same thought cross Grace's mind as her eyes met mine and then snapped away toward the gate. Draig commanded us all to hurry. To me, that sounded like we had more to worry about than he was giving out. Grace swung to the rear to guard our flank, urging everyone forward, her weapon in her hand.

Resa grappled my fingers more tightly into hers. I glanced aside and down, anticipating—I didn't know what. An explosion, maybe. But she looked me in the eye. Right in the eye. As if to reassure me. Something was changing with my sister. Carina and Grace were a part of it. I didn't know how, but they were. Like the legend, the three of them tied together. The warrior, the witch, the thrice-gifted child.

Also, the Darkness. I hadn't told them about that yet.

Yeah, I had my own secrets.

I smelled the *conjure* before I saw them. The animals huddled together in an open-sided shed. Blowing flakes coated their hides. They resembled massive, snow-covered boulders rather than living creatures. Except the horns. Those long, deadly, corkscrew appendages couldn't be mistaken for anything else. Not if you'd seen them in action. I hadn't really understood how lethal they could be until Chauncy skewered a beast brought down from Emerald with his. He'd saved Grace's life. I'd never call him derogatory names again.

We pressed ourselves into the sheltered area along with five or six warriors who had hurried from the tavern after we did. They, too, carried packs, prepared for the ride ahead. At a thrumming in the air, I turned, looked back.

"What's that noise?" I didn't care who answered. I only wanted to be told it wasn't what I feared. Because I knew that sound, and if a ship were in the air, a ship that had followed us here, we were not getting away.

It arrived, lights cutting through the snow above the trees. I shoved Resa behind me. As though that would do any good.

Grace stepped in front of us both, her weapon parallel to the ground. She stared up at the craft for a mere second before whipping around to face Draig.

"Is it yours?"

He shook his head. It wasn't one of Tiran's

ships either. I glanced behind me to Mika. He had gotten a good look at the cargo ships from the Lyoness' glass fields. "Recognize it?" I shouted at him.

"No. No, I don't." All eyes in our group turned not to Draig, but to Grace.

"What do we do?" I said to her.

She narrowed her eyes one more time at the vessel hovering in the air, then looked to the *conjure* shifting and starting to rumble beneath the shed roof. "Follow me."

Draig reached out a hand to stop her, dropped it to his side and fell in behind. His warriors did likewise. We shuffled through the snow into the *conjures'* midst. One lifted its head at sight of us and bellowed. Grace hurried to its side. With a sweeping movement, she cleared the snow from its hide with her arm. It shook his head and looked back at her, showing a white-ringed eye in its ferocious, ruddy-brown face. Chauncy.

Without the need for words, we lifted the shorter girls onto his back, packs and all. Grace addressed Draig hurriedly. "We need two more of these. Will they permit it?"

It seemed a need for discussion had ceased between them. I figured it was a warrior thing. He didn't argue, just lifted his hand and pointed to one beast and then another. Mika and Ren went straight to the nearest and scrambled up. I got onto the other, extended my hand to help Grace onto its back. I should have known better.

She mounted unaided, settled onto the creature's spine. It made a funny noise deep in its throat, almost welcoming. I don't think Grace even realized. Draig heard it though. He eyed the beast and then Grace in a swift up and down.

"Will you stay to fight?" she asked him.

"Yes."

"We will wait for you while we can. Which way should we go?"

"There is a small gate at the rear wall. Go straight over the mountain. With the morning's light, you will see a pass in the next ridge. Head there. You will find a village, abandoned now. Sweep your trail as often as you can, then hide there."

"And if you don't come?"

"I will be there," he said, fiercely.

"If you don't come?" Grace repeated.

He made a face, angry, I thought, or perhaps just concerned. "Keep moving toward the setting sun. Someone will find you again."

"We don't want the wrong ones finding us," I said.

His gaze shot to mine, held on with an intense expression I didn't quite get. He nodded. "Understood. You must be careful."

His eyes then moved on, to where Carina, Resa and Hannah sat. Without speaking, he walked around the *conjure* we straddled and over to Chauncy. Resa reached out, touched his face with her open hand. He nodded at her and backed away.

My mouth dropped open. "What is that all about?" I whispered.

"I don't know," said Grace. "But we have no time to find out. We need to go now."

I swiveled to get the ship still above the trees into view, saw villagers running with weapons or running to hide, the warriors surging toward the front gate. Draig took the few who'd been planning to accompany us and trotted across the trodden snow. My confidence we'd see him again felt pretty non-existent, which meant we'd be on our own again. Grace didn't ever seem troubled by the solitude of our mission. She should be. It was only going to get harder.

The *conjures* shoved their way toward the open area beyond. Lights from the ship flashed across buildings and trees, seeming to search for something. Us. Of course, us. I mean, it could have been seeking out Draig and his warriors for a reason I couldn't fathom. I didn't think so, though. We'd been perpetually hunted by something or someone since the day we managed to escape the facility on Emerald.

In front of me, Grace spoke encouragingly to the others. She kept her *lathesa* upright, pointing toward the sky to avoid, I supposed, the risk of cutting anything or anyone nearby. I'd always liked the way she held that thing. Effortless. Assured. Like it was an extension of herself. I still felt awkward with a weapon in my hand. Maybe one day we'd continue our training, all of us, and she could show me a better way.

Not that I really wanted to use one. I dreaded the day I might have to wield the glass cutter, the blade, any other lethal object against an actual person. But that day was coming, whether I looked for it or not. I had to be prepared. We all had to be prepared. I hated the necessity, but I also did not want to fail my friends when they needed me most.

Carina turned toward me from Chauncy's back, drawn alongside. "You've never failed us, Duncan," she said. "Never."

I smiled at her, more a grimace really, in gratitude. What I wanted right then was something on my head other than my hood and torn blankets, some seriously thick, strong hat that could block her from reading my mind.

"A hat?" she said, chortling. "Really?"

At the sound, Mika glanced over at her. Their eyes met with something so intimate and understanding in the contact I felt my face heat. I did not want to know these things, did not want to see them. They made me uncomfortable, especially with Grace so near.

Quickly, I tried to think of something else. I focused on the snow swirling, the shadows, the shapes they made circling before my eyes. Anything to keep Carina from zeroing in on the thoughts in my head.

This weather is fascinating, I thought, filling my mind with it. Nothing to see here, Carina.

A few moments later, my efforts didn't matter. I stopped worrying about infiltration into my most embarrassing reflections. Things happened. Multiple things happened.

The first was the sight of the rear gate standing open. *Open.* That couldn't be right. The second was a great crashing sound at the front gate behind us as wood and stone collapsed, splintered, shot against the buildings all around. The third was Grace shouting, "Hold on!" Without context, we obeyed anyway, digging fingers deep into the *conjures'* thick, coarse coats. Carina pressed Resa's hands there, held them with her own, leaning forward to keep them both in place on Chauncy's back, while Hannah took up the rear, gripping Chauncy's red-brown fur for all she was worth.

The fourth thing? Those great, lumbering beasts took off in a full gallop, straight for the narrow, rear gate, a gate I'd have bet Carina would have been hard-pressed to walk through unimpeded, let alone monstrously huge animals burdened by the likes of us on their backs.

We went through first, Grace and I, for a reason that became evident straightaway. The barricade shattered on impact, wood cracking and flying out into the darkness beyond. The *conjure* wheeled about as the others came through. Suddenly, its great horn started tossing things about. Men, I realized, in dark uniforms. They lay like black shadows on the snow and didn't get up.

"Keep going!" Grace yelled as she leaped from our *conjure's* back.

I didn't think. I just did. Not going, but following. I slid down from the *conjure* and landed right beside Grace, whipping the glass cutter from my belt with my undamaged hand.

Apparently, the time I feared coming was already upon us.

Chapter Five

I'd barely raised the glass cutter to disarm the nearest soldier when a great, ice-filled energy pulse rushed past me from behind, tumbling me to the ground. Grace pounced on top of me, holding me down in the snow. With a start, I realized she was attempting to protect me with her body as an onslaught of debris flew past, battering those soldiers who had been left standing after the *conjure* did its dirty work.

Not Draig's warriors. I was glad to see we hadn't been so thoroughly betrayed. But whose soldiers they were, I had no idea. I peered out from beneath Grace's arm, watching the soldiers rise into the air, spinning in a manner I recognized.

Resa.

Before I could analyze my weird sense of pride, or the grief that followed, the soldiers suddenly disappeared, propelled over the wall and into the enclosed village beyond. I struggled up under Grace's negligible weight. She rolled off me, grabbed my arm, yanked me to my feet. I looked back to where Chauncy stood, massive legs foursquare for balance. Carina reached both her hands to Resa's uplifted arms, closed her wrapped fingers over my sister's wrists. Behind them, Hannah looked like she might have peed herself. I hoped not. She didn't possess a change of clothing. None of us did.

The cyclone ended when Carina made contact. Snow and branches and some weapon lost from a soldier's grasp plummeted to the ground. I grabbed the latter, stowed it in the pack I'd shirked from my shoulders when I'd clambered down off the *conjure*. It looked like it might be broken, but if I ever had the time I would try to fix it.

"Let's get out of here," I said.

Ren and Mika had dismounted not far from where Chauncy had come to a stop. They climbed back on when Grace and I hurried to our placidly waiting *conjure*. She allowed me to help her up. In a second, I saw why.

"Crap, Grace! What the hell?"

I reached for a large sliver of wood, as thick as two fingers, sticking out through a bloodied tear in her trousers. She stopped me before I reached it, shoved my hand away.

"It happened when we charged the gate. Leave it until we are far from here. It needs a pressure bandage or something. You pull that out now, there will be a trail of blood in the snow for all to follow."

I swore and ground my teeth, staring at her impalement. She tossed a blanket over the wound, as much to stop me from gaping at it as to prevent blood from spattering the ground.

"Mika will fix it," I said, more for my benefit than hers, and climbed up behind her. My stomach clenched. My eyes kept going to the place her injury lay hidden. It looked serious. I only hoped Mika did have the knowledge to help Grace now. He certainly had the know-how for bones and treating burns and reading us when things were not going well. But this wound of Grace's was likely deep and dangerous.

"Grace," I whispered.

"Shut it, Duncan," she growled. "I'll be fine."

I laughed, because I was meant to, but at her tone, my clenching stomach plummeted. The *conjures* took off, galloping toward the wooded hillside without command. From Grace I heard the occasional pained grunt, soon followed by a more alarming whistling through her teeth. As soon as the animals slowed beneath the trees, I flagged down Mika.

"Grace is hurt!" I shouted.

"Don't yell," Grace hissed at me.

"How bad?" Mika asked, softer, calmer, avoiding having Grace chastise him, as well.

"Bad," I said. "Really bad."

"Not that bad," Grace mumbled, followed by a quiet keening, cut short. "We must not stop yet."

"Grace…"

"We won't stop yet," she ground out. I could feel the effort it took for her to speak.

I looked at Mika, who looked back at me. Their animal had drawn close enough for both Mika and Ren to hear what Grace had said.

"Grace," Mika said to her. "How far do you think you can go on?"

"An hour," she answered. "Let's try for an hour. If I am still alive then, we will try for an hour more."

"Not funny, Grace," I snapped.

"Not meant to be," she whispered back and reached around, grabbing my hand, giving it a small squeeze. My heart performed an erratic beat in my chest, kind of like the ones I used to hammer out on every available surface back when…well, when I thought my life would somehow turn out differently. When music seemed an option, and mapmaking seemed an option, and everything seemed an option, until I was approached by the Grif-Drifs right after my tenth birthday. Or was it my eleventh? It didn't much matter. My path had changed, then, been sealed, and it had seemed the right choice. Not now. Not considering where it had led me.

The blanket Grace had tightened around her leg a short time ago, maybe to keep the stick from moving too much, bloomed black with blood in the night. I realized suddenly I could smell it, her blood, a sharp metallic tang on the frigid air. I wondered the *conjures* didn't react to it. They were carnivorous, after all. So were other things in this forest mountain range.

"Mika," I said, "we don't have an hour. We've got to find a place to shelter quick, so you can help her. As long as it keeps snowing, our trail should be covered over." I looked at Ren. "Is that how it works? Snow fills in the holes? The hoofmarks?" He nodded, wide eyes shifting to Grace—who, scarily, had given up complaining about any suggestion to stop soon—and back to me.

The *conjures* picked up speed, perhaps sensing new urgency. We all bent low to avoid being swept off the creatures' backs by low-hanging branches. I had full support of Grace now, holding her, protecting her as she'd tried to protect me. As she always protected me.

I clutched Grace's limp body, the only sign she hadn't passed out or died on me an occasional, breathless expletive. The darkness beneath the trees deepened. The *conjures* began to hurtle around patches marked by dense undergrowth. I wondered if they knew where they were going, if, with their uncanny sense, they understood what we needed now.

Without warning, they thundered to a halt. I looked around, narrowed-eyed, and spotted a crevice in the hillside, darker than the stone around it, far darker than the snow that managed to glisten even in the shadows. A small cave.

"No way," Ren said from behind Mika. "I'm not going in there."

"The *conjures* brought us here. It has to be safe. It will be safe," I added in conviction.

Mika dismounted, pushed his way forward through the snow-seized growth. "I can't see a thing," he said, looking back at me.

"I've got it," Hannah announced, sliding from Chauncy's back. Hurrying to Mika's side, she produced the flame-ball she'd taunted me with in the past and held it high, casting its bright light across the stone and inside. Not to be outdone, Ren threw himself muttering to the ground and stomped over to them.

"Too bright," Grace said, so low I barely heard her. I knew what she meant though and warned them to shield the light. Rather than flap on at me about telling her what to do, Hannah complied, cupping the heatless manifestation closer to her chest.

"It looks empty," Mika called quietly to me. "Deep enough for us all to fit inside."

I climbed down to the ground and pulled Grace from the animal's back. I tried not to jostle her leg, but failed. She cried out and staggered. Ren hurried back and hooked her other arm over his shoulder. He ducked his yellow head close to her dark one. Deliberately. Whispering something I couldn't hear. I bit my tongue and kept any sarcasm to myself. Now was not the time.

Once we managed to get her inside, we settled her down on the blankets Carina had piled on the ground. Hannah had deposited the sparking flame on an outcropping of stone directly above, providing light for Mika's examination. He prodded the crimson-soaked fabric of Grace's trousers aside and bent close. His brow furrowed. He looked at me. I sucked in a breath.

"You can help her, Mika. You can. Can't you?"

He nodded, a small movement. I wanted to believe him. I needed to believe him. But my hands started to shake. He glanced at them and back up to my face.

"I need fire," he said. "A small one. We'll have to risk it. Could you and Ren gather something and get that started?"

"Okay." I jerked my head toward the opening and spoke to Ren. "Come on."

Outside, I found the *conjures*, including Chauncy, had formed a semi-circle before the cave entrance. We eased past them to hunt up fallen wood. It would be hard to light, given the dampness, but once it caught the dead stuff would burn well.

"What's he want fire for?" Ren asked, holding his arms out while I piled sticks and branches into them.

"To boil water, maybe?" I suggested. "To keep everyone warm? I don't know. I'm not questioning him though. He knows what he's doing." Please, please, let him know what he is doing.

Voices drifted from the cave. A word here and there, uttered by Mika and Carina. Hannah and, of course, Resa remained silent. So did Grace. I hurried through our task.

When we returned to the cave, I piled the wood near the entrance, to prevent smoke filling the cave. I hoped the scent wouldn't travel far. Glancing back at Grace, once, twice, probably a dozen times while I worked, I set about lighting the kindling with an instrument Kerrick had given me. Carina sat opposite Mika, Grace's head in her lap, her hands on either side of Grace's face. Near the wall, Resa clutched Hannah's hand. My sister, who never accepted anyone new. She had changed. She was still changing.

"What do you need, Mika?" I asked.

"Do you have one of those glass blades handy? I would say a cutter, but I don't know how to change the settings."

I tugged the glass knife blade from the small holder in my belt and held it up.

"Stick the blunt end in the flames. Get it hot."

Wrapping my sleeve around the blade, I did as I was told. I figured he wanted to sterilize it by fire. I didn't want to imagine for what.

"Carina," Mika said, "are you ready?"

I glanced back, saw Carina nod, her eyes wide and black as the night sky.

"Mika, what—"

He ignored me, speaking only to Carina. "I'm going to pull this out and then I need to probe, quickly, to make sure there are no pieces left inside."

Carina nodded again, preparing, I realized, to shut Grace down.

"After that, you, Duncan," he said without looking at me, "need to get that blade to me while it's still smoking hot."

"For what?" I began, and then I understood. My stomach twisted and dropped.

"I won't stop the bleeding otherwise. I don't have a choice," he said.

I closed my eyes. No, no, no.

At Grace's cry, cut short, I spun to face them. Carina was perspiring, shining salt liquid sliding down her face. I'd never seen her so much as sweat a single drop before. The huge segment of splintered wood lay on the cave floor, blood still dripping from a gruesomely sharp end. Mika performed something with his right hand, his head turned aside as though he operated from feel rather than sight. Which, I supposed, he did. I glanced at Ren, who looked a little green.

"Now?" I asked.

"Now," Mika said.

I rushed the blade to Mika. The conditions weren't ideal, could very well be bad, indeed, but I trusted him. "I trust you," I said out loud as he took the blade from me, hardly aware I'd done so.

"I trust you," I ground out again when the fire-heated glass handle contacted the penetrating wound. A tendril of smoke and stench rose up, straight into my nostrils, making me gag, my eyes water. I vowed in that instant to change my diet. I vowed in that instant to never leave Grace's side again. I vowed to be better, so much better, if only, please only—

"Put your hand here," Mika directed. He slapped a piece of clean cloth into my palm, pulled me down so hard my smacked knees on stone, and pressed my hand over the cauterized wound. Mika struggled upright and crossed to where his pack lay. He fumbled through it, pulled out a glass bottle filled with clear liquid. The shape looked familiar.

"Did you steal that from the bar?" Ren asked, echoing the thought in my head. He still appeared a little off, as if he might vomit.

"Yes. It was the closest thing to medicinal alcohol I could find. I grabbed it on the fly. I didn't dare use it in the wound itself, but I'm going to clean up a bit around the outside area and then apply a padded bandage." His eyes finally shifted in my direction. "Duncan, she'll be all right."

My eyes closed again in silent thanks to whoever was listening out there in the cosmos.

*   *   *

Despite Grace's feeble insistence, or maybe because of it, Mika adamantly refused to move from where we were until he felt sure she wouldn't start bleeding again. I only left her side once, to retrieve more wood with Ren. We'd decided to build up the fire a bit more until daylight, when the smoke might be seen. Once the flames had been fed, we sat huddled together, all of us, eating a bit from our supplies and melting snow until it was hot, drinking it like flavorless tea. Mika sat with Carina against the far wall—far being an exaggeration, since they were only about eight feet away. He had his arm draped over her shoulder while she broke pieces from a slice of brown bread and handed them to him. He looked tired and rather pleased with himself. I couldn't blame him there.

"Your dad would be proud of you," I said and wished I hadn't. I knew better.

Mika stared at me for a long moment before shrugging. "Mom would have been," he said, and left it at that.

Resa had fallen back asleep, using my knee for a pillow. I couldn't imagine any comfort in the position, but she lay there with her mouth open, her hand wrapped around my ankle. Ren and Hannah sat as far apart as the cramped space would allow. Hannah's silver-blue eyes kept moving from me to Grace and back again. She had something on her mind, but I had no idea what. Ren watched only Grace. My thoughts went to his earlier whispers to her. I had no plan to ask him what he'd said, though. I wouldn't give him the satisfaction.

Like Resa, Grace slept open-mouthed and exhausted. She'd eaten. I'd made sure of that. Yet immediately afterward she'd dropped off, sinking like a rag into water. I wouldn't have been able to wake her even if I'd wanted to. She'd lost a lot of blood. I doubted she'd have the strength to continue the journey anytime soon. I really didn't know what our next move would be.

Outside the cave, something rumbled. A *conjure*. They'd been doing that on and off, like they were talking to each other. They lay in the snow close to the opening, blocking the wind, the cold. The firelight. I held no foolish notion they stuck around for us. Chauncy was Grace's, no matter what she said on the matter. The other two followed his lead. Or they were hers now, too. What did I know? Nothing.

Leaning my head back against the stone, I listened to the crackling wood, the popping embers. Hannah's light had been extinguished some time ago, leaving only the flickering glow from the fire. We were supposed to meet Draig and his warriors, if any remained to him, in the abandoned village at the pass in the next mountain. We'd barely crested the ridge of this one. Grace hadn't the stamina for traveling, let alone fighting. Looking back, I couldn't believe she'd faced those soldiers at the wall with that stake sticking in her thigh. Adrenaline. Adrenaline could fuel even the weakest among us.

But not Grace. Not right now.

I drew in a long, deep breath, released it slowly, pushing the thick splinter standing in Grace's leg from my mind. Up until now we'd all been lucky. Bruises, cuts, burns, broken fingers, injured ribs. All minor, when compared to what we'd been up against. Yes, all lucky, but perhaps our luck was running out. Shane's surely had, way back there on the Emerald. What had made us think we could avoid serious injury, death?

We hadn't really thought about it, I guess. At least, I hadn't. Not that I could recall. We'd just kept right on. Determined. Following Grace. Grace, who now lay in what I could only hope was sleep and not something worse.

I glanced aside at her, her warrior's tattoo stark on a cheek gone as flat in color as sun-baked mud. Again, blood loss. No getting past that. The blanket soaked in her blood had been tossed against the wall. We'd have to leave it behind. Some hunting animal would surely get wind of the smell otherwise.

"I wish we could stay right here."

I looked in surprise toward Hannah. "What, like forever?"

"It's cozy," she said, "and safe."

Ren snorted. "Don't be stupid."

I shifted my hips on the hard floor, careful not to disturb Resa. "She's not being stupid. Leave her alone. We're all feeling a little bit of that right now."

Ren grumbled and turned aside, whipping his blanket up over his shoulder. Hannah grinned at me, a seriously wide grin. Her eyes sparkled with…tears? Crap.

Treat her gently. That's what Grace had said to me, or something like it. I hadn't understood what the heck she meant, but now I did.

Hannah liked me. *Liked* me. I gave her a little nod, looked away, trying not to hurt her feelings, trying not to panic.

Crap, crap, crap. This could get awkward. It probably had been, all along, for Hannah anyway. But now that I knew, or guessed, or suspected, or… Crap.

Grace, I thought, *wake up. Tell me what to do.*

Gods, had I become that pitiful? I didn't need Grace's instruction in my love life. Well, my like life. Neither of which could exist while we were on the run like this. Not true, though. Mika and Carina made it work. But they—they were like an old married couple, somehow. All the painful, rushing, clumsy stuff seemed to have skipped over them.

Besides, I didn't like Hannah. I didn't not like her, just didn't like her in that way. If, in fact, she did feel the way I suddenly assumed she did. And why did I think she did? Because she'd cried when I stood up for her?

Swearing silently, I closed my eyes, pretended a sudden need for slumber.

When I opened them again, Mika stood over me. The fire had been doused. Smoke hung heavy in the air. I shook the hair from my brow.

"Did I fall asleep?"

"Yeah," he said. "But it's daylight now and we need to figure out what to do."

"Right," I said, swiping the drool from my mouth. I looked to Grace. Still out. Not good.

We'd gotten so used to Grace being the answer, leading us, directing us, saving us, for crying out loud. I moved my legs, remembered Resa, and looked around for her, too. She stood by the erstwhile fire, following the curling smoke with her eyes. Outside, the *conjure* had moved away from the opening but I could still see their shadows, hear their soft, grunting calls. Such gentle language for beasts that could rip your head off. I remembered how afraid of them we'd all once been. Everyone but Grace, of course.

Of course.

"What can you do for her?" I asked Mika. He didn't question who I meant.

"I was thinking about cutting up that blanket of hers. Leaving the bloody bits behind and wrapping her leg with the rest, so she can't really move it."

"She'll hate that," I said.

He looked me in the eye. "Too bad."

I nodded agreement and stood. Together, we took the glass blades and sliced through the blanket's thick weave, tossing good strips to one side, blood-blackened strips to the other. Fortunately, more existed to the first pile than in the latter, leaving plenty to work with. We carried the strips over to where Grace lay, eyes still closed, breathing labored. Mika bent down, touched her forehead with the back of his hand, held her wrist for several seconds with his fingertips. His lips compressed.

"Mika?"

He shook his head, turned, and removed the bandage, taking some time examining her injury. Hannah walked over, stood beside me.

"I have this," she said.

I glanced at her. She held out her hand, not to me, but to Mika. "What is it?" he asked, eyeing the packet on her palm.

"My dad gave it to me before he left. For fever, he said. She has one, doesn't she?"

"A small one," Mika answered her. "The wound looks clean still." He took the packet from Hannah, opened it carefully, frowning at the powder inside. "How much do I use?"

Her mouth twisted. "He told me a small bit. Only what would fit in the cup of your hand if you curled it up tight, like this. He showed me. Here." She took the package back and poured a measured amount into her hand. "You mix it in water. Can you get some?"

The last she directed at me. I hurried to grab the container I'd been using for heated water and quickly melted some more snow in the embers. We had water in our packs, but were trying to keep it for scarcer times. Right now, snow lay everywhere and so long as we could melt it, we would be okay. She dumped the powder into the cylinder when I returned and swirled it around. Mika took the container from her, brought it up beneath his nose, smelled the mixture with a dubious expression.

"My dad's a doctor," Hannah said defensively.

"Mine, too," Mika said. "Do you know what's in this?"

"It's made from the bark of a tree that grows near the water. That's what he told me. That's all I know."

Mika drew and released several breaths before nodding. "Duncan, can you give me a hand?"

I rushed to Grace's other side and hoisted her into a sitting position. She grunted and opened her eyes, pushing at Mika's hand holding the metal cylinder to her mouth.

"Drink it," I whispered. "Please."

"Why?"

"Because you must."

To my surprise, she did, swallowing in deep gulps, emptying the container. Her nose wrinkled. "That was disgusting."

"You have a fever," Hannah said to her. "This should help."

Grace's face screwed up in confusion. She looked around. "Where are we?"

"Don't you remember?" I asked. "Your wound? We had to stop. Mika…Mika saved you."

"I didn't—" he began and let the sentence drop. I understood then how bad, how close it had been.

"Thank you," Grace said.

Mika wagged his head. "Don't. You're going to hate me in a minute. Duncan and I, we're going to wrap that leg up, make it immobile."

"Fine," she said, her tone gruff despite agreement. "Just tell me what to do."

"Don't move, don't complain and don't contradict me," Mika said. Ren laughed. I studied him with a quick frown. I hadn't even been aware he'd come near. Carina crossed the floor to gather Resa from her continued observance of the smoke. Everyone understood the minute we finished readying Grace for the journey, we had to leave. We needed to put much more distance between us and what we'd left behind.

The *conjures* were ready when we exited the cave, as if alerted through some freaky telepathy. Chauncy made his way over to Grace where she stood supported by my arm, and planted himself there.

"I guess we're on you this time, eh?" He dropped to all fours. I handed Grace over his broad back, then took a seat in front of her. She protested. When I lifted her bound leg up against my thigh and clamped my hand around her ankle, she understood. Her injured leg couldn't be allowed to dangle. Mika had insisted. Worked for me. I didn't want her getting it into her head she could leap right down on a whim.

Because she would. First sign of trouble and she would.

What the rest of us might do in her stead when that trouble came, I couldn't begin to envision, except we'd do what Grace would do. We had to.

Chapter Six

Having crested the mountain, we'd plodded on down the other side toward a valley before mid-morning and without incident. Smoke rose in the distance from what might have been a clearing, spotted through the flakes before disappearing into cloud cover. We planned to avoid it, deciding to take no chances, no matter what the cause.

Grace drifted in and out of consciousness. Due to her random awareness, she was repositioned, her back to my back, and bound there. Her leg, too, was strapped into place after a brief objection on Grace's part. I understood her mumbling-voiced apprehension. If she or I needed to move quickly, we couldn't.

This weighed on my mind as much as hers. Only difference was she complained about it incessantly when awake, and continued to mutter about it when not quite with us. Mika had given her a second powder dose in water. Since he didn't exactly trust the dosing or the concoction, he possessed his own concerns. Everyone else kept silent. We were all worried. Somehow, despite no cognitive thought as to direction, the *conjures* proceeded without missing a step. Perhaps they adhered to their own agenda. I had no way to tell. None of us did.

The beasts kept to the trees, which meant we couldn't be seen from the air. It would have been hard anyway, because this snow stuff continued to fall, coating the bare branches, and piling up in those apparently always green, no matter the season. Occasionally a great pile would slough off and crash down onto an unsuspecting head.

I was getting pretty sick of it. The precipitation had been fun for a while, back when only a few inches lay on the ground, when we'd been tossing frozen balls at each other. The clothes Kerrick had provided were treated with a waxy substance from some berry which made them repel water and keep in body heat, but I expected the fabric had its limits.

My gaze went to Ren and Hannah on the black *conjure*. They rode with a precise distance between them on the animal's back, one that went beyond the boundaries caused by the packs they wore. Even though they'd coming looking for us together however many days ago now—it was hard to recall—they acted like strangers, like two people who'd met waiting for ground transport. I couldn't even tell if they liked each other at all.

I remembered my earlier revelation and looked away before Hannah caught me watching. I didn't want to give her the wrong impression.

Puffing out my cheeks, I blew a long, frosty breath into the air. Now I'd recalled that moment, I knew I'd be stuck with it. Things making me uncomfortable often kept the tightest hold. I didn't want to be uncomfortable. I wanted to be cool and nonchalant. Not dismissive, though. That would be…mean.

"What's wrong?"

I nearly jumped at Grace's voice behind me, startingly clear and lucid.

"Nothing," I said. Too hastily.

She snorted. "Not worried about me, are you?"

"No. Well, yes. Just not right this second."

"I'll be fine." Already, her voice sounded weak again. "So, what is it?"

"Drop it. It's no big deal. Really."

"You'll tell me later?"

"Sure," I said, "yeah." But I wouldn't. I knew I wouldn't. Somehow sharing my non-dilemma dilemma with Grace didn't seem appropriate. Odd, because since the very first instant we'd actually met, I'd shared more with her than I had with anyone. The desert warrior I thought might kill me in retaliation for what I'd done had instead became my closest friend.

Maybe more than that.

Yep. Not going there now. I had enough demanding space in my head. So did Grace.

A few seconds later Grace relaxed against me, spine to spine, back asleep.

"She okay?" Ren spoke, the *conjure* carrying him and Hannah beside me now. Mika and Carina, Resa between them, had dropped a little behind.

Funny, how the seating had changed. Ren didn't appear particularly happy with his arrangement, but he hadn't been thrilled to be riding with Mika, either. I supposed he'd wanted to be in my place, with Grace. Like hell.

"I hope so," I said.

He nodded. "Me, too. We all do. We need her. And she's a good friend."

Hannah seconded his statement from behind him. I eyed them both askance, somehow surprised by their sincerity. Why should I be? Perhaps because I found myself harboring a cynicism worse than Shane's had been, sometimes. I needed to amend that. For Grace's sake, if nothing else. I looked at them both.

"She is, and we do. You're right."

"We're not stopping until we get to that abandoned place, are we?"

"No," I said, "we're not. We'll find shelter there, or so Draig said. It's best we go straight to it."

Ren and Hannah agreed quietly. Without argument. They were treating me a bit like they had treated Grace. Like I was the de facto leader. Given Grace's condition, someone had to be. We had all looked to her in that role. She'd taken it over, early on, unwavering and unquestioned. We'd let her. Perhaps we were all smarter than I reckoned. But I realized, feeling her body leaning slack against my back, it hadn't been fair.

Thanks to the *conjures*, we managed to give the village with its rising smoke a wide berth, descending into the valley and crossing a crackling, near-frozen stream to a point where we felt safe enough to pause for a few minutes to see to necessities. Once back on the creatures, we ate as we went, rather than take the time while dismounted and vulnerable. Mika risked another powdered dose for Grace, a half-dose, he said, mumbling how he wished we had more of the stuff because we were bound to need it at some point. He didn't mean for Grace. He meant for any one of us. We really had been lucky so far.

I kept an ear out for anything indicating Draig and his warriors might be in the vicinity, heading for the pass where he expected us to be. We couldn't be sure he was even coming. Not anymore. But we'd wait for a day or so. Grace had told him we would. If he didn't come, well, we'd figure out what to do. Heading into the setting sun wasn't an option at the moment. We couldn't see it through the falling snow. We had spotted the pass, though, in a brief break. I wasn't quite sure we still headed in the right direction. Grace would trust the *conjures* to find it, or at least Chauncy. We'd decided as a group to do the same.

"Duncan?"

I turned my head, speaking over my shoulder. "Grace."

"Where are we?"

"You mean like a place name? I have no idea."

"Not a place name," she said. "A point of reference."

She sounded grumpy. I'd dealt with Grumpy Grace often enough. Sometimes Sad Grace, too. Never Defeated Grace. Honestly, even now she didn't sound defeated. Tired, yeah, and weak.

Maybe a little miserable and like she didn't want to be any of those things. I could understand. I reached back to give her arm an encouraging squeeze and accidentally backhanded her thigh with my knuckles. She swore. My rushed apology didn't begin to reflect the guilt I felt.

"It's all right," she interrupted me in a testy tone. "Point of reference?"

"Valley," I said. "We had sight of the pass earlier but it's snowing too hard now to see it."

"Where's my *lathesa*?"

"I've got it here." I patted the long, wooden weapon where it lay across Chauncy's back. "Why?"

"Can I have it?"

"What?"

"I'd like my weapon back."

"Are you sure?" Stupid question. "I mean, do you think you really need it right now?"
Silence. "Grace?"

"Give it to me."

I whipped it up and over my head lengthwise. She tugged at it and I let go.

"Thank you."

"Grace."

"Yes?"

"I've been worried about you. We all have."

Again, with the silence. I figured she had no plan to answer, but her head turned, rolling across the back of my own. "I was worried about me, too," she whispered. "I'm going to be fine, though. I promise you, Duncan."

I smiled into the wind. Icicles from my moist

breath broke free from the torn blanket wrapped around my face and dropped onto my hands. It would be nice to get under cover again, away from the weather. I said as much to Grace, felt her moving around behind me.

"It's cold," she admitted in understatement.

"What are you doing back there?"

"Attaching the *lathesa* to my waist for now."

I said nothing for a moment. "Until it's required?"

"Until it's required."

"But you're not—"

"Don't say anything else, Duncan, please. I cannot fail at my duty. I won't allow it."

"Okay," I said. "Understood."

Two minutes later she'd fallen asleep once more. Damaged Grace, determined to save us all.

"We've got your back, Grace," I said, though I knew she couldn't hear me. On the *conjure* plodding along beside Chauncy, Ren heard, however. Heard me just fine and looked at me with a long, slow nod.

"Darned right, we do," he said. "Always."

A second later something swept him from the *conjure's* back, slamming him hard.

*　　*　　*

"Man down!" I shouted. It was a phrase I'd heard once, I couldn't even remember where, but for the first time it made sense. Hannah let out a scream and disappeared, too. Chauncy wheeled around. I wrestled with the length of torn fabric binding me to Grace. Abruptly freed, I tumbled clumsily to the ground, the glass cutter appearing in my hand without conscious thought. Scrambling across the snowy terrain, I headed for the opposite side of the black *conjure*, weapon raised.

I found Grace had gotten there before me.

Pale beneath her bronze skin, breathing hard, she stood with all her weight on her good leg, the padded one at an awkward angle. She held the *lathesa* spear-like, the crystal shard pressed against the chest of a small…boy. I cocked my head to the side. She withdrew her weapon slightly. Ren pushed himself up off the ground, glaring at the figure still sprawled in the snow by Grace's feet. Nearby, Hannah stood, both hands clapped to her face, her eyes wide.

"What happened?" This, from Mika, who had come running. I glanced around for Carina and Resa, found them still on their *conjure's* back, then into the trees, checking for more of whatever this thing was. A boy. It looked like a boy, but in the instant before Ren was thrown backward, it had appeared to come from the branches above like an animal.

"Can you speak?" Grace asked it. Him. Whatever it was.

It nodded. The little thing seemed quite hairy. Narrowing my eyes for better focus, I realized it/he wore animal fur as clothing.

"Speak, then. Why did you attack him?" Grace nodded at Ren, who was attempting to get his headgear back on over his yellow hair.

"Didn't," said the thing. "Fell."

"I didn't fall," Ren growled.

"I fell," said what I had to finally conclude was a kid. He looked up. "From there. I was hunting."

At the word 'hunting', I took a step nearer, eyeing his extremities for any weapon. Beside him in the snow, a strange implement lay. It possessed a "Y" shape and appeared to be made from wood. A band of material with a shallow cup formed in it stretched across the two arms. What I assumed to be the bottom had been wound around by cloth, maybe for a better grip. It didn't look dangerous. Didn't look like something he could hunt with, either. My brow puckered.

"Hunting what?" Grace asked him.

"Trat," he said. At least, it sounded like *trat*.

"In this weather?" I scoffed. I couldn't help myself. He shot me an insolent glare from his dark eyes, as if questioning my sanity. Mine. When he had supposedly been hunting some creature through the snow-heavy trees in the frigid cold with no visibility worth a darn and that weird…stick.

"Ain't nothin' wrong with this weather. In the cold and snow, trat get slow and stupid. Kinda like you."

My mouth dropped open. Before I could get a word out in protest, Grace laughed and couched her weapon in the snow by her wrapped leg. She extended a hand to him. He eyed it for a split second before reaching out and taking her fingers. She yanked him to his feet.

"Will you give me your name?" she asked him.

"Brand," he said. Again, I had to assume this

was the word. He had a mumbling form of speech, although he'd been quite clear with the slow and stupid remark.

"I'm Grace," she said.

"Yeah," said Brand. "I know."

Grace didn't miss a beat, didn't allow the smallest expression of surprise to show on her face. "I thought you might. You probably know a lot of what goes on in your territory here. Does everyone else know, too?"

"O' course. We were told to keep an eye out for you."

"And stop us?"

He shrugged. The snow on his furry shoulders tumbled to the ground. "Nah."

"Are you allowed to help us?"

"If I want," he said.

"And do you want?"

"Yeah, sure. I can tell you where not to go."

"And where might that be?" Mika asked. Brand shoved his hood back in order to give Mika a long study. He turned his back on Mika, crossed his arms, tipped his head to one side to answer Grace. His attitude made me wonder if he really was as young as I thought.

"How old are you?" I charged in before he could reply to the question asked.

"Old enough to hunt." The way he said the words, they sounded like *ol-nuff-ta-unt*. Somehow, though, I managed to understand him.

"Where are we not to go," Grace said, recalling his attention to her, "and why are we not to go there?"

The energy burst that had seen her successful leap from Chauncy's back seemed to be flagging. I started toward her. She stopped me with her eyes.

"You mean to go t'other side of the valley and into the mountains again," Brand said. "You might not want to."

"Why?" I asked.

He looked at me. His face twitched. "The weather."

Grace snorted. "How long before the weather improves?"

He shrugged again. "Day or so. Maybe longer."

"Will your people give us shelter?"

"Expect so," Brand said. Carina and Resa had climbed down and now stood side by side near Mika. Resa's gaze was on the Y-shaped apparatus sticking up from the snow. She made her way over to it, snatched the tool up. Brand whipped around. His intent to snag the thing from her flared in his eyes and died there. Instead, he shuffled backward.

"Don't be afraid," Grace whispered.

He shook his head. "If you say so."

"We don't need to inconvenience anyone," Grace went on. "If there's a barn or something, we can bed down there. Would you take us to speak with your elders now?"

"I can't come back empty-handed." His eyes shifted again to the implement in Resa's grasp. I went to her and retrieved it for him. He reached into his pocket, drew out something dark and roughly round and fit it into the indentation on the band, after which he pulled the band back and released it from his fingers, firing the projectile into the branches above our heads. In utter silence, a white-furred creature as long as my arm dropped to the ground and didn't move again. Brand lifted the animal and tossed it across his shoulder.

"We can go now."

Okay, so I'd been wrong. The Y-shaped thing was both dangerous and deadly. Same as the kid. After I helped Grace back up onto Chauncy's back, I walked beside him. I wasn't taking any chances.

Skelly

Chapter Seven

Welcome back, Grace. I didn't think you were going to make it. I bet you didn't think so either. Not exactly touch and go, but I could see your thoughts while you were out of it. I can always see them. I know your fears. Honestly? I was a bit scared myself. Because, hell, if you bite it, what happens to me? That's not something we've addressed yet. That's not something I want to face. You?

Of course not. You're too busy worrying about the useless clods. Well, not totally useless. The freak, Oaks' sister, has come in handy a couple of times, hasn't she? Is that why you keep her around? You don't exactly trust her. You worry she'll hurt your precious Duncan, or one of those other dolts. But she's the least worry you've got.

While we're on the subject—oh, weren't we? Well, I am, Grace, and you're going to listen. You need to stay away from that place you were told to go. I'm not talking about the Sleeping Myth place. That could be interesting. It really could. I'm looking forward to it. I get a sense it's not what everybody thinks.

No, I'm talking about the abandoned village. Because it isn't. Abandoned. Not exactly. The hunter kid, his thoughts are loud. Somehow, I'm hearing them. Not sure what his trick is. He could be, you know, *different*. Still, I figure you might want a heads up. Something lurks in the village.

Some *thing*.

I just thought I should share.

Signing off, now.

Your good buddy, Skelly Shane.

And no, I'm not laughing.

Much.

Grace

Chapter Eight

After having avoided the area, we were now heading back in the direction from which the smoke had earlier been seen rising. I supposed it still did, but it was harder to tell with the snow falling thick and heavy. The boy, Brand, led the way in silent efficiency, Duncan stalking at his side. Twice now, Skelly had been trying to tell me things, to unnerve me. I kept pushing him away, down into silence. I couldn't afford distraction. In my present condition, I needed my wits about me even more than usual.

My injury had weakened me. I wouldn't deny it, as much as I wanted to. I refused to let the knowledge hamper me beyond the physical. The mind played an equally important part in any defense. I had not been able to guard myself against my wounding, because no opponent had been involved. It had been, unequivocally, an accident. A galling, foolish, unforeseen, possibly preventable accident, but an accident nevertheless.

My leg pounded, the whole length of it. I needed this wrapping removed, although not until we were somewhere safe and out of this ridiculous icefall. I wanted a good look at the wound myself. I trusted Mika, I truly did, yet I could not be comfortable, could not be reassured, until I saw for myself the wound was clean and not festering. I'd had a fever. I knew that. With a clearing mind, I hoped it had gone.

I looked again at Duncan, striding alongside the young boy with his snow-covered game swinging from his shoulder. Duncan appeared to be taking his self-appointed place in the front quite seriously. A place where I should have been. I had let them all down; let them down when they were all following me into a place far from their homes, into possibly more danger, into uncertainty.

They wouldn't see it that way, I knew they would not. We relied on each other. I counted on them as much as they did me. Still, I could never shake the warrior's embedded responsibility despite my recognition of how capable they all were in their own right.

Duncan, after all, had been the driving force in the escape from the glass mines. He and Mika had saved many, including Ren. As for Carina and Resa, together they were a force to be reckoned with, powerfully symbiotic. I, on the other hand, had allowed myself to get injured in a way that endangered us all. I had brought them into The Wilds in the first place. Before that, I had made decisions on my own that had nearly cost us everything.

Now you get it, cupcake, Skelly whispered in my head. He snorted and my lips twisted, almost as if the sound came from me. Sometimes I believed it did. Sometimes I felt as though Skelly Shane and I had become inseparably intertwined. Perhaps I should go on by myself, leave my friends here where they had some semblance of safety. I was the one who required answers, not them. They just had to survive.

"We survive together, not alone," Carina said, my thoughts drifting into hers. She reached precariously across the space where the *conjures* bumped together and took my hand, pressed my fingers, let them go. "Besides," she added, straightening back up with Mika's help, "you need us."

I nodded. The tears I blinked back threatened to freeze on my lashes. I ignored Mika's questioning look. No doubt, Carina would explain the reason for her words to him in a more private moment. Or she might not. Mika could be content to leave well enough alone. I shifted my focus back to Duncan, to the snow clumped like fungus on his headgear and his hunched shoulders as he bent slightly forward to talk to Brand. I could not hear their conversation, but I saw Brand point to the branches overhead and Duncan's gaze follow. I looked, too, spotting several white-furred creatures observing our passage. Brand whipped out his weapon and took down another to add to his catch. His lips moved with a brief word to Duncan as they continued walking.

I wondered if Brand ventured out into these horrid conditions every day to secure fresh meat for his family. I thought him young for such responsibility, but what did I know about the customs in the territory we now found ourselves? What did I know at all? My life among the tribes had been privileged and protected compared to those my companions had led and to many I had met.

My shoulders slumped. I ached all over in a way I could not quite describe. Bone and sinew, tissue and soul. We had been taught young as warriors that if we must lead, we must lead by example. I was no example to my friends now. How could I serve them like this? Because leadership was also service. We had learned that, too.

I did not look aside at Carina. If she probed my mind right then, she would have been aware of my wretchedness anyway, without witnessing it in my eyes. Yes, I kept wanting to blame my injury for the way I felt, but I knew better. The wound was only physical, after all. Something else plagued me. Something I did not understand.

I began to shake. Fever burned through me again. My limbs felt tight and loose at the same time. I turned to Mika, found his *conjure* had dropped back on the narrowing track, taking him, Carina, Resa, away from me. Ren and Hannah rode farther behind. Duncan and the boy seemed impossibly far to the fore, like I'd stopped and they'd kept moving. I dug my hands into Chauncy's fur, curled my wrapped fingers around the thick, coarse strands, held myself upright as the world started to tip. I continued anyway, following it further and further to my left as though I had no choice in the matter. I suppose I hadn't.

I tried to make my mouth listen to my brain, shaping it to expel the words forming in my head. Warning words. Frantic words. Words about the shadowy, writhing darkness closing in on me. Closing in on them, too. Turning up into down.

My face smashed hard into a cold nothingness.

*   *   *

Whispers flitted through the air, back and forth in hesitant, halting, incomprehensible questions. I tried to turn my head but it felt weighted down. My arms, too. Lashing out, I caught someone or something, hard; heard a grunt; felt a warm, sudden grip on my hand.

"It's all right, Grace."

I knew that phrase, heard so many times, so many more than I could ever count. "Duncan," I said and then thought I hadn't. It did not sound like me, and yet the voice I heard had been in response to my desire to say his name. I swallowed, felt myself grimace. Someone lifted my head, pressed a cool thing against my lips. Not Duncan. He hadn't released my hand.

I drank water, water laced through with a taste I didn't recognize. I started to fight, but Duncan gave my fingers an encouraging squeeze. I took a few more sips before turning my head away. A damp something fell from my brow onto my shoulder, allowing light to filter through my eyelids. I wanted to open my eyes. For the moment, I could not.

"Is everyone…here?" I managed to rasp.

"They're not all in this room," Duncan said, "but they're nearby."

"Are they safe?"

He didn't answer right away. When he did, the word came softly, slowly, so that I wondered at the truth of it.

"Yes."

"Duncan…"

"They're safe," he said.

I forced my lids up, felt the lashes come unglued from each other. The first face I saw belonged to him, to Duncan. His hair—longer than mine, I realized at a tangent—stuck out in so many directions it looked as though he had been sleeping on it for days.

"How long have I—"

"It doesn't matter," he said.

"It does. We were meant to meet—"

"It doesn't matter," he said again. Stubbornly. Shutting me up. I couldn't help but question why. Not out loud, as caution crept in. I started to turn, to look around, to take measure of the room and whatever people were in it. I had not moved my head very far when another face entered my view. Mika appeared enormously relieved to find me awake.

"How do you feel?"

I had to think about that. My eyes started to close. I forced them open again. "Weak. Stupid. Curious. Scared," I said, whispering the last. Duncan's fingers tightened.

"Do you think you could sit up and eat?" Mika asked.

I nodded. Again, someone not within my sight acted, put an arm behind me, pulled me up, settled a soft pillow behind my back. I looked and saw a stranger. A tattooed stranger, not with the tribal markings I knew, but in a severe coloration designed to make the face look angry, fierce, even though her mouth curved up and her eyes were soft.

"I am Lyric," she said, in response to my stare. "This is my village." The statement made me think she perhaps possessed a matriarchal position within it. "I am also a physician." Ah, that explained things a bit. "Your friend did well," she added with a nod toward Mika, "with what he had to hand."

"I am—" I began, but she cut me short.

"I know who you are. You will eat now. Regain your strength. You are underweight. You all are." She frowned around at someone, her expression matching her startling tattoos. I had not drawn a complete breath before someone appeared in response to her look. The girl carried a four-legged tray with something steaming from a bowl on top. Duncan released my hand, helped me to sit up straighter.

"I'm not an invalid," I grumbled.

"For now," he said, "you are, so shut it."

The girl, perhaps as young as half my age, lowered the tray across my legs and then inclined her pale head. She shot a glance at Lyric, whose lips curved in a smile. "Thank you," Lyric whispered. They shared a profile, those two. I figured the girl might be her daughter.

Suddenly, painfully, I thought of my own mother. I bit my lip, swiped at my crusted lids.

"Eat," said Lyric, rising.

"Wait. Please."

She looked down at me where I sat on a simple, narrow bed, my back against the wall, a pillow cushioning my spine. "Yes?"

"What news do you have as to the lands beyond your boundaries?"

"Sporadic," she said. "You worry about your people?"

I nodded. "All of our families." The scent from the bowl hit my nose and I began to salivate. I did not yet pick up the spoon, however, waiting on her answer.

"I do not know individually how fare your families. I do not know enough about any one of you to obtain that knowledge, even were I able. I can tell you, though, that the desert peoples are fighting, Grace Irese."

I thanked her quietly, picked up the utensil and began to spoon a rich, flavorful broth into my mouth as she and the female child left the room. They exited through a door to my left, pulling it closed behind them. I waited to hear a lock click into place. I heard none.

After consuming several spoonsful in rapid succession, I slowed my eating and took time to study my surroundings, aware Duncan and Mika kept a close eye on me. I considered the low-ceilinged room with its dark, heavy beams above, the pale, uneven walls. Interior shutters covered one window and an arched fireplace like the one at home held a small, crackling fire. A lamp stood on a table with a circular ball of flame inside the glass not unlike the fireball Hannah liked to make except smaller and contained. Other than me, Mika and Duncan, the room held no other inhabitants.

I'm here, too, or have you forgotten me?

A few drops of broth dribbled down my chin. I swiped them away with my sleeve, allowing my hand to drift casually toward my throat. I did not touch the bag I could now feel resting against my skin but laid my fingers against my collarbone before lowering them to my lap.

I had forgotten. For the first time in so very long I had forgotten the existence of whatever Skelly had become. I felt the weight of him now, though. In fact, for an instant he seemed to steal my breath.

"Grace, are you okay?"

I nodded at Duncan and went back to eating.

"Where are the others?" I asked between mouthfuls.

Again, that hesitation, like when I had asked whether we were safe. Both Duncan and Mika looked at me, mouths slightly open, no words coming out. I lowered my spoon onto the tray and released it.

"Duncan? Tell me."

He remained silent.

"Mika?"

"They're fine," he said. "They're helping with food preparation."

"Even Resa?" I asked, shocked, although it made sense she should remain at Carina's side.

"Even Resa."

My gaze slid back to Duncan, surprising an expression there which he quickly tried to rearrange. I reached for the cloth once lying on my forehead, scrubbed at my crusted eyes with it, my face. The material held a somewhat herbal scent in its damp weave. I wiped my hands, too, and then dropped the cloth beside the bowl on the tray. I pushed the tray away with slightly shaking arms, pulled my legs out from beneath it. Instead of the damaged trousers I had been wearing, my lower half was now covered by a lighter, softer pair, with the fabric rolled up on the damaged leg to well above the wound. Clean bandages encircled my thigh. When I moved that leg, it only hurt half as much as I remembered. I wondered again how much time had passed.

"You mustn't get up," Mika said.

"I want to see them."

"Not now," said Duncan. "Not yet."

"Yes, now," I said, maneuvering my legs over the mattress edge on the opposite side, so they couldn't stop me. Duncan got up from whatever he had been sitting on and scurried around the bed. He bent down in front of me, meeting me eye to eye.

"You can't go anywhere without help."

I scoffed, a small grunting snort from a still-dry throat. He looked past my shoulder for assistance from Mika.

"Let's get something on your feet," Mika said, as if he spoke to a toddling child. I bit my tongue to keep from lashing out. He rounded the bed with a pair of boots that were not mine. They had been fashioned from animal hide with the fur still attached, lined with the same. I eyed them with distaste, realized my feet were freezing and grabbed them from him, slipping my bare feet inside, into warmth and softness. He then retrieved my coat from near the fire and held that out to me, too. Gratefully I took it, shoving my arms into the sleeves and reveling in the flame-warmed interior.

"Thank you," I said.

Duncan moved to one side, extending his arm to help me up, to aid me, no doubt, in simple locomotion across the floor. I shot him a look.

"I'm not going anywhere," he said, "so don't think a sneer is going to chase me off. You're stuck with me."

Oh, please, Skelly whispered in disgust. I pushed him down.

I wasn't going anywhere either. Although apparently, I almost had. At least it seemed so the way these two were treating me. As if I had broken. To be honest, I had. I felt it. I knew it. And so did they. My friends, looking after me. I couldn't stay angry.

Even so, I knew we had to leave this place soon. Although I possessed no true understanding regarding the circumstances of the attack in the other village, I recognized how imperative it was we leave this one behind. What had happened in the village where Draig had brought us could easily be trailing us into the deeper mountain wilderness. Whoever lived here, in this place, would be in danger. They needed to be warned. Very likely, Duncan had already done so. I would ask him as soon as I caught my breath.

"Lean on me."

I glanced up at Duncan, realized for the most part I had already taken up that position, my weight solidly up against him. I drew a few deep breaths and released them, all through my mouth. Not the correct way to breathe, but all I could manage.

"How long have I been like this?" I whispered against his arm.

"A few days."

Mika rustled around behind us. I did not look to find out what he might be doing. All I really wanted at that moment was to climb back into the bed and close my eyes. My mind drifted to my last training days before I attained my warrior status, to my mentor's voice. Never give up. Never give up.

I straightened, pulled away from Duncan, pushed my unkempt hair from my eyes. The fire felt warm on my right side, the heat grazing my face, my limbs through my garments. "A few days? Have you told them about—"

"They know," he said.

I took another breath, a proper one this time, and continued toward the door, hearing distant, unclear voices as I approached it. "Where's my *lathesa*?"

"In the corner by the bed," Duncan answered.

I started to turn around. He touched my arm.

"Leave it."

Mika stepped past us to turn the knob. He pulled the door wide. A slight chill blasted in, yet I could see we weren't headed outside. The corridor before us lacked both heat and light, but at the far end I detected the latter. It was from there the voices came. I saw people moving about and hesitated again.

"It's fine," Duncan said. "Come on."

I heard something in his tone, though; an underlying stress, a concern. Still, he moved forward, taking my hand in his. Mika strode at my back, oddly protective, I thought. Such realization did nothing to reassure me.

At the corridor's far end, I limped into a vast space with a high, arched ceiling. Part of the ceiling was glass construct, smeared with snow sliding off from the heat in the room beneath. I recognized the place as an area for meal prep, filled with tables, ovens, several stoves, a hearth at either end. People milled about everywhere, handling food, shifting it from place to place, cutting, cleaning, cooking. I spotted Hannah's spiky, red hair and Ren's yellow head beside her. So, I had not been lied to—they were involved in preparing food. I couldn't see Carina and Resa anywhere. Not entirely surprised due to their height, I kept looking, Duncan's arm hooked under my own in support.

Eerily, and little by little, conversation stilled. Heads turned our way. Both Hannah and Ren pushed through the crowd to my side, Hannah throwing her arms around me, Ren standing behind her wearing a grin.

"You're alive," he said.

Duncan shifted his weight from one foot to the other. "Was there ever any doubt?"

They exchanged a glance, a long one, leaving me to understand there had been. Nerves abruptly combined with exhaustion, causing my knees to shake. Duncan reached around to support me but I refused to let him. I went forward to a counter and put my hand on it, palm flat, holding myself up, spine straight. No coddling. I needed my strength back as soon as possible.

Conversation started up again, but most attention remained on us. I looked past the two Wildron before me, searching again for Carina and Duncan's sister, unnerved by their absence, our recent confinement at the Lyoness's pleasure still potent in memory. The focus in the room shifted. People started shuffling sideways to let someone through. Carina came first, her tiny body swimming in the clothes Kerrick had provided to Duncan for us, her usually flowing hair restrained in a long, white braid. Her eyes, her transmutable eyes, met mine in a shade like smoke, pupils large and black. Behind her Resa followed wearing clothes I had never seen before, an embroidered, beaded dress, boots like the ones on my feet, a long coat. She had always looked younger than her age to me, but in her present attire she appeared strangely older. Resa turned her head and looked up and back. Only then did I notice the woman walking beside her, dark-haired and amber-eyed and somehow familiar.

I sucked in a breath. A footfall sounded beside me. Duncan's hand lifted, settled on my shoulder.

"Yeah," he said. "It's my mom."

Chapter Nine

A breathless word slipped past my lips. I looked at Duncan, really looked at him, finally recognizing what I had not since regaining my full senses. Pain. Confusion. Distrust. Not of me, not of our situation, but of the woman approaching us. The mother who had forsaken him and Resa both.

"Duncan," I whispered.

He shook his head at me. I pivoted, returning my attention to his mother, a woman not as tall as I but considerably taller than her daughter. She walked with her amber gaze so much like her son's glued to him. My shallow respiration quickened, anger on Duncan's behalf firing through my blood.

Carina reached me first, took my hand, closed her fingers around mine. She said nothing, spinning on her heel to face Resa and the woman with her. I recognized a warning in the touch, a warning I did not understand but also did not question. After all we had been through, I trusted Carina. Resa continued toward me and joined Carina, leaving her mother standing alone, facing me.

"Grace," she said, "I'm glad to see you are up and around."

I cleared my throat. "Thank you."

Her gaze swung back to Duncan. "Duncan, aren't you going to properly introduce us?"

My breath caught. Duncan's grip tightened on my shoulder.

"Grace, Marcella. Marcella, Grace."

Her face twitched, much the way Duncan's did when annoyed or staving off anger. "I am Duncan's mother," she said to me. "And Resa's."

"I figured that out," I responded, without respect, unable to contain my curt reply. A breath hissed out her nose.

"You're defensive, for my son's sake."

Odd, how she left out Resa. Or maybe not so odd, considering the way Duncan held firm to my shoulder.

"I am not surprised by that," she went on. "I—"

"Why are you here?" I interrupted. Her presence seemed an improbable coincidence, and yet I had experienced others even more bizarre. I knew nothing more than what Duncan had told me about his mother and he'd had no idea where she had gone after she left him and Resa that final time. It seemed unlikely he had ever expected to find himself in her company again, but he'd probably possessed some very private imaginings about what such a meeting might be like. It had never been this.

I felt sure it hadn't.

Marcella cocked her head to one side, her hair dipping over her collar bone and the decorative pin she wore there. "I don't understand your question."

"How did you come to be here, in this place, at the same time as your son and daughter?"

Marcella straightened. She squared her shoulders. "This is my home."

Her home. I didn't dare look at Duncan. My lips moved, preparing to ask another question, but I caught movement behind her skirt. A small boy stepped out, a very young boy, no more than five or six years old. He slipped his hand into Marcella's, his brown eyes wide, his dark hair ruffled, disheveled in the same way Duncan's often stood about on his head. A funny pain burned through my chest.

"You didn't desert this one, I see," I said.

"Grace!" An exclamation in unison from both Carina and Duncan.

"I'm sorry." But I wasn't. I truly was not. I knew how much pain she had caused Duncan. As for Resa, I had no clue what Duncan's sister felt most times, but I could well imagine. I understood what I would have suffered in her place.

"What is it you think I've done?" Marcella asked.

I experienced a prickling, a bristling, coursing along my skin. "You left them, your children. Is this one more to your liking?"

"Grace, don't," said Duncan, voice cracking. I glanced back at him, caught the glitter in his eyes, whether anger or hurt, I could not discern. Possibly both. It would have been both, had it been me. "I'm sorry," I said again, directly to him, and this time I meant it. He released my shoulder and eased past, stopping before the boy, where he dropped to one knee.

"Toma," he said, "come and meet Grace."

Duncan held out his hand and the boy—his brother—took it. The pain in my chest flowered into something else, something that nearly choked me. My respiration stilled to nothing as they approached.

"Hello," I finally managed, looking down into eyes more like Resa's than Duncan's. Did they have the same father? If so, was he here? I still held myself up on the counter, but I extended my other hand toward him. Toma took my hand and shook it, the way certain people did in greeting.

"Are you feeling better?" he asked.

"I'm starting to, yes," I said, even as a quaking began anew in my knees. I pulled out a nearby chair and sat, hating my weakness, worried about it, too. Leaning forward from my new position put us more at a level, Toma and me, eye to eye. I realized Resa stood hardly more than an inch or two taller. I also realized how closely she watched us from behind him and recognized she knew, or had been told, who this boy was, who the woman, Marcella, was. I still could not, however, glean her thoughts on the matter. Her expression in observance remained oddly bland. Carina stood at the ready beside her, indication enough regarding Resa's sentiments.

Toma dropped my hand, looked at Duncan. "Is she angry at Mother?"

Duncan flinched at his question, quickly controlled, expression smoothing, lifting into a smile, albeit a forced one. "I'm sure she's not," he said. His eyes met mine. I nodded. Whatever Duncan's feelings or mine on this matter, he had no desire his little brother should be pulled into it. As well he should not. Such things were between Duncan and his mother and not meant to stain her relationship with her youngest.

Resa would be another matter altogether. Whatever grievance she held could come out in dangerous fashion.

I wondered if Marcella understood that.

She certainly understood something about Resa's condition. She had left her daughter to her mother's care—and her son's—for that very reason. Duncan talked about it little, but he had said enough for me to appreciate how hard it had been for them, especially when they finally had to give her up to the Sisterhood as her outbreaks became more than they could manage. When we had rescued Resa from Stone Tiran, we had been fortunate. We had Carina. Since then, through Carina's influence Resa had started to change. I thought I had been imagining it, but Duncan had also noticed, had made mention more than once. This fact gave credence to the myth, the supposed prophecy, linking Carina and Resa, the witch and the thrice-gifted child. It seemed likely to me Marcella and the others here had heard the prophecy. Perhaps Marcella suddenly valued the daughter she had abandoned because of it.

Goodness, said Skelly from inside the crystal,

you're starting to sound like me.

I hoped not and tried to keep that thought away from him. A pointless exercise, because I suspected no process in my mind remained hidden when my guard was down, and in my present condition the barrier remained non-existent.

Whatever the circumstances here in young Brand's community, we would have to stay long enough for me to heal. I chafed at the truth to our situation. With what was coming, we must not allow ourselves to be trapped here, or worse, imprisoned. I had no idea the villagers' plans. They, too, might seek to use Resa if they had any idea about the forces pursuing us, the intentions of the power-hungry, their armies' extent. Duncan said the people here knew about recent events, but I doubted they had been told everything. They would need to be. Despite my mistrust and apprehension, I could not leave them without providing knowledge for their defense. But I would not leave them with Carina and Resa. I would not leave them with Duncan.

And if they want to stay? Skelly whispered.

My heart squeezed. I could barely comprehend going on without them. And yet, if they chose to stay here, what right did I have to ask them to do otherwise?

You could stay, too, and release me. We could stop the armies here. Together.

"No!"

Duncan and his little brother gaped at me. Marcella narrowed her eyes beyond them. Carina, with Mika now at her side, opened her mouth and shut it again without speaking.

"I am sorry," I said, for the third time in as many minutes, and said no more, unwilling before strangers, before anyone, to explain what releasing Skelly into the world meant. Not just to them, but for me. Hannah and Carina had witnessed the damage for themselves, but I did not believe Hannah understood from whence it came. Unleashed, Skelly wanted to be free. He had tried to sever the bond in the City of All Dwellers, attempting to drain the life from me to achieve his freedom. I had no trust for his motives. He desired nothing more than to wreak havoc. Furthermore, only Carina possessed some knowledge of Skelly's existence. The others had thought the manifestation a release of Resa's powers. No one else could know. If those with ill intent, or even good, thought Resa a boon, they would be even more inclined to mistakenly believe Skelly, his wicked power, the power I carried with me, would save them.

"Maybe you should rest again," Marcella said tightly.

"Yes," I agreed, "maybe I should."

I rose from the chair with a formal little bow in her direction. Why I did so, I could not say. Perhaps to call a truce between us. I knew I had antagonized her, mother to Duncan and Resa, and for the sake of their relationship I needed to keep my emotions in check. I did not particularly want to, though.

"I'll walk you back," Duncan said. He took my arm.

Once out of earshot, I spoke my mind. "Why are you not furious?"

"Who says I'm not?"

I studied him with a frown. "And?"

"And what? People do things they regret, that they're sorry for later."

I knew he was referring also to his own actions, but I would not let it go. "Has she said as much, your mother?"

"Drop it, Grace."

My mouth opened, but at his next words I clamped my lips together.

"As my friend, Grace. Please."

We walked the remaining corridor in silence. Behind us, conversation resumed. Scents from food being prepared followed in our wake. In typical fashion, Duncan's stomach growled. I wondered if his mother knew this about him, that he was always hungry. I wondered if she knew anything about him at all.

"Whose room is this?" I asked as we entered it. I made my way straight to the bed and lowered myself wearily onto the mattress. The tray holding the broth-filled bowl still sat at the far end. Listing sideways, I grabbed the dish and brought the spoon to my lips, waiting for Duncan to answer. He moved to the fire. Crouched before the hearth, he started placing logs in the flames.

"It's part of an infirmary," he said without looking at me. "Where those who are most ill are kept. I think it's near to the kitchens so someone's always available to look after the occupant. You were in bad shape, Grace. I won't lie."

I swore, softly. For some reason, I didn't want him to hear me. "So," I said, more loudly, almost jovially, watching him study the crackling flames, his longer-than-mine, disheveled dark hair rimmed in gold reflection. "Are we safe here? I know I asked before, but no one else is here, now."

"Do you think I wasn't truthful before?"

I said nothing. His shoulders slumped. He picked up a stick, prodded the embers.

"I don't know," he said. "We can't go on until the weather breaks anyway, and until, well, until you're better. We're never going to be safe anywhere, really. You know that."

"But no one is—"

"Aggressive? Threatening? Not yet."

I swallowed the broth. The concoction had grown cold, felt sticky and rather unpalatable on my tongue. I recognized my need for sustenance in order to regain my strength and I kept going, spooning in more.

"My mom," he said, still with his gaze averted. "I had no idea where she'd gone. Gran didn't either. At least not that she'd said. But Mom has been living in this village nine years. Had another kid. One she kept. One she stuck around for." His voice trailed off.

I remained silent. I knew better than to interrupt him now. My heart hurt at his tone, his words, the stillness in his body. The stick he held hung limp in his hand.

"Things happen for a reason, don't they?" he went on, so very softly. "The universe intervenes somehow. We could have passed right by, headed to that empty village to meet Draig, but we're here instead. And she's here, and Resa and...and Toma."

I managed to get up and cross the floor. I stood a second looking at him, at his bowed head, his hanging shoulders, before dropping to my knees behind him. I put my arms around him, leaned my cheek against his hair, his skull's warm curve. I pretended he did not cry. I knew he wouldn't want me remarking on it. I just held him without restraining him, hoping the shaking, the stifled gasps, would seem to go unnoticed.

Chapter Ten

"You must return to bed."

My head shot up, jerking toward Lyric with her strange and unsettling tattoos, so different from my own. I had not heard her come in. I dropped my arms to my side and wriggled away from Duncan, who jammed his palms against his eyes, swiping the moisture from his cheeks.

"You shouldn't have been up as it is," she said. "I heard you went to the kitchens."

Scrambling upright, I took a step toward the rumpled mattress. "I wanted to see my friends," I said.

"And now you have."

Duncan rose also, more slowly, taking the time to compose himself. He pivoted on his heel to face the physician. "She's a hard one to say no to."

Lyric's cheek twitched. "I imagine that's true.

However, she needs rest. It's best we leave her alone, now."

My brows lowered. I felt like a child being dismissed without the bother of direct address. Pointless to react, though, because they were both right. I turned and stalked over to the bed, feeling a twinge in my leg each time it supported my weight. After kicking off the borrowed boots, I threw myself down onto the mattress and pulled the blankets up over my shoulders, burrowing into their warmth. I heard Duncan say my name as I fell asleep, but I might already have been dreaming.

When I awoke, I had lost all time-sense and possessed no clue how long I had been unconscious. The tray with the bowl had vanished. I peered out from beneath the blankets, eyes narrowing at the flames dancing brightly on the hearth. The shadows in the room lay empty. I had been left alone.

Throwing back the covers, I sat up, swung my legs over the mattress edge. I glanced around for the trousers I had been wearing, the garment provided by Kerrick, warm and waterproof and not nearly as flimsy as those covering my lower half now. I would need them once we were again on our way. More immediate, I had kept things in those pockets I wanted to assure had not been lost. Hannah had entrusted me with safeguarding her tiny figure of the Crone. I had been intending to return it to her since our escape from All Dwellers. It meant something to her, the figure did. She had only given it to me because she hadn't expected to survive.

So many had not.

Determined, I stalked around the chamber,

searching under extra blankets lying across two chairs. I presumed Mika and Duncan had been using them while they kept watch over me. Near the hearth, I finally located the garment, neatly folded. The bloody stains had been cleaned from the fabric and the jagged tear neatly sewn. All items had been returned to the ample pockets: the brilliant feather I had picked up on the mountainside before the snow started to fall; packets of dried food I carried around mostly for Duncan's benefit; Hannah's icon.

I turned the latter over and over in my fingers before the fire, observing the flames' light glinting from its dark surfaces. For us in the desert, the Crone represented the beginning and ending of all things. For Kerrick and his brother, the female represented harmony. I really had no idea what it represented to Hannah, although I assumed a mystical or spiritual attachment existed, perhaps relating to the Far Seer, or perhaps the place she spoke of, the place we sought, the Cavern of Sleeping Myth.

Following a quick glance into the room's shadows, I removed the lightweight trousers and slipped carefully into the pair I had been wearing before treatment. I felt my muscles relax in the garment's confines, warmed by their proximity to the fire. Unable to locate my boots, I shoved my bare feet into the fur-lined set and skirted the bed to retrieve my *lathesa*.

When I went to speak to whatever elders existed here, I wanted to appear formidable, capable, a reminder I was, indeed, a warrior. I wanted to give the impression not of recovery, but strength. I wanted to make sure they were convinced danger pursued us, and then I wanted to leave.

The fact I didn't know where to find anyone might prove the first impediment to overcome. Resolute, I headed out into the corridor with shoulders back and a conscious effort not to limp.

*   *   *

The vast kitchen at the far end showed only a small glow. No voices drifted to me. Whatever meal they had been preparing earlier seemed to be finished and all had moved on from the large room. Unless I had been unaware, which would not have been surprising, it appeared none of my friends had returned to the chamber where I slept. As I saw no other hallways or doors leading off from the corridor, I continued into the kitchen. Food smells were strong here, churning up my stomach acids. I wandered over to a sink, turned on the faucet and took great gulps from the flowing, cold water. The fires had been banked down to embers and a chill permeated the area. Overhead, the snow no longer slid off the glass but covered it in a white blanket. Turning off the water, I listened hard for any sign someone was nearby.

Besides the final drips into the basin, the shifting embers on the various hearths and the snow blowing across glass, I heard nothing. Panic quivered in my nauseated belly. I adjusted my grip on my *lathesa*, stepped into an open area and spun the weapon several times, assuring myself I still possessed the skills to which I had been trained. The crystal-tipped shaft whistled, cutting the air.

Nearby, palms slapped together in three, slow, concussive claps. "Bravo," said Marcella's voice. "You are what they say you are."

I pivoted to face her, dark in the shadows where she must have been standing motionless. The fact I had not noticed emphasized my weakened state. "And what is that?"

"A warrior."

"I am a warrior," I stated. "Why would you doubt it?"

"I don't," she said, "but you are young."

"I attained official warrior status on my sixteenth birthday. There is nothing unusual in that accomplishment."

"Perhaps among your people there isn't," she said.

"Your people have a child hunting meat for the table," I reminded her. I did not say more than that, although I wanted to.

She shrugged, causing the long cloak she wore to shimmer in the faint illumination. "Brand is very good at what he does."

"As am I."

She had started across the floor, but stopped. "I don't doubt it."

I drew a deep, quiet breath, released it.

"Brand does not fulfill a prophecy, however," Marcella said in measured tones. "You do. You and the tiny island mystic and my daughter. Oh, are you surprised I know these tales?"

"Not surprised," I admitted, for I had assumed

as much. "Dismayed."

"Why?"

Already growing tired, I lay my weapon across a scrubbed counter, put my hand on top as if to hold it there, although the act was more to keep myself upright. "Because there are those who will use us to attain their goals. Use your daughter. I will not allow it."

I expected disdain, disbelief, anger. I saw none of those in Marcella's expression. "So, I have heard," she said. "And I am grateful."

"Grateful?"

"Yes."

I tipped my head, studying Duncan and Resa's mother in the darkened room. She was old—well, not old I supposed, but likely somewhere near her fortieth year. Younger by far than the battle-scarred Nimue, Lyoness of the Wildron. I don't know why I compared the two. Maybe because I had no trust for either of them. Yet, Marcella's gratitude seemed real enough.

I straightened, faced her dead on. Marcella possessed a certain bearing similar to what I had noted in Duncan. I had been thinking he must resemble his father in stance, but I now saw I'd been wrong.

"Why did you leave them?" I asked. The question echoed in the room's silence. Marcella blinked, dark lashes lowering over amber eyes the only sign she had heard me. Her expression didn't change.

"Your friends are waiting for you," she said, turning away. "I promised I'd retrieve you.

Otherwise, I would have left you to your rest."

Her statement rang false. I couldn't tell which part. Perhaps her words were untrue in their entirety. I knew one thing only for certain. She did not plan to answer me.

Snatching the *lathesa* from the counter, I followed her, my stride frustratingly slower than hers. She paused to wait at a door at the kitchen's far end. I quite understood the smug expression flashing across her countenance, since I had been less than respectful from the moment we met. Yet remembering Duncan weeping at the fireside, I told myself she had no right to any consideration from me. Or from her son.

As soon as I caught up, Marcella moved on without speaking. Thin flames danced in sconces along the wall, their color more than their shape reminding me of Hannah's talent with the flame-ball she could produce. I looked more carefully at the apparatus holding each one, the light hovering above the metal cup beneath without connection, floating in the air behind glass. I listened closely for any hiss from gas or mechanical hum. Except for our footsteps, our breath, fabric's rustle, all was silence.

We reached a staircase, leading down. I paused at the top, staring at Marcella's head several feet below me. She stopped, glanced back.

"Can you—"

"Yes," I said, and started down in a hop from step to step, to keep the weight from my bandaged leg. "Where are we going?"

"Underground passage," she answered shortly.

"Between structures. Keeps us all out of the weather."

I hobbled along a few steps behind her. "I imagine the winters are long."

"I don't think you really can imagine it, desert dweller," she said.

I frowned at the back of her head, trying to continue conversation, for Duncan's sake. "You could be right. I have never been so cold. I had never seen the snow before, either."

"Are you cold now?"

"I'm all right." I did not want her sympathy and her tone had been almost sympathetic. In truth, I wished I had brought a blanket along to drape around my shoulders and back. The chill fought through my clothes, making me long for the coat from Kerrick. He had been gracious in providing us with garments both remarkably warm and impervious to outside moisture. Now that I considered it, the coat had no longer been anywhere in the chamber where I had been healing. I would not ask Marcella. I would find it on my own.

The passageway began to brighten, illumination's source appearing in my weariness to be quite far away. Voices flowed along the stone walls, too. One, a deeper, grave tone, rose above the rest. Drawing closer, I spotted a staircase leading upward. The light and conversation came from above.

I took my time climbing the steps, arriving at the top if not breathless, at least somewhat winded. I swore silently.

"Leave your weapon at the door," said

Marcella.

"No," I said. "I have learned better."

"It's customary."

"It's not going to happen."

She stared at me for a long, strained moment before shrugging. "You're impossible."

"I have been called worse."

"I'm sure you have."

In that instant, I came close to liking the woman. Although she had given in, she hadn't really backed down. She weighed choices quickly and altered her plans as necessary. Like a warrior. For the first time, I wondered where she had been born, raised. I had been assuming she spent her childhood on Riley but, quite honestly, I had no idea. I only knew her history from the little Duncan had told me. Duncan had been raised on the gambling planet by his grandmother, Marcella's mother. I had, again, assumed his Gran had always lived there. Foolish of me. I should have asked.

This realization I had drawn mistaken conclusions and held onto them threw off my mental balance for several seconds. I stood gathering my wits and taking in several breaths, my gaze travelling over the people inside the vast chamber as I sought out Duncan and the others. I found them standing at the far side before a raised platform, seeing clearly only the taller among them due to the people pressing near. A long, rather ornate table had been positioned on the platform with five equally lavish chairs behind it. Four were occupied. The man in the center snared my attention.

"Is that—" I stopped myself. Marcella turned her head, following my gaze.

"Who?" she said. "Who do you think he is?"

"He resembles a warrior I recently met," I advised with a strange reluctance. "A man called Draig."

"The man you see before you and Draig are estranged," Marcella said. "They are brothers. Aeron is my husband."

My breath caught, fluttered out. "Does he…does he possess ancestral mage blood?" It seemed he must, because although I had heard mention of gifts such as Resa's among various peoples, never had they been as strong as hers.

Marcella nodded, solemn, thoughtful in countenance.

"And is he—"

Anticipating my question, she answered before the words filled the air between us.

"Yes," Marcella said. "Aeron is father to my children."

"To Resa and Toma," I said.

Marcella looked at me. Her eyes held mine. "To *all* my children."

Duncan

Chapter Eleven

I didn't much like interrogation, especially from a man I'd been advised was my father. My *father*. The same as Resa's. Had someone told me we had different parents, or had I only assumed? And where the heck had he been when Mom went off-world to give birth, not just to me but later to Resa? I used to imagine he'd died or something, anything that would provide a good enough reason he'd never looked for me. I didn't quite believe this guy, this mage-blood Elder—Aeron—could be my dad anyway. We didn't look a thing alike.

The family resemblance glared when it came to Toma and Resa, though. Anyone with half a brain could spot it. Aeron, however, hadn't yet publicly acknowledged us as offspring, despite the fact many knew. He made no effort to act it. Or perhaps he made an extraordinary effort not to. Either way, his battering-ram questions began to irk me, big time. I wanted to walk out. For my friends, I wouldn't.

He hadn't denied parentage when my mother told me who he was, right in front of him. And since he was my father, mage blood ran in me, too. I couldn't quite wrap my head around this revelation. Knowing this odd truth didn't make me feel any differently. Like many among the Wildron, old abilities had passed me right by. Ordinary Duncan Oaks, me. While I contemplated what gifts Toma might have, I lost track of Aeron's rambling, powerful voice until I realized it had ceased speaking.

I glanced up at him. His attention had been caught by something at the back. Conversation rippled behind me. Heads turned, on the platform, at the walls. I followed suit, looking to the rear.

Grace. Grace and my mom. One expression made itself clear on both faces. Not happy.

Grace broke away first, left Mom standing in the doorway. Grace walked slowly, less graceful than her usual lanky stride, her pain obvious despite her efforts to cover it up. Yet, even with the pain, she made her way straight to me, forcing people to move aside merely by her presence. I grinned.

"Grace," I said, as soon as she drew near enough to hear me.

"Duncan." She took my hand, the unbroken one, curled her fingers around mine. I hoped she'd hold on for a bit, but she didn't. Releasing her grip, she turned to face Aeron. Something in her eyes, the way she held herself, caused the hair at my nape to shift.

"You are Grace Irese," Aeron said. His deep, booming voice often caused a person to step as far away as possible. She didn't. I hadn't, either. I'd stood right in front of him and hadn't moved. The whole time he had been questioning me, questioning us, I'd thought about Grace and how she would have conducted herself without a tremor. She had always been brave. I remembered her facing me down in the corridor her first conscious night in the facility on Emerald. I remembered how she rescued me from the creatures on the planet, outnumbered and alone. How she had challenged Stone Tiran, how she had challenged the Lyoness, how she stood up to everyone she met. Even my mom. Not that she needed to. Not my mom. I figured I would work it out with her. Or not.

Likely not.

Letting out a long, slow breath, I turned my head a little, looking for my mother. She appeared different than the Mom I remembered. Then again, it had been twelve years and when I had thought about her in the intervening time—if I'd thought about her at all, I told myself—she most often came to me in a likeness similar to the framed image Gran had hanging on the wall. Mom possessed the same face, naturally, although older, her dark hair showing the occasional white strand, as well. What struck me most was none of those things, but the way she carried herself now. Back then she had been…I don't know. Antsy. Defeated. Angry. She wasn't like that here in this place. Still angry, maybe, but somehow steadier, stronger.

I turned my head front again. Grace stood with her chin high, observing the people on the platform. I spotted the *lathesa* in her fist. How I had missed the weapon when she first walked up beside me, I couldn't fathom. Aeron's gaze went to it, too.

"I hear you are mending from your wound," he said to her, pulling his gaze away.

"I am. Thank you. For everything."

I shot a glance at her. She didn't quite sound sincere. Something was up. I wondered if perhaps we should be readying ourselves to flee or fight. My muscles tensed. I cast a sideways eye at Mika and Ren, Hannah, Carina and Resa standing behind them. Carina's eyes met mine, whatever she tried to convey to me unclear.

All our weapons had been stored in a closet in the room where Grace recovered. We had given them up voluntarily as a sign of good faith. Since no one had actually disarmed us, taken the weapons away, I'd thought there'd be no problem. A naïve, stupid, possibly costly mistake. I had insisted Grace's *lathesa* remain by her side, though, because I thought she might sense it there, lie more easily as she healed. Now she possessed the only means for defense.

I took a small step nearer to her. Our companions did the same. The change in position did not go unnoticed.

Aeron straightened in his chair, fingers curling over the arms. "I was questioning your friends," he said to Grace, "about recent activity."

"You mean war," Grace said.

"Yes," he admitted, "war."

Grace turned to me. "How far did you get?"

"I was trying to go in order. I was just getting to specifics about the creatures from Emerald," I said.

"So, you haven't yet told him about Draig and the warriors with him?"

The sibilant whispering in the room suddenly stopped. I had a suspicion this had been Grace's intention. To instigate something or maybe to uncover a truth. In the silence I heard footsteps and found my mom approaching the platform. She stepped up onto it and took a seat next to Aeron. My brows lowered like a weight pressing down across my eyes.

"Draig is no longer a member of the Ryder Clan, whatever claim he made to you," Aeron said slowly.

"He and his warriors saved us," Grace said. "First from wild animals and later from soldiers. Soldiers whose garments, weapons, I did not recognize. Their uniforms were black, like Citadel guards, but different. Were they yours?"

One or two gasps sounded behind me. Grace ignored them, meeting Aeron's gaze. He considered his response. My mom leaned forward.

"We would not send soldiers against you," she said.

We. My guts bounced down into my boots, my gaze shifting back and forth between her and the man seated beside her. My dad, I had to remind myself. I shouldn't need to do so. If he had been in my life, if I had known anything about him, perhaps I wouldn't. Mom lifted her hand, placed it across his to calm him. *We.* I hadn't figured on her being in an elevated position. One more stupid conclusion on my part. Aeron was an Elder. She was his wife. They were *we.*

Grace took a step forward. "My question remains unanswered. Were they yours, these soldiers? Set against Draig and his warriors perhaps, since not against us?"

A muscle leaped in Aeron's jaw. I could almost hear his teeth grinding together. Resa left Carina's side, moved to mine, took my hand. Aeron observed the action with scant attention, glanced at my face, returned his focus to Grace.

"I would not do that," he said.

"Again," said Grace, "my question is not answered."

Gods, I admired her. Admired her nerve, her ability with words in the heat of the moment. I noted straightaway Aeron's surprise at her persistence. I would have crossed my arms in anticipation of the show if I didn't have Resa's hand in my own, if I hadn't been worried I might need both my arms quickly.

Aeron leaned forward. "My brother and I are estranged, it is true."

Wait. What? I really needed to start paying closer attention. I recalled Draig's appearance, planted his features mentally over Aeron's, recognized the similarities. As I should have done right away.

Resa's actions with Draig were perhaps better understood now, considering the blood relationship, except she'd been with only us, me and Gran, since not much more than a baby, and later with the Sisterhood. She didn't know Aeron, didn't know Draig, wouldn't even remember our mother. Not clearly, anyway. Still, this was Resa. Anything could be possible. Who knew what she had seen in her way through the years?

I'd often wished she could show me, share her perceptions, her strange knowledge with me. Not so I would have it, too, but so I would understand.

Aeron continued, quiet in the stillness. "Draig has chosen his life and his loyalties. He serves another, not me. I would not attack him for it, however. I have no cause."

"Do you, then, command an armed force here? One that you did not choose to deploy against either us or your brother?"

"Your questioning is impertinent." My mom spoke, not Aeron. Aeron's eyes narrowed. He seemed to be gauging Grace, her intent.

"We lost all our warriors a long time ago," he finally said. "The few remaining to us left with Draig, seeking excitement, opportunity, employment, where they understood it would be found." His shoulders slumped beneath the heavy fur robe he wore, unintentionally, I felt sure. He seemed a proud man, one who would not want others to sense anything but his strength, his position, but I recognized a broken one, too. Still, I refused to feel sorry for him. I didn't know him. I didn't know anything about him. I wasn't sure I wanted to.

"No protection? That's not good," Mika said in an undertone.

Grace echoed a similar sentiment, loud enough for all to hear. "A bad position to be in. With what is coming, you, your people, are undefended."

"The mountains protect us," Aeron ground out. "Our isolation protects us."

"I am not sure that is enough," Grace persisted, undeterred. "We are being hunted, my friends and I, by more than warriors and soldiers. I am not referring to the Lyoness' replicants, if you are aware of them. They aren't real. They are only a psychological advantage. Nor do I refer only to the unknown troops which converged upon the village where we rested. Stone Tiran has brought down genetically manipulated creatures from Emerald. Creatures that will twist your minds and then shred your helpless bodies into pieces."

With her last statement, Grace's hand jerked up to her throat. Her mouth stretched, grimaced. She closed her eyes. I moved closer, reached for her elbow, grabbed it, felt her weight shift into mine.

"I've got you," I whispered.

She nodded, a brief movement, and then straightened. She pulled away from me.

"That sounds like suicide," Aeron said.

"I agree," answered Grace. "The mutants cannot be controlled. They will not distinguish between those who seek to use them and those who run."

Aeron waved a hand. "This is too fantastical. Do you have proof to offer these things exist?"

Grace scrubbed her fingers over her trouser leg. "No. You have but our word as to what they are and what they can do. We have seen it, Mika, Carina, Duncan and I. We lost…we lost one of our number to them."

My stomach twisted in memory. Skelly's screams, his ravaged body, his remains tossed up onto the cargo ship like a bloodied animal skin. I hadn't liked the guy. He had been arrogant, even cruel, and probably less than sane well before sinking into prison-sanctioned addiction. He hadn't deserved what had happened to him, though. No one would have.

Aeron stood. "Then possibly the best strategy is for you all to leave straightaway," he declared, too loudly, aggravated by Grace's bold speech. Beside him, Mom jolted forward in protest. He glared at her and spoke again. "If you are being hunted, we should not be sheltering you. As you have pointed out, we have no defenses."

Mika sucked in a breath at my shoulder and called him a coward. Not loud enough for anyone but me to hear.

Squaring her shoulders, Grace took another step closer to the platform. The narrow lights in the room flickered across the crystals on her weapon. I think it had been momentarily forgotten by all those gathered. Aeron looked at it now and jerked back.

"Recall your brother to your side," Grace said. "Your brother and all those who may still ride with him. Make amends. We will depart as soon as we are able, but do not believe for one minute our leaving may save you from what is coming."

Her voice reverberated in the room like one who spoke with foreknowledge. She didn't possess the gift, but I wouldn't blame anyone for believing otherwise in that moment. A ringing truth existed in her words. A certainty and a determination marked her posture. The old, fierce, undaunted Grace shone in her eyes.

Our absence would not prevent war from coming, if those who waged it decided otherwise. I knew that. This man, my father, should also have recognized the fact. As for the creatures being utilized by Tiran, well…no one would be safe.

I turned my focus to my mother. Her amber eyes had gone wide and wild, darting from the man at her side to me, to Resa, to a point beyond us where, perhaps, Toma stood. I spoke, said words I never expected.

"Mom, you and Toma, come with us." My teeth snapped together the instant the plea exited my mouth. I'll never know how she might have responded because behind me, almost immediately, a woman screamed.

I whipped around. Grace somehow beat me to that position, her *lathesa* already raised. Cold air blasted into the room from an open door, white flakes swirling like smoke around the dark shapes rushing in. My heart nearly ripped from my chest. I shoved Resa behind me. I probably shouldn't have. I became airborne before I knew it.

With more than a dozen others, I fought to keep from bashing against the ceiling high above. Below, Aeron still stood by his chair, my mom beside him.

The other three Elders shared the ride with me, though, cloaks flying, arms flailing. Ren, too. The rest up here, strangers from the gathering, gaped in silence as they spun and fought the forces, apparently too startled to screech. My sister stood front and center in the maelstrom, arms raised, hands out, dark hair whipping about her head. Carina hovered about six feet above the ground, gripping Mika's shoulder with one hand to anchor herself, legs flapping in the air behind. Her other hand stretched toward my sister, oddly holding back from contact. After a quick second I understood her hesitance. Those caught in the whirlwind had a long way to fall.

The figures who had pushed in through the door stopped, staring. Not the creatures from Emerald—my initial, heart-exploding thought—but Draig and his warriors, brilliantly-colored, snow-spattered clothing bloodied and damaged by battle. Despite her spontaneous reaction, I believe Resa recognized Draig, even if she didn't understand the significance of weapons kept sheathed and belted. Rather less slowly than I would have liked, the suspended in the room dropped. I landed with a grunt and a sharp retort from my knee striking stone.

Growling out a few crude phrases, I clutched my kneecap a moment before rising. Ren shoved his straw-colored hair from his eyes and reached out a hand to me. With a glare warning him not to mention it later, I accepted his help.

No one spoke. Which was odd. I would have expected some questions to be flying about, if not actual screaming.

"Is anyone hurt?" Good old Mika, the doctor's son. Had his dad only encouraged him, maybe he wouldn't be in this mess. Then again, Mika's decisions had been his own. As mine had been. Grace's, too. Even Ren, Hannah, likely Carina beyond the strange life in which she'd been fostered. I pulled my lips in between my teeth and released a long breath through my nose.

Draig and Aeron stared at each other across an expanse filled with somber, frightened people. People who began to shuffle backward, as much to make way for Draig and his warriors as to put distance between themselves and my sister. Calm, Resa stepped in Draig's direction, hands lifting again. Carina darted forward, but I stopped her. Resa's fingers, hands, arms began moving in their fluent, silent speech. I went to stand beside her, concentrating hard on the changing configurations. After several seconds, I addressed Draig.

"My sister says she saw you coming through the forest."

Draig nodded, his eyes showing white all around like a wary beast as he observed her.

Resa continued. I frowned and looked up again at Draig. "She says you are not yet pursued. But…" I scowled in concentration, watching her hands. "But they are coming."

Someone sucked in a ragged breath nearby.

"How long?" Draig asked.

I asked her, turned back to Draig, ignored my father behind me, sputtering now with his own questions. "She does not know," I said. "What she does is not foretelling. She sees distant places and events as they occur, the way I see you standing before me."

Resa stilled at my elbow, Carina beside her. Mika, too. I glanced aside to find Hannah and Ren had joined us. Grace stood on my other side, weapon in hand. Without a word, we had all gathered, ready for whatever came next. This response had become habit. One that had saved us more times than I could count.

"Can she regulate what she sees," Draig asked, "seek it out, find it?"

"I don't know," I admitted. "I don't fully understand her gift. I never have."

Draig nodded, raised his eyes to look past me to his brother. The floor vibrated beneath my boots. A heavy hand fell on my shoulder.

"Step aside," Aeron said. "Keep the child under control."

The child. As if he didn't care about her, or choose to recognize her as his own. He behaved as though what he had just witnessed didn't surprise him, either, didn't frighten him, didn't intrigue him, but like Draig, his eyes showed white all around. I touched Resa's shoulder. Together, my companions and I moved out of Aeron's path. The villagers nearest scuttled in every direction. Aeron descended on his brother like a dark and rumbling thundercloud. Tensed and ready, Draig stepped back. His warriors pressed closer. Aeron scowled at them.

"Do not threaten me in my own hall," he snarled.

"You are not being threatened," said Draig. "We are here because you need us, whether you will admit to it or not."

"And what of *she* who commands you?"

My ears perked up. I had been curious whose bidding Draig followed since first mention. I was not, however, to be enlightened.

"I have come at her command," Draig said, without giving a name.

"Not because you have regained your senses? Not from loyalty to me, to us?"

"I have never been disloyal to you, my brother. I am here to protect you all from what is coming."

"And what, exactly, is coming? I have heard tales from these children—"

I stiffened. He didn't care. He didn't care at all that among 'these children' existed two of his own.

"Tales that are doubtless true," Draig cut in.

"They would know the truth better than anyone here."

Someone tugged at my sleeve. I glanced aside to find Grace there, her dark skin almost ashy, darker circles beneath her eyes. "I've heard enough," she whispered. "Haven't you? Come on. We need to talk. And we need our weapons."

We all slipped away aided by Aeron and Draig's raised voices dominating all attention. Certain eyes followed us, but none tried to interrupt our departure through the doorway at the stairhead. On the steps to the underground passage, Grace struggled, one hand on the wall, her gait uneven until halfway down, where she paused and swore.

"That's our Grace," said Ren. I shot him a look he ignored.

"I'm all right," she said, head bowed. I stood two steps above her and still managed to hear her shallow, pained breathing. I huffed out a breath of my own and scooped her up without warning, throwing her over my shoulder, bracing myself for her angered outburst and the fist she pounded into my back.

"Stuff it, Grace," I said. "You don't get a choice. We haven't got all night."

I didn't care if I offended her. Whatever headed our way, we were in it together. Nothing could change that. Unfortunately, at least until Grace healed, we were also stuck here, right here, in this cold, ridiculously inhospitable land.

With my parents.

I might have laughed if the shock of it all would have let me.

Chapter Twelve

"No, Grace, you're not up to it."

I was glad Mika had taken over, because she sure hadn't been listening to me. Not only that, but she'd been insisting she would go on alone, leave us here where we had shelter, food, maybe safety. I reached out and touched her forehead, checking for fever. She'd knocked my hand away.

"We have to stay together," Ren added.

In a chair by the wall, Hannah leaned over her knees, her tone almost imploring. "I know we said you needed to go to the Cavern, but you can't make the journey by yourself. You mustn't." She straightened, her expression turning defiant. "We won't let you."

I noticed only Carina remained silent. The gaze

she fixed on Grace had turned a very strange color. In all the transformations I'd witnessed, I didn't recall this one. Her eyes closely resembled Hannah's at that moment, a pale, silvery-blue, but I could swear I saw white smoke moving in them.

"Tell them, Grace," Carina said now. "Tell them what they need to know."

Grace sat on the hearth, her back to the flame's warmth, her injured leg stretched out straight before her, her face stubbornly set. At Carina's words, she blanched, looking suddenly... I don't know. Frightened.

My stomach flip-flopped at the sight. I lapsed into total silence, my fists squeezed between my knees, waiting. When she didn't speak, I prodded her. "Yes, tell us, Grace. Whatever it is. Please. Maybe then we'll understand." A lot of things required understanding, for me at least, like what had been troubling her for days, weeks now. Something that haunted only her.

"Besides," I tacked on, "we go where you go. You know that."

She reacted in the last way I would have imagined. She broke down in tears.

I leaped up from the mattress edge. "Crap, crap, crap," I muttered, hurrying across the floor and lowering myself next to her on the hearth. She smashed her face into her cupped hands, horrendous sounds coming from behind them. Helpless, I glanced guiltily around the room at the other occupants and waited for the torrent to end. "Grace," I said, bending close while she mopped her face on her sleeve. "What is going on?"

She drew a deep, fluttering breath, lifted her chin. Shaking hands went to her throat and loosened the fastenings on her shirt, reached inside, drew out a bag hanging from a silk cord. I recognized it, remembered briefly holding the tiny sack back when we were traversing the long, tunnel-like cave through the mountain. Recalled, too, the way it had felt in my hand. Painful, like waking up a sleeping limb. I'd figured I had imagined the sensation. Now, seeing Grace slip the cord over her head, raise it in her fist with the bag swinging from the loop, I started to wonder.

"What's inside there?" I asked.

She turned from me to Carina, gave her a long, steady look. Carina stared back, unflinching. White smoke continued to swirl in her ever-changing eyes.

"Grace, it's time they knew," she said.

"Knew what?" said Ren.

Hannah straightened against the chair back. "About what happened, right? Back there in All Dwellers?"

Whatever had transpired while Mika, Ren and I had been separated from the girls, struggling to return to them, they had been reluctant to talk about it. The escape had been big, I knew that much, and naturally it involved Resa, which made perfect sense since they would have needed her gift when surrounded by the Lyoness' people. Yet, Grace in particular appeared to be holding something back. I understood not wanting to talk about the nasty stuff, the stuff not worth recounting because it didn't do anyone any good, but I suspected a secret being kept. By the looks still being exchanged between

Carina and Grace, it was a bad one.

I slipped to the floor, pulled my knees up, wrapped my arms around them and settled in, like a creeping dread hadn't suddenly begun clawing its way around my anxious stomach. The glass cutter attached to my belt clanked on the wooden surface beneath my hips.

Grace turned her head away, looking past me at nothing in particular. Her hands twisted on her thighs, the sack on its cord flopping back and forth. The action brought to mind a Gran-term: wringing one's hands. Never a good sign. I hadn't seen Grace do that before, not ever.

"Grace," I said. She lifted her pointer finger up, a quick, knife-like movement. I understood and pressed my lips together, saying nothing more. Her gaze shifted to me.

"Do you remember when we escaped Emerald, when we sensed something around us, you and me?"

I nodded, the claws reaching out through my skin and gripping my spine. She couldn't be about to tell me that had been real. She couldn't.

Although Carina had confirmed a suspicion about that. I remembered now. How had I forgotten? Probably because I never wanted it to be true. Once I no longer sensed anything, I had dismissed the notion Grace and I were targeted by something, by something unnatural. I had figured that particular darkness had gone on its merry way. Convinced myself as much, anyway.

"Is it here?" I asked.

She raised her left hand, indicated the bag with

her right. "Right here."

My breath rushed out. "What do you mean?"

"It's trapped in a crystal, one of those from the original orb. Duncan, it's Skelly."

Those reaching, gripping claws suddenly turned to ice. I looked to the others, found Ren and Hannah confused, curious, maybe a little afraid, but Mika stared at Grace, expression frozen, stuck in place. Resa sat on, content to watch the flames, unaware of a conversation I had not shared with her. I turned back to Grace.

"Shane? How?" was all I managed.

"I don't really know. His...entity appeared back at the compound. Honesty, it saved me, but I knew right then that without being stopped he would lay waste to everything. Somehow, I called him down into the crystal and have been struggling to keep him there. I don't know what to do now. About him, about many things. These are the answers I seek."

I remained silent for a very long time. We all did.

"That's old magic," Ren finally said in awe.

"Can we see it?" Hannah asked. Ren told her in no uncertain terms to shut up.

"I hear him," Grace went on, as if Hannah and Ren hadn't spoken. "He talks to me. He wants to be let out. Sometimes I feel his despair, his contempt, his rage as if it were my own."

"Oh, Grace," Carina whispered.

"He believes he can tear down this world and everything in it. I have no idea if it's true or not, but I have seen the damage he's caused. I cannot control him. And I can't, I won't, let him out again."

"Again?" I echoed.

Grace nodded. "In the City of All Dwellers. I didn't intend to. He destroyed so much. Even now, he hounds me with promises to crush the armies pursuing us."

"Then why don't you let him?" Hannah once more. It fell on me to tell her to shut it, because Ren said nothing. For all I knew, he might have been thinking the same as she.

"He nearly drained my life back at All Dwellers," Grace said. "I believe, given free rein, he would do the same to every one of you. And I do not want you to die. I will not let him do that. I also do not want the responsibility of any death on my conscience. Among those warriors and soldiers are people like us."

"I doubt their goals and ideals are guided by a conscience such as yours," Mika said, but quietly.

Grace's face shone with tears. I hadn't noticed she'd begun crying again. "What would you do?"

"Thank the gods that decision isn't mine," Mika answered.

Hannah opened her mouth and closed it when Ren's hand slapped down onto her knee.

"What do you need from us?" I asked.

"For one, keep my secret. Others would willingly take advantage of what I carry, no matter the consequences."

I nodded.

"And second, stop arguing with me about my leaving. I have to keep going, find the answers or at the very least take this crystal far away from everything and everyone."

"And do what with it?" Carina questioned.

Grace slipped the cord back around her neck, tucked the bag inside her shirt. "I don't know. To destroy it would mean the release of what is inside. Drop it into the biggest, darkest hole and bury it? I don't know." She shook her head from side to side, grimacing as if in pain, then sucked in a ragged breath. In those seconds, we witnessed the inner battle she had been hiding from us for a long time. Hiding from me. I frowned.

"Grace," I said, "you're so much better than you were a few days ago, but you're not strong enough to do this on your own, no matter how stubborn you are."

Her lips curved. She swiped at her cheeks.

"And do you really want to leave us? All of us? I mean, Ren you might do without, but…"

She laughed, shot Ren a look to show she understood I didn't mean it.

"But I don't want to take you away, back out there. You are all warm here, fed, sheltered," she said, repeating her argument. "There are warriors ready to fight, to protect the residents. Your parents are here, Duncan, and your little brother. I heard what you said to your mom."

I ducked my head, picked at something smeared and dried across my pant leg. Looked like gravy from dinner. I didn't want to think about what Grace said, didn't want to think about leaving behind the little brother I'd never known, leaving my mom to the danger surely coming, no matter that she'd left me and Resa years ago. My father had already shown himself a man I didn't like and certainly didn't know. I really felt no connection to him. Besides, his brother had returned. Draig had access to more warriors, based on what he had said to us shortly after we met him. Surely, they could fight, if need be, or flee.

"I'm not sure Resa is safe here," Carina said into the momentary silence. "Not after what everyone witnessed tonight. Mika and I will be coming with you. We will take care of your sister, Duncan, if you want to stay behind."

"Count us in, too," Hannah said. I glanced up in time to catch her waving her thumb between her shoulder and Ren's. "We sought you out for a reason. We can't drop out now."

"But you will have to wait, Grace," Mika added. "You'll be a hindrance to us all in your present condition. We'll help you on the journey, sure, just give it another day or two."

"I don't know if we have another day or two," Grace said.

No one voiced any disagreement with Grace's statement. After all, how could we? We all felt the same, all understood that leaving in a day or two might be too late. A small part of me wriggled in indecision, though, despite the declarations I'd made. I needed a conversation with my mom I had never thought to have.

*   *   *

The others had finally fallen asleep in the room

where Grace recuperated. We'd spent more time talking after gathering all our scattered possessions and weather garments from the various places we'd been housed. No one stopped us. The few people we saw appeared unnerved and said nothing. I couldn't blame them. Resa had done her thing. Word about that had to have spread. My father's brother had returned—my uncle, I reminded myself—and an enemy was possibly on its way into their borders. So, no, I didn't blame the folks here for being anxious. Still, all the sidelong gazes, ducked heads, compressed lips did little to help my own nerves.

I decided to make my way to the large meeting chamber, not because I expected anyone to be there at such a late hour, but because it would be the best way to my parents' living quarters. I had only been there once, yet I did recall which door led to the covered walkway ending at the clustered dwellings, one of which was theirs. The third on the left, I reminded myself. I didn't want to be knocking at the wrong home. Especially with the sun not yet up.

I had already considered I would likely be waking them. It seemed strategic, somehow, to catch my mother off guard. I wanted some honest answers from her.

The lights in the underground passageway had been extinguished. I shook the kinetic torch I'd pilfered from the kitchen until it began to glow and slowly made my way down the stairs. Water dripped somewhere, slow and steady, far steadier than my pulse. Lately I'd been wondering how I managed all those cons without uncertainty or the smallest, telltale tremble, looking marks in the eye as if I were honest, as if I could be trusted, fooling them all. My mom, of course, had no idea what path my life had taken. I doubted she'd even care. Even so, I didn't want her to find out.

The crunch from my boots on the stone floor echoed off the timber-shored walls, steps lagging as I neared the stairs leading upward to the meeting hall. Sleepless contemplation had done nothing to aid me in finding the words I wanted to speak. I only hoped the man Mom had called my father would not be present. I had never known him, never needed him, had no desire for his counsel or interference.

I climbed the steps slowly, the torch in my hand throwing my shadow across the walls. At the top I opened the door, stepped inside, and stopped.

In the puddled, yellow light from a nearby lamp, papers, actual old-fashioned papers like the kind you could still sometimes find in books, were spread across the table on the platform. A free-standing monitor sat on the table, as well, not switched on. Beyond the light my father sat in the shadows, head bowed, looking lost in study of whatever writing presented itself across the paper sheets. Before I could back away, he looked up.

"Don't go," he said, picking up on my panicked intent. "Come. Sit next to me. We should talk."

He kicked back the nearest chair with his right foot, the sound ridiculously loud. I flinched, recovered, and crossed the floor hoping my reluctance wouldn't show. I eyeballed the chair he had shoved out for me, my mother's chair, and sat.

The papers spread across the table's surface appeared quite old, handwritten words scrawled across them. I stared at the pages as if nothing interested me more. He turned his attention back to the pages. For a full two minutes we sat in silence.

"You and your friends don't have to leave here," he finally said without lifting his head from his work. "I spoke in haste."

"What's changed?" I asked.

"Draig. Draig and his warriors. Whatever happens, we'll make a stand."

I speculated how much this had to do with Resa and decided not to ask. Not yet.

"Grace is still recovering," I said. "Provided we can, we'll leave as soon as she's able."

He shot me a look from dark brown eyes like Resa's, like Toma's. Not like mine. I really saw nothing resembling my own face in his features.

"What are those?" I indicated the papers.

"Ancient charters. I don't know why I'm looking at them now. I needed something else to think on, I suppose."

For some reason, I believed him, at least in part. Whatever he sought in the writing before him did not concern me, however. "You mean something other than the fact war may be coming?" I prompted.

His lips turned down. "Nothing can free my mind from that, I'm afraid."

I nodded. He returned to perusing the documents. I sat on for another two or three minutes, then started to rise.

"I'm sorry," he said.

I sat down again.

"I heard your words to Marcella earlier, to your mother. This is why you are here, isn't it? To discuss this with me? You think you need to save her in some way. That's not your job. It's mine."

I didn't answer. How absurdly his mind worked, that he believed I would need to discuss with him anything I wished to speak with my mother about.

He went on. "I'd like to tell you a few things. May I?"

His demeanor, his attitude, struck me as odd, so different from the man who had shown himself to one and all these past few days. I inclined my head in agreement, still silent.

"Many years past, I did not hold the position of head Elder among our people. In fact, there was one who was considered lord of these lands, as ruler over all within this valley and the mountains surrounding it, crowned by birthright. That man was my father. Your grandfather, I suppose. That hadn't occurred to me." He checked, raised his head, stared at the wall a moment, thick, dark brows lowering.

"Is he—"

"Dead?" he said. "Yes."

I felt no grief, only a small shock at Aeron's tone. Gran's image passed quickly through my mind. Her, I would miss. Her, I would grieve. I pushed the thought away. It hurt too much to even contemplate.

"While he was alive, my father kept Draig and I at odds as to who would inherit the title. Neither of us was allowed to marry. I left for a time, traveled, met your mother. She returned here with me. We wed in secret, but I feared for her and for any children we might have. My father was a cruel autocrat. I sent her away when it was known she carried a child, both times."

"But she returned to you and left us behind," I reminded him, in case he tried to excuse what had happened.

He sighed. "Yes. She did. And then my father…died."

A little alarm bell dinged in my head. After what we'd been through recently, the hesitation in his statement set off all manner of suspicion. "How?" I asked.

"Don't look at me like that."

I hadn't been aware I'd been looking at him in any offensive way. I rather thought I had been schooling myself to a calm, maybe mildly curious expression. One you reserve for people you're afraid might fly off without provocation.

"It wasn't me," he added, surly now, annoyed, even though I'd said nothing. "There was an insurrection. My own mother left and set up court elsewhere. Draig followed her. Here, we reformed the way our community is run. I was elected head Elder. Things changed."

"And Toma was born," I said.

"Yes."

"And my sister and I remained forgotten." I had to say it, the obvious truth. I struggled to keep anger from my statement, any petulance to tick him off.

He sighed again, a long, drawn-out noise. "No. Not forgotten. Only better off where you were."

I stood, crossed the floor, came back up onto the platform, unclenched my fists at my sides. "That's not good enough," I said.

He stared at me. The flush on his brown skin darkened from a windblown red to something resembling muddy crimson. I knew I had probably pushed him too far but I didn't care. Yeah, life with Gran had been both hard and good, and I had no major complaints there except, well, where I'd ended up, but that had been my own doing. Resa's life had been different. It still was. It always would be. Had they not considered that?

Yet, who knew what it would have been like here among my father's people. Could they have helped her any more than the Sisterhood? Would they have accepted her, been frightened of her, used her abilities in ways my friends and I struggled even now to prevent?

I didn't want him to be right. His maybe being right in whatever convoluted way angered me more than anything. I would be glad when we left here. I truly would.

My thoughts abruptly returned to what he had first said.

"Save my mother from what?" I asked.

He looked minutely confused and then shrugged. "You asked her to come with you and your friends when I said you had to leave. Why would you do that unless you thought you could keep her safe from what may be coming to us here?"

I shook my head at him. "Didn't you see her face when you spoke? She was afraid. Afraid for me and Resa, for Toma. Right then, I thought she cared. About all of us."

"She does care."

My breath exploded from my lungs. I turned on my heel and strode away from him without another word, headed straight for the stairs to the underground passage back to the kitchen. I shook the torch until the glow lit the steps beneath my feet. The light prismed, glittering in the idiotic tears clinging to my lashes, the ones I didn't want Aeron or anyone else to see. I swore several times under my breath, dashing my knuckles across my eyes.

She does care.

I had been of two minds about hearing from my mother exactly what my father had just said to me instead. What the hell. The knowledge didn't make anything easier. If anything, it turned decision-making into a nightmare.

I swore again, kicked a loose pebble out from under my boot, sent it clattering against the wall. I would have to be upfront with Grace and Mika and Carina, try to work this out. We had a couple of days. At least I hoped we did.

Climbing the stairs leading to the kitchens, I heard a sound like something sliding along the floor above. I paused, listening, figured someone had come in early to get the stoves ready. Odd, how the entire community prepared and ate communally in shifts for the morning and evening meals, dining in the same room where meetings were held. I supposed it saved energy and resources, made us all "friends." Frankly, it made me darned uncomfortable. Everything too noisy, too close, too overwhelming.

Hearing nothing more, I continued upward. I didn't want to be detained, didn't want small talk. I wanted to get back to my actual friends, maybe catch an hour of sleep before getting down to the deep stuff with them. That didn't seem too much to ask.

Apparently, it was. Way too much to ask.

Chapter Thirteen

Chill air blasted me when I entered the kitchen. At the far end, the huge, double doors stood wide open. I doused the kinetic torch and yanked the glass cutter from my belt. Moving quickly in case I had been spotted, I dashed to my left and crouched behind a wooden block table. Enormous shadows shifted back and forth beyond the open doorway. One broke away from the others, made its way inside.

At that exact moment I heard another noise, saw further movement to my right where the passage led from Grace's room. A figure appeared wrapped in a blanket, pushing hair from its eyes. From her eyes. Grace.

I bolted upright and charged the thing suddenly bearing down on her. The large shadow moved, swung, caught me right across my middle and sent me flying. I landed on top a nearby counter and scrambled upright. Through the ringing in my ears, I heard someone shouting.

"Grace!" I cried and leaped down in her direction. Immediately I found myself sprawled across the floor. A hand reached down, snagged my wrist, tugged me to my feet. I met Grace's green eyes in the dark.

"What do you think you're doing?" she hissed.

"Protecting you," I said, wondering why she sounded angry, wondering why we weren't running.

"By bringing them in here?" I followed the direction her arm took, suddenly recognizing a smell in the frigid, swirling air. I looked up toward a corkscrew horn on a massive head that had surely slammed me in the stomach twenty seconds earlier. A white-ringed eye studied me. Still outside, two more animals shuffled back and forth, one a mammoth black and the other slightly smaller with a soft, brownish coat. They appeared hesitant to follow Chauncy inside. I jerked my arm from Grace's grasp.

"Even I have the sense not to bring a *conjure* into a kitchen, Grace," I snarled.

Grace's shoulders jerked, I thought in offense, until I recognized the accompanying noise as laughter. My lips twisted in response.

"It's freezing," said Grace. "We've got to get him back outside and shut the doors."

Easier said than done, I thought, recalling how often Gran said those exact words to me. I had tried her patience a lot, I knew. Chauncy seemed set on trying Grace's patience now. He refused to budge.

Grace stopped pushing and coaxing the *conjure* and turned to me. "Duncan."

"Yeah?"

"Why are they here?"

"What? I told you I didn't—"

"No, I mean *why* are they here? Why have Chauncy and these two broken out from wherever they were housed and come here? Something's wrong. Something is very wrong."

One intemperate word sometimes serves the purpose of half a dozen more. Grace's expletive matched my own.

"We've got to wake the others," she said. "Get our gear on." She glanced around the still dark kitchen. "Gather supplies."

Chauncy rumbled, deep in his chest, and backed toward the open door. I needed nothing more than that to tell me Grace was right. We pushed the damaged doors closed, Grace and I. I knew Chauncy and the other two *conjures* would be waiting in the snow on the other side when we returned.

In the infirmary chamber, I relit the torch and slapped it down on a table. In its light and the golden glow from the hearth flames, Grace and I woke everyone but Resa, prodded them in the direction of clothes, outer gear, packs. For now, adrenaline fueled Grace, but she would be flagging soon, requiring help. We would give it, all of us.

"What's going on?" Ren asked a second time, no longer satisfied with Grace's exhortations to hurry.

"We don't know," I said. "The *conjures* broke into the kitchens. Chauncy refused to exit until Grace understood we had to leave. Okay? Good enough?"

We all had experience now with the *conjures* and their strange ways, with the animals' ability to glean things we couldn't. Ren clamped his lips shut and hustled. Carina shook Resa gently awake and attempted through thought to convey the urgency to her without overdoing it. Resa turned and looked at me.

I slowed down, carefully signed as best I could. She shook her head, returned a single signed word which took me only a moment to translate. Brother. She didn't mean me.

Right. I hesitated. *Do you want to stay with him*? I asked, fingers moving awkwardly, reluctantly. She couldn't, it wouldn't be safe for her here, she—

No. She wanted him to come with us.

Suddenly, so did I.

*   *   *

I hurried through the kitchen, down the stairs, back along the underground passage and up into the meeting room. My father had gone, taking his papers with him. The lamp no longer burned and I stumbled over the platform in my race to the door leading outside onto the covered walkway. When I reached the clustered lodgings, I counted the doors and pounded on the third. The sound caught the notice of an armed warrior walking the perimeter.

Before he could reach me, question me, stop me, the door opened, yanked inward by Aeron.

"What's wrong?" He grabbed my elbow, tugged me inside. The door shut behind me. We stood together in a stairwell, a dim light burning at the top. A shadow appeared in the opening above. I looked up.

"Mom."

"Come upstairs," said Aeron and spun on his heel, leading the way.

I stomped snow from my boots on a mat before following. Mom stepped back. Catching movement behind her, I spotted Toma in her shadow, sleepily rubbing his eyes, tall for his age and young, maybe a little frightened as he stared up at me. The self-righteous fervor that had sent me barreling over here deflated a little. He didn't just appear young. He was young. Too young to be on the run with us.

"We're leaving," I blurted out. Maybe even this was wrong, telling them. All three stared at me in awkward, momentary silence.

"Why?" Mom asked.

"The *conjures* came to collect us—"

"They did what?" This, from Aeron, from my dad, his brow furrowed.

"They broke through the door in the kitchen. Something is coming. They sensed it. Chauncy—" I waved a hand before I could be interrupted with questions. "The *conjure* known to Grace would not back down until Grace understood we had to go. So, we are. There's no guarantee our leaving will lead whatever follows away. Consider yourselves forewarned, because… because it's so much more than this. There's a darkness coming to all the lands. I met a man in The Wilds who shared this with me. It is known, recognized, among his kind." I turned, feeling sick. Toma's gaze followed me. He scurried forward, grabbed my hand.

"Stay with me," he said.

I crouched down, my face close to his. "I can't."

"Then I want to go with you."

My mother cried out, snatched at his shoulder but he stepped aside. In my mind, I saw again the crumpled boy, not much older than Toma, lying in the glass fields. I thought of the mines, the struggle of our escape. I recalled the hardships, the very real, constant dangers I and my friends had been exposed to for many weeks now. "You can't," I whispered.

I heard a sound like a sob. From my mother, I thought. It didn't seem likely Aeron would make such a noise. I rose.

"Is there some place where the little ones can be hidden?" I asked.

Mom nodded, pulling Toma back to her side.

"Bring Resa to us," said Aeron. "We'll keep her safe, too."

I wanted to believe him, to believe his motives altruistic. Yet, he had witnessed what she could do. Even if he hadn't, I wouldn't leave my sister behind. It was she they wanted, our pursuers. It had been all along. I began to better understand why Grace kept silent about the thing inside the crystal. Together, especially with Carina's help leveling out Resa's unpredictability, they possessed the ability to form a dire weapon.

The warrior, the witch, the thrice-gifted child. I hadn't fully understood Grace's position in that triad. I doubted any truly did. We would have to make darned sure they never learned.

I shook my head. Aeron straightened, slid one foot forward. "I could make you—"

"No," I said, facing him, "you couldn't."

He backed away. My mother watched us both, her gaze finally settling on me. I wanted to hug her. Not like I had when I'd been little more than Toma's age, clinging tight, bawling like a mad creature because she was leaving us. This time, the harsh reality was different. There were more immediate reasons I might never see her again.

I gave her a nod.

"You know where to find me now," she whispered. Tears glittered in her amber eyes, the eyes like mine.

I shook Toma's hand. I'd seen him do so with others, with Grace, with Mika and Ren. He squared his narrow shoulders, accepting it. Releasing his hand, I cupped my fingers around Aeron's shoulder.

"Keep them safe," I said.

I had gotten halfway down the stairs when the door below me flew open. A guard, a warrior, whatever his title, rushed inside. He pushed past me with barely a glance, taking the steps two at a time.

"Elder, the scouts! They have been attacked. Only a handful have returned—"

I didn't wait to hear more. I pounded down the stairs, rocketing back the way I had come. In the kitchens I skidded to a halt. Once again, the door lay open, almost battered from its hinges. I raced down the passage to the infirmary, burst inside and found it empty. None of my friends were there. All their gear had vanished, too.

At a footstep behind me, I pivoted toward the sound. Draig stood framed by the doorway.

"They're gone," he said. "They're all gone. I sent a handful of my warriors to guard them on their journey."

Yanking my own pack off the floor, I tossed it over my shoulder and started past him. He stretched an arm out, blocking my way.

"They are moving fast. You aren't going to catch them."

"I can sure as hell try." I shoved his arm aside. He grabbed my sleeve, spun me until we were facing each other. I had to tip my head back to look him in the eye.

"Not alone," he said, "and we can spare no one else. You will stay here and fight. With your family, nephew. Where you belong."

Chapter Fourteen

The *conjures* galloped through the snow, sending an icy spray into the forest, obscuring our trail. Looking back for the hundredth time, I wondered how Duncan and the rider who was to accompany him would be able to follow us. I had wanted to wait, demanded five more minutes, but we were not to receive it. Not from Draig's warriors, not from the vicious sounds drawing closer. Even so, I would have stayed; would have gone looking for him; would have done anything to have him here with us, with me. Instead, we had left him behind.

My heart sank like a leaden weight, deeper and deeper into my bowels. Mika, Carina and Resa rode the big black *conjure*; Ren, Hannah and I, Chauncy. As each minute fled past, it seemed more and more likely Duncan would never catch up to us. We couldn't slow down, however, because even if Duncan didn't find us, something else would.

I swore.

"What's that, Grace?" Ren asked, the question nearly unintelligible through his chattering teeth. Not from cold, I knew.

I shook my head, not inclined to repeat myself. My wounded thigh pained me. My ill-used muscles protested every move. I wanted to lash out at our escort, but bit my tongue as I caught the expression on the warrior nearest me. Seeing his face, I looked past him, around him, to the others. Grim-faced, they numbered one to every member of our party. Anticipating trouble, I supposed. I figured from whatever army marched into the large valley, but I supposed it could equally have meant from us. Narrowing my eyes against the ice pelting my face, I studied them. Two were the very same male and female who had attempted to bait us at Draig's table in the tavern. Spotting my gaze, a look passed between them. They dropped back.

My breath huffed out through my face covering, melding with the ice crystals already caught in the weave. I looked to Carina, finding her eyes seeking out mine. She nodded, acknowledging my sudden unease.

"Where are we going?" I asked the warrior to my right. Safely away from the fighting would not serve as a destination anymore. I wanted a real response. Although I welcomed the opportunity to get Resa far from any who might wish to make her a killer, I needed to know what we faced.

"To the deserted village, as our commander first directed," said the warrior, delivery stiff and less than eager. Kan was his name, or something sounding like that word. "We will tarry overnight to await further instruction and if none come, we continue on."

"Continue on to what place?"

"To the Lady's court, there to gather more men and decide how best to proceed."

I did not trust his answer. I sensed a lie in it and turned once more to Carina. Mika had diverted her attention. She didn't look at me.

Returning my gaze to the warrior, I watched him a moment longer before speaking. I did not think he meant a court of law. In history lessons forced upon us even in warrior's training, we had learned about courts such as I believed he referenced. They were considered both feudal and extinct. In fact, as students we had been told in plain words they no longer existed.

"Who is the Lady?" I persisted, seeking more information. "Where is her court? What lands does she rule?"

He snorted in impatience at all my questions. "You sound like the child you are."

My teeth chomped together. The ice forming on my wrap sprinkled down onto the blanket draped across Chauncy's back.

"Then enlighten me," I said, controlling anger.

"She is Lady of Gabrilon. Her name is not yours to speak. She once lived where you were recently housed, when that place was stronger, larger, more powerful. She is the honored parent of our commander."

"Draig's mother?" I blurted. The warrior shot me a look. His hands bunched into two gloved fists on his *conjure's* blanket.

Draig's mother. Considering the resemblance between Draig and his brother, Aeron, she was the Elder's as well, and therefore also Duncan's grandmother. A far cry, I would willingly bet, from Duncan's beloved Gran.

I wondered if Duncan knew any of this, if he might have learned through conversations with Marcella, with his father. *The universe intervenes somehow.* He had said that, Duncan had. I began to believe it true.

I also believed something else to be true. These warriors were not our friends. They possessed their own agenda, one that did not necessarily wish us well. I needed to pay attention, needed to alert the others somehow, to make certain they maintained their guard. I had no idea what we faced ahead. We had to be prepared for the worst.

*   *   *

By the time we reached the empty village, I could barely dismount. Forgoing my usual leap, I struggled and slid sideways, using Chauncy for leverage until my feet touched the ground. I could put no weight on the leg I had injured.

Mika appeared beside me. "You okay?"

"I will be," I said.

"Your leg's not swollen, is it?"

I shook my head. "Just oddly numb and sore. It will be all right."

Carina and Resa pushed their way through the snow to join us. The six of us stood for a moment in silence. We were meant to be seven. I felt Duncan's absence as keenly as a missing and necessary limb.

"Why are we just standing around out here?" Ren asked.

"Beats me," said Hannah, although the question had been addressed to me. I didn't know, either. Nearly hidden beneath snow and wind-beaten vegetation, the village remnants dotted the hillside pass. Our attendant warriors had halted outside the broken teeth which had once been a wall and stood a small distance away from us, discussing something in quiet voices. I heard a distant howling roar, and then another, I hoped too far away to be any concern to us.

Don't count on it.

Skelly's sudden voice in my head caused me to jump. I ignored Mika's concerned frown.

Why? I asked back. *What are they?*

How would I know? Think about it. How?

Even he seemed agitated. I pushed him down, concentrating instead on the returning feeling in my leg. I would not let him frighten me with nonsense. If he had something worthwhile to contribute, I might listen, but I had been through this before with him. Goading me, especially at my weakest. Despite my injury, I felt far stronger than I had. I would not allow him to provoke me now.

The weak winter sun did nothing to warm the air through the swirling flakes. In the gray morning, cold bit deep without the *conjures'* warmth. As if called, the two shuffled closer, blocking the shifting wind from both sides. I patted Chauncy's neck first and then the black one.

"What's his name?" I asked Mika. "Did anyone tell you?"

"Vigor," said Carina.

"Thank you, Vigor," I said softly.

"Why are we here?" Ren asked. "I know this is the place Draig wanted us to go, but that was before, to avoid occupied habitation, wasn't it? We don't need to wait for him now. I mean, why don't we just go on? There's a lot more daylight left. We could get pretty far."

"I don't know if I'd used the term daylight," Mika murmured.

"Draig planned to provide us with a more accurate direction for travel, I think," I said. "Even so, we can't go somewhere Duncan won't be able find us. We have to wait for him."

Ren wanted to argue. I could see the warring emotion in his glare, his eyes the only part of his face showing above the heavy wrapping covering nose, mouth, and throat. I didn't care what reasons he supplied. We went nowhere now without Duncan. He would catch up. He had to.

I understood Ren's anxiousness, though. We needed more distance between us and the place we had fled, needed also to travel while we could. Except we couldn't. Not until Duncan arrived. We had all been separated before. I would not let it happen again.

"Somebody should talk to that crew," Ren said, jerking a thumb over his shoulder toward the warriors still in earnest converse. "Find out why they're making us stand around in the cold instead of finding shelter."

"I'll go." I braced myself for the bitter wind and tensed the muscles in my leg so it would support me without faltering. I'd appeared weak enough in the dismount.

As I made my way around Chauncy, I slid my *lathesa* out from the blanket's weave, carrying it loose but ready in my hand. I paused at weapon's length from the group, set a crystal tip gently into the trampled snow.

"Should we not find somewhere out of the weather?" I asked, throwing the query out in a general manner. I had no wish to appear aggressive despite the weapon I carried.

Kan turned at my question. "Why? Are you cold?"

"A bit," I said, my hackles rising at his tone. "As are my friends. None of us is used to this weather."

He turned away to address a whispered comment from a companion.

"If there are no plans to seek shelter," I said, "then we shall move on. Thank you for your kindness in seeing us this far."

We were not moving on, but I hoped to force the warriors into action. They seemed to either be ignorant to our actual need for a warmer environment or they simply did not care. I would have led my friends immediately into the village if not for my worry the buildings might be ready to fall around us. These warriors were familiar with our surroundings and therefore should possess some knowledge as to any peril.

Kan jerked around to face me. "You'll need to split up, search for a suitable place, one with an intact roof and walls and not inhabited by beasts."

"Very well," I said, "except for one thing. My friends and I will stay together."

He frowned. I waited, considered his expression and the possible thought processes behind it. Did he want to divide us? If he did, why? I hated being so suspicious, but I possessed good reason. How many times had I thought I could rely on a person, a moment, a thing, and been proven wrong? The only ones I could truly count on were my companions.

"Do you not trust us?" Kan asked, echoing my thoughts, perhaps reading them in the scowl on my face.

"It is hard," I said, "to do so, when everyone around either lies, seeks to use us, or treats us like we are too young for the truth."

His eyes widened. A muscle danced in his jaw. "Ah. I see."

Do you, I thought? I doubted it. In my present frame of mind, I doubted it very much.

My group had made their way up behind me without my notice, another indication how distracted I had become. The *conjures* followed them, huge bodies dark at their backs, standing together, somehow threatening in solidarity.

"Come on," said Ren, "we'll find a place to get warm and wait for Duncan, then we'll continue on." He jutted his chin at Kan. "No reason why we can't, is there?"

The warrior exchanged a brief look with his comrades before answering. "None," he said.

I looked past them all to the nearly invisible tracks we had left when pounding up the hillside to the pass. Any trace would be obliterated soon. So long as Duncan's escort knew the way to this point, he would be with us soon, but if we went on, it didn't appear likely we could be followed.

"Let's set up camp for the day, then," I said. "When night comes, I'll take first watch."

"No," said Hannah, "I will. You need to rest."

I wished she hadn't said that in front of the warriors. I would have preferred no further attention called to my debilitated state.

We entered the village together, leaving the warriors outside. Kan had sent two back the way we had come, presumably seeking out Duncan and the rider with him. The other four took up a stance outside the damaged perimeter. I experienced some relief seeing them assume a guardian position, hoping I had misjudged surliness for hidden duplicity.

We all carried our weapons openly now, remembering what Kan had said about wild animals. I still heard those distant growling calls. The *conjures* followed us in, for which I was grateful. They provided protection and comfort and, if necessary, warmth. I feared we might sorely need them for that soon, as the buildings upon entry into the village were derelict, indeed. Roofs dipped slack as hanging cloth, exposing beams and blackened wood through stark white accumulated ice. The three boys preceded the rest of us, pushing snow from the path. Being taller than the other girls, I might have joined them, but I knew I had not the strength. Not yet.

Will you ever?

Please, Skelly, not now.

He laughed. I found the noise escaping my mouth.

"Grace?" Carina's white brows dipped down.

"I'm fine," I said.

Liar.

Shut it.

Let me out, and you'll never have to deal with me again.

Let you out, I thought back at Skelly, *and we'll all be dead. We'll never have to deal with anything again.*

So, there is an upside. Think about that.

I deliberately returned my focus to the uninhabited settlement. We had been trudging along the broken, snow-covered lane for more than five minutes. I looked back toward the wall and Draig's warriors. In the swirling, ice-filled air they appeared far away, misty and warped, like a scene viewed through the bottom of a glass. I wondered if I might be feverish again. I didn't think it likely. My mind felt too clear, my body more like my own, not dominated by flaring temperature. Ren said something I didn't quite hear. I searched him out, realized he had moved ahead of Mika, arm raised, pointing. We all hustled a little closer to where he stood waiting for us.

"Have you found something promising?" I asked.

"Right here," he said, waving his hand.

I saw nothing but more dilapidated dwellings. "Where?"

"Oh, for crying out loud, Grace," he answered, "here!"

I scanned the others for their reactions, found them as confused as I. Carina sucked in a breath. "No," she whispered.

I spun back toward Ren. He pointed at me, took a step, a single step toward me, and vanished.

Chapter Fifteen

"Where are we?"

We all rushed after Ren as soon as he disappeared, I with the thought his sudden departure meant he had dropped down into a hole. I did not know what the others believed had happened, or if it really mattered. He had vanished before our eyes and therefore needing finding. Now, so did we. I turned to Mika with the best answer to his question I could muster.

"I don't know."

In fifteen steps it seemed the world had gone from day to night. Everything we could see prior now looked shadowy and distant. In addition to the strange, sudden transformation, we all glowed. No one had yet commented on that fact. We did not glow as lanterns do, but more as if every visible follicle on our bodies had become a vehicle of light, like filaments. The two *conjures* had also thundered after us and been equally affected, the shaggy coats not blocked by congealed snow and the blankets they wore flickering with thin, white, heatless flame.

"Ren!" Hannah called, agitated, near panic.

"Hush," I directed, listening hard. Her voice hadn't carried. Neither had mine or Mika's. Until a minute ago, sounds had been echoing across visible stone walls. No longer. Everything had become muffled, as if we existed beneath a heavy blanket.

I didn't even swear. Right then I did not wish to hear the sound that was my lifeless voice.

We all stood quite still. I glanced aside at the *conjures* and realized their breath did not frost in the air. Had it gotten warmer or was there simply no breath to be seen? It occurred to me in horrifying clarity I could be dying from the cold right now and all this no more than a figment prompted by my fading imagination. Each one of us could be in the same predicament.

Something touched my hand. I, well-trained warrior, almost screamed.

Carina spoke softly. "It is real, Grace. Be calm."

"Do you know what this is?" I whispered.

"Hannah does. She's afraid to admit it out loud."

I forced my legs to move in Hannah's direction, the left one still stiff, still painful. If nothing else, that much remained real. "Hannah," I said, "what is this? You know. Carina says you do."

Hannah nodded, movement spasmodic, her respiration whistling from her nose. "I-I've heard t-tales. I can't b-believe they're true."

"What tales?" I pushed.

"M-mage craft," she said. "This place is warded."

"Warded?" I had not heard the term. "What does that mean?"

"Bound by magic. S-sealed."

"Not sealed very well," I said, rather flippantly all things considered. "We got in."

"Perhaps we were m-meant to."

I considered her words, their implication. "Like a trap?" I finally asked, my stomach pushing bile up into my throat.

"Cou-could be."

I patted her arm, hoping to quiet her, to help stop her stuttering. She drew a deep breath, released it slowly.

"We have to find Ren," she said.

"I agree." I turned from her to the others. "But we cannot blunder around blindly. We don't want to pass him in the dark, and we aren't splitting up to search either. We stay together. If it would not impede our walking, I'd tie us together at the waist. He can't have gone far, though."

"Unless there are some differences in distance now?" Mika suggested.

I shook my head, not wanting to think about the possibility. "We will start right here. He has to be somewhere close."

Shirking my pack from my shoulders, I allowed it to slip to the ground and reached inside, searching for one of the kinetic torches we'd appropriated from the kitchens. Duncan had insisted we bring them. He'd said—

I closed my eyes, pulled out the torch, shook it, keeping my head bowed, away from observance. If we were in such a place as Hannah suggested, and I had no reason given our predicament to believe she might be wrong, then Duncan would not find us. He could charge right into this place and not find us. We would lose each other in this strange, warded realm.

"Grace?"

I waved my hand, turned my head, wiped my cheek on my shoulder. "I'm going to plant this right here," I said, lowering the torch to rest on the cobbled lane. With a start, I realized no snow covered the road's surface. The clumped precipitation still clung to our clothing, to the *conjures'* hides, but the road was as clear as if no snow had ever fallen.

"I know," said Mika, watching me. "I just noticed it, too."

Unnerved, I stood with a small struggle, glancing around at the shadow-dark buildings. No snow there, either. Yet I still felt cold. Useless, I knew, to attempt to make sense regarding what I could not understand. I decided not to try and washed my hands of perception.

One step, one thought at a time.

"We'll leave the torch there, as a beacon," I said, "and search in a circle, always keeping it in sight. Agreed?"

They acknowledged me with grunts and single syllables. We moved in an oblique orbit around the torch. Chauncy and Vigor remained where they were, their hulking, comforting, glittering shadows hovering near the light a good marker for our progress and for our return.

The small glow from everyone's hair follicles distracted vision, made us each believe we had spotted something, despite the light from the fireball Hannah produced. Frustratingly, we found no obvious sign of Ren in the outside areas, on the road, between structures, behind odd boxes and barrels. The bright orb highlighted buildings intact but empty. Glass panes threw the light back at us, as well as our reflections in unexpected movement. Nerves stretched thin.

"Carina," I said, "can't you sense him?"

"I'm trying." At her side, holding tight to her hand, Resa watched the shadows. I wondered what she saw there, or if her mind had traveled to some foreign land, some distant place we would never see. With her cognizance as to her immediate surroundings waxing and waning, I wondered, too, if Resa even knew her brother remained absent from the group.

"We'll have to go inside," Mika said, indicating the nearest building with a nod.

Although we all knew this to be true, we stood and stared for an entire minute at the stout door. Finally, I hefted my *lathesa* with a quick toss, balancing it in my grip. The hum from Mika's glass cutter seemed overloud in the silence following my action.

I went first, trying not to limp, lifted the latch on the door, shoved the barrier open. It flew back noiselessly until it struck the wall. I swore, shoulders jerking, half expecting something to jump out at me in anger. When nothing happened, I stepped inside. Hannah followed right behind me, holding the brilliant orb above our heads.

"No. Oh, no, no, no," she whispered.

I spotted what she did at the exact same second.

"It's not him, Hannah," I said. "Look at the clothes."

It could not have been Ren anyway, could it? I figured not only the clothes but the condition of the body precluded it being him, but if something like time ran at a different rate within the warded boundary, Ren's body might well have been reduced to a pale brown skeleton and even the clothes could be his. I hurried over and bent from my waist to study the body, frowning, biting my lower lip. A ruby ring glittered on one bone finger. On close examination, I saw the garments were not any style I recognized, and definitely not the utilitarian garb from Kerrick we all wore.

"Not him," I said again.

"Then who?"

I shook my head. The clothing might once have been a different color, an odd fabric or perhaps fur, but the color had faded, browned, become almost desiccated.

"What the heck is that?"

I glanced back at Mika. "A dead person," I said unnecessarily. At least he didn't speculate out loud whether it might be our lost companion. I straightened, catching sight as I did the thin, dark brown hank of hair still clinging to the skull. Definitely not Ren.

Turning slowly, I studied the room. A tavern, I thought, albeit a small one. Bar, shelves, chairs, tables, everything empty. Webs from disuse hung from every imaginable edge, corner, crevice. And yet it looked as though it had never been anything more than empty, a shell for who knew what reason.

"I can't see any obvious cause he died," said Mika, scrutinizing the body from a distance with lifted chin and a frown.

"Maybe he died because he was stuck here," I said. "There is no food, nothing to drink. We're lucky we have what we brought in with us. We need to find Ren and then a way free from this place."

"Do you think Draig's warriors knew about the warding?" Carina asked. "Maybe that's why they didn't pass through the outside boundary. Maybe that's why they made us go in alone."

The thought had occurred to me, as soon as I realized the warded place might be a trap, in fact. I had not wanted to hold onto the suspicion. I could not help its return now Carina had spoken. Believing this could be true only made our position more precarious. Duncan's too, once he caught up with us. I began to worry he might never do so, if Draig planned to separate us. If I had agreed to Kan's demand we split up and search for shelter, would the warriors have divided us male and female and pushed Carina, Resa, Hannah and me toward the warded territory? And done what with the boys? I refused to speculate on that. I needed a clear head. In this place, a clear head would be hard won.

"Ren!" Hannah shouted.

I didn't like the sound, the deadened, flat, failing sound. I resisted the urge to clap my hand over Hannah's mouth, listened to her call again and again. "Enough," I said. "We're going about this the wrong way."

"What do you mean?" Mika asked.

I eyed the dead man on the floor. "It seems this place is designed for trickery. I'm still freezing, actually shivering, yet there is no snow, no ice, no wind to be seen or felt. Is it possible we are all still standing outside in the village and only our minds are here?"

Mika cocked his head in thought. "All our minds, together? Is that possible?"

Shaking my head, I turned and started for the door. "I don't know. Maybe I'm only seeing all of you, and you're each seeing something else. No connection, only different, what, illusions?"

Mika made a desperate sound, reflecting exactly what I felt. Desperation. Confusion. A clawing panic. Carina hurried after me, Resa in tow, and closed her fingers on my wrist.

"It's real," she said. "This is real."

"You would say that, though, in my head, wouldn't you? It is what I want to hear."

Carina tightened her grip. My breath stilled in my chest. The dark places around me shifted into black as she shut me down.

*   *   *

I stirred to warmth, to a glow against my shut lids. Opening my eyes, I found myself close to leaping flames and sat up, scooting away. To be honest, once I had, I knew I had been in no danger, but for the briefest instant upon awakening I had imagined myself burning.

"Where did you find the wood?" I asked, though to no one in particular. I couldn't see anyone. I did not look around, as I feared I might find myself alone, or worse, with someone or something I didn't know.

"We broke up some chairs from the tavern." I glanced up at Hannah, shuffling over to the fire with her arms filled with shattered wood. She placed the pieces into the flames one by one, eyeing me sidelong.

"I feel the heat," I said uncertainly.

"Do you still believe this to be some sort of mind construct?" Mika questioned, coming toward me now holding out the battered cup from my pack filled with some steaming concoction. He forced it into my hands. I felt the warmth from it, too, seeping into the wrap around my hands and fingers.

I frowned down at the contents. "What else can it be?"

He sighed. "Listen to yourself, Grace. You, who by your very heritage, knows mage craft exists. Why are you questioning this?"

Because I don't trust any of it, I thought. Not even you, Mika.

Good girl, Skelly murmured.

I shook my head like a beast bothered by an insect. Mika and Hannah exchanged a quick, uncertain look.

"Where are the other two?" I asked.

"Resting," Mika answered.

"And Ren? Have you found any sign of him?"

"No," said Hannah.

"Not yet," Mika added quickly.

I brought the cup to my nose, took a small sip, pushed the liquid around inside my mouth, swallowed with great reluctance. "How long have I been lying here?"

"A while," Hannah whispered. She began shoving embers around with a stick, causing them to flare beneath the newly added wood. Her vivid red hair stuck out like the serrated leaves on a *crerberry* bush. I imagined mine looked about the same. Not that I cared. I wasn't caring about much right then.

Mika lowered himself onto the ground beside me. "You know what I've been thinking?"

I can't imagine, said Skelly. I squeezed my eyelids shut, opened them again.

"What?" I prompted Mika, even though I would have preferred he go away.

"Remember you told me they were making the replicants at All Dwellers?"

Listless and disinterested, I nodded, took another drink from my cup, then wondered why I had.

"Grace!"

"What?"

"I've been talking to you and you're not even listening."

"Yes," I said, "you asked me if I remembered the replicants they were manufacturing at All Dwellers."

Hannah looked back at us from the fire, where she continued to toy with the flames. "That was about five minutes ago."

I dropped my face into my hands, breathing deeply the air drifting between my fingers. "I'm sorry. Would you mind repeating what you said?"

A silence followed my request and I peeked between my pointer and middle finger to find them exchanging another look. I told you so, Hannah mouthed at him.

"Go ahead," I said, slapping my hands onto my knees. "I'm paying attention."

Mika twisted his mouth. I noted scraggly hairs along his jaw, near his upper lip. He had removed his headgear so close to the fire. His once bald head sprouted with fine, golden-brown hairs. I tried to remember clearly how he first appeared to me, showing up at my cell door with Skelly Shane. He hadn't looked as healthy as he did now, if I recalled with any accuracy. The hardships we had faced had toughened him, made him stronger. I supposed everyone had become more like that with each passing day. Except me. I had obviously gone backward.

Before Mika could speak, a soft, almost noiseless step fell to my left. I turned to find Carina gazing at me, her eyes the same color as the flames.

"Stop feeling sorry for yourself, Grace Irese," she said. "This isn't who you are."

"Is that what I'm doing?" I said, meeting her vivid gaze, my sarcasm evident.

She ignored my mockery. I was glad she chose not to latch onto it. Deep down inside, I remembered I didn't treat my friends this way.

Carina crouched down beside me encased in her oversized suit from Kerrick, her natural grace undiminished. "We want to help you."

"I don't need any help." I wondered at my obstinance even as I spoke. Carina's gaze dropped to my jacket front, to the place where the bag and its crystal hung beneath my clothes, heavy and burning against my breastbone. I knew what she was thinking. She believed my distress arose from the thing I carried, from Skelly. She could believe what she wanted. Something else tormented me, far beyond the entity in the crystal, beyond my injury, beyond Duncan's absence and Ren's disappearance, beyond the darkness in which we found ourselves.

Sucking in a breath, I shimmied around to face

Mika. At my movement, Hannah ceased her fussing with the fire and faced us, too.

"What about the replicants, Mika? What were you trying to tell me?"

"I wasn't trying," he said. "I was."

"Okay. Understood. Won't you tell me again? I—I somehow missed what you were saying."

"Too late," he muttered, turning to look over my shoulder. Carina grasped my sleeve.

"We can help you," she repeated, her gaze once again on the place where Skelly lay hidden. "But you have to give it up freely in order for us to carry it for you."

"What? No," I said, jerking my arm away. Quite suddenly, I realized we no longer glowed, not even the *conjures,* their shadows hulking beyond the firelight. I drew up my knees, both knees as if the pain in the damaged leg did not exist, and pressed my forehead hard against them, attempting to think.

I was not the only one affected by this place. My friends were all tainted by it. Off, somehow. I had never known Mika to be petulant. Not since being together at the facility, anyway, and that had only been once or twice. Carina was not aggressive in nature, and Hannah...well, Hannah baffled me as to her difference, but it existed. I sensed it. Oh, yes. Right. Except for the heatless flame-ball she created, the only magic bequeathed to her by genetics through her mage ancestry, she feared fire.

I shot to my feet, the pain in my leg suddenly back in force, causing me to stumble sideways. I swore. My voice no longer echoless, words seared through my brain like a scream. Not only my words, my voice, but others. I looked around, desperate to find their source. One hand dipped into my pocket, the other began to stray toward the crystal around my neck, as if I had no control over them. My gaze fell on Resa, whose mouth had opened. Whatever she had been about to say disappeared in thunder when the world exploded all around us.

Chapter Sixteen

Resa couldn't speak. I knew that. Why had I expected her to? It didn't matter now. They were gone, all my friends. The darkness, too. Light shone everywhere like the brightest day, but suffused somehow, as though I lay behind a gauzy screen. I remembered tales from when I was very young about a place such as this, light and airy and without pain. I knew I had not gone there. Everything ached, right down to the hairs on my head, a feeling that had grown quite familiar to me. I moved toes, fingers, twisted my neck from side to side with care to assure myself my extremities remained intact, my head still on my shoulders. Which, of course, it did. I possessed awareness, after all, and not only could

I see the white expanse of nothing, suddenly I could hear.

"Gods, Grace, please wake up." I recognized the voice straightaway. Ren's face appeared in my line of vision.

"Ren," I said. "You're here."

He straightened, stood against an utterly barren white backdrop. His clothing, his face, even his ridiculous yellow hair looked dark against it. "I never went anywhere," he said.

"You did."

"No," he said, "you did."

His response had nothing to do with a typical Ren argument. He meant what he said. Believed it. Was right?

"Just me, or all of us?"

"Just you."

I moaned, dropped my head back, shut my eyes. "And where am I now?"

"Right where you were when I was talking to you."

I considered this for a short time. Shivers coursed through my sore body and an understanding dawned that the white I saw all around had to be the snow. I turned my head, looked right, narrowed my eyes to bring decrepit buildings into focus, dark against accumulated drifts.

Something uncomfortable rested against my spine, forcing me into an awkward position. My pack. It had to be. I raised both arms, asked something it galled me to request. "Could you help me up?"

Ren complied in silence, yanking me upright without grace or form. I stood a moment gaining my legs, spotting something in the trampled snow where I had been lying. I bent, scooping the object into my fist.

"What's that?" Ren asked.

"It belongs to Hannah," I said, shoving the icon back into my pocket. "Where is everyone else?"

"We split up to look for you. I volunteered to stay here, in case you returned to the same place you'd vanished."

I closed my eyes, shook my head again in short movements. Split up. No. "How long have they been gone?"

"Not very. A minute or two?"

My face screwed up in concentration. I felt the cold skin pucker and pinch. "And how long was I not here?"

"Five? It was weird. You went down as if a heavy net had been thrown over you and just vanished. Totally vanished. I checked the ground where it happened, in case you'd slipped into a hole. Nothing was there. Not even you."

I had worried the same thing had happened to Ren. Maybe he had said something, therefore influencing my thoughts. Unnerved, I looked first one way up the snow-covered road and then back again, to the place where Draig's warriors should be, outside the broken-down walls. They were there, still pacing beside their animals. Kan turned in my direction and then away.

In the other world or consciousness or whatever I might finally settle on calling it, I'd been thinking they had been aware we entered a dangerous place and had deliberately stayed outside. Would I find that yet to be true?

Expelling a breath, I returned my attention to Ren. "Where are the *conjures*?"

He jerked his chin. "There," he said. "They haven't moved. I think maybe they were waiting."

I spun and looked. Chauncy and Vigor stood snow-covered beside the nearest building, their heads down but eyes on me, each horn tapping the other's, scraping along serrated corkscrew edges, making the noise I'd been hearing in the place I had gone, like voices. Calling me back? Because I was back. I understood I had returned to reality, experienced the knowledge in my body's every cell. But where had I been? And how?

There's danger here, Skelly said quietly. *I tried to warn you. You were determined to ignore me.*

I clapped my hand on Ren's arm. "We have to find the others now." The words had only passed my lips when I heard my name and turned to find Carina and Resa hurrying toward me, Resa in the lead, dragging Carina behind her. I met them halfway. Resa began signing frantically. Unlike Duncan, I couldn't understand her rapid-fire speech. I indicated as much, hoping she was paying attention enough to catch it. Her fingers fluttered to a halt, folded together. She lifted her gaze to my face, her eyes moving back and forth, searching for who knew what. Abruptly, she threw herself forward, wrapping her arms around my waist.

"You're safe," Carina said.

"Yes," I said, "quite."

"No," Carina corrected me, "I am telling you that you are safe now. This is what I am getting from Resa. You are safe now."

I crouched, staring into Resa's face, into her dark brown eyes nearly hidden beneath the dragging snow on her headgear. Her wind-chapped skin showed ruddy pink against the brown. "Did you bring me back?" I whispered to her, articulating the words carefully. Sometimes she could tell what a person said, if the words were made clear on the lips speaking them. But she had no response.

"From where, Grace?" Carina asked, eyes wide, pale face blanching beneath the cold-induced purple blush. "Bring you back from where?"

"I don't know. You were all there—all except Ren—but I started to realize no one was real, they were not you, not the people I know, somehow. Like a dream, a lot more time passed than the five minutes Ren said I was gone." I stared hard at Carina. "But I wasn't dreaming, was I?"

She shook her head, mouth opening and closing while she figured out what to say. "Maybe you were dreaming, but you weren't here. You had vanished."

I swore. I really had to stop doing that.

"Mika!" Carina abruptly called out.

I glanced over my shoulder. Hannah and Mika pushed their way through the snow between two buildings and hurried over.

"We were so worried!" Hannah cried. "Where were you?"

"Right over there," I said with a toss of my head. "I never left. At least, I don't believe I left. Hannah, what does 'warding' mean? As in something being warded."

She gave a little gasp, eyebrows arching. "Grace, I—"

"You told me the village was warded in my dream, or whatever it was. Is this something you know about?"

"You weren't dreaming," Hannah said. "You were gone."

"Gone and dreaming," said Ren, who had come up behind us. Reaching around, he handed me my *lathesa*, which I assumed had been somewhere on the snowy ground. I thanked him with a wordless nod.

"And I don't know how you heard that," Hannah added.

"Were you talking about warding?"

"No," she said, "thinking about it."

I turned to Mika. "You, were you thinking about the replicants?"

He jerked, startled. "Well, yeah, I had a theory that maybe you hadn't disappeared at all and we were under the influence of some perception filter. I mean, the replicant application seemed to rely on perception, didn't it?" He frowned at me, his brows twisting like tree roots.

I didn't understand anything that had happened. Had I, in whatever state I had been in, found myself able to listen in on my friends' thoughts? Was such a connection the reason they populated my dream, if, in fact, it was a dream?

"Grace," said Carina, "this is real. Be calm."

"You said that, too," I shouted. I didn't mean to shout. I held no anger, only fear. I would need so many questions answered when we finally reached our destination.

"I'm sorry," I said to Carina at her wounded expression, then turned to Hannah, still standing beside Ren. "Hannah, how big can a ward be? An entire village? Or only a single person?"

She shook her head, shoulders lifting and falling. "I've only heard tales. Many of us have. I've never met anyone who had the ability to do what you're talking about."

"I don't like this place anyway," Ren said. "I don't like the way it feels. We should just move on, leave them behind." He tossed his hand up in a rude gesture toward the warriors outside.

"We can't," I said. "We wait for Duncan."

For a full second, no one spoke, until Carina reached out and tapped my hand. "But not here, I think? We'll find shelter nearby."

I had no desire to argue, and everyone else appeared more than willing to find a place beyond the damaged village walls to settle until Duncan came.

If he comes.

Skelly, I don't want to hear anything more from you.

But you do. You'll be begging for me to talk before long.

No, I won't, I shot back at him, despising myself for letting him reduce me to the last word. I shrugged my pack into a more comfortable position and led the way away from Draig's surly warriors to a higher elevation at the village's far end. From where we had been standing, I had spotted trees closely grown. They would serve. We had sheltered in worse.

*　*　*

We watched in rotation, leaving those not involved in the task to stay close to the fire. I'd have thought the smoke would call Kan and the others near, but possibly seeing it they assumed rightly that we had camped. Even so, I could not understand why they stayed below. The snow had ceased to fall and I clearly saw them settled down right where they had been, but without the benefit of fire to keep them warm. Their *conjures* had circled around them, however, and they had taken refuge within the snug boundary.

Standing guard with Hannah—it had been decided no one would stand alone—I chewed on a bit of bread slathered in some viscous stuff and toasted over the flames. As with the actual campsite, the heavy greenery in the branches overhead had kept the ground around us clear from snow. I stood with my back against the large trunk, letting it support me as I took the weight off my wounded leg. A few minutes earlier I had pushed myself a bit too far in my attempts at exercise.

Hannah had positioned herself on the opposite

side so we had a view in all directions. She talked quite a bit despite the tree barrier between us. I had not expected any less, although I could not always hear her words and only answered sporadically. It seemed she didn't require my answers anyway.

Chauncy and Vigor had each taken a turn disappearing into the forest to hunt, returning bloodied and sated. They hadn't left the campsite since. Their proximity reassured me, as I could still hear those distant, howling growls. The sounds had not gotten any closer, but actual hunting might be performed in silence.

The blue shadows had grown long while Hannah and I stood watch. Night would be upon us soon and still no sign of Duncan and his escort. I wondered if he would come at all and hastily pushed back at Skelly before he commented on my thought. But depending on how fierce the battle breaking out around his parents' settlement, perhaps he couldn't. Perhaps even now—

I pushed that thought away, too.

I should have stayed, would have if not for the *conjures* strange behavior and the arrival of Draig and his warriors to see us away. I had trusted Chauncy and Vigor's motivation, as unfathomable as it might be. I did not quite trust the purpose driving the warriors, though. Their behavior struck me as just so odd.

I remembered Draig urging us to ride on to this

abandoned place. For shelter, he said. Yet his own warriors appeared reluctant to enter it. I couldn't blame them. Whatever had happened to me in there unnerved me still. But they had not stopped us when we went in search of a place to hunker down and had not accompanied us either.

Ren was right, we should move on, but without Duncan, without some word Duncan would not be joining us, I refused to budge.

Don't wait too long.

Is there something you know, Skelly, that you'd like to share?

Of course not.

I shut my eyes, opened them, responded to something Hannah had said, realized my words were inappropriate when she came around the trunk and frowned at me, head cocked to one side.

"I'm sorry," I apologized. "I wasn't paying attention."

"That's for sure. I—" Her eyes widened, looking past me. My head snapped around to follow her gaze. I shoved myself away from the tree, took a few steps forward, sweeping a snow-laden branch aside with my arm.

In the streets below, the midnight blue snow-shadow darkened, congealed, became quite black. It grew as I watched, spreading like water, like a slowly rising flood, over the streets, the buildings.

"It's them, isn't it?" Hannah whispered. "Those

creatures, like the one Chauncy killed."

I shook my head, watching a dome form, expand, lift higher into the darkening sky. "No, not them," I said, impatient. "Those creatures walk like you or I, but horribly. Look at it, Hannah. It's one thing, expanding. Is it possibly a ward? Something designed to encapsulate the village? Maybe to trap us?"

She sucked in a breath. Her fingers slapped down on my wrist. "It could be. I don't know. But it is growing. Who's to say it won't reach us here?"

I told you. Or tried to. You need to learn to listen, Grace.

Grabbing Hannah's hand, I tugged her back to the campsite, kicking snow over the flames upon arrival. A hiss filled the air. Smoke billowed. I waved it away.

"What gives?" Ren demanded, reeling back and swinging his arms around.

"Throw everything into your packs and mount up. We're leaving."

"Going where?" Ren again. I did not respond. I helped Resa and Carina onto Vigor's back, once Mika had thrown the blanket over the *conjure*. Mika leaped up behind. Chauncy went down on all fours for me. I ordered Ren and Hannah on first, taking a minute to tie a strip torn from the cloth about my face to the nearest tree, the knotted side facing uphill.

"What's that for?" Hannah asked.

"For Duncan," I said. "To let him know he's going the right way."

The right way meant he would have to come straight through the village. It couldn't be helped. I had no way to warn him off. All I could do was hope that if the warding had been set as a trap it hadn't been set for the likes of him.

Duncan

Chapter Seventeen

I'd not been born a fighter. I rarely got into scuffles growing up. While Grace had been in warrior school or whatever they called it, I'd been hitting up marks in the casinos and surrounding environs without so much as a scraped knuckle. So, when I looked down, spotted the blood on my clothes, I figured it belonged to me. It couldn't have come from someone else. I didn't do that, didn't cause blood to bloom from another, despite my occasional fantasies about punching Ren in the nose. Thus deluded, I began to prod my body, searching for injury. Finding nothing frightening there, I felt my face, my head. No wounds.

"Oh, hell," I said and sat down abruptly in the snow. I didn't look around, kept my eyes averted from the skirmish nearby as the last of the attackers succumbed to death, fear or surrender. Many had retreated, running away into the woods, perhaps to regroup and return. I'd heard the attackers referred to as a vanguard. Forerunners, I supposed to a further army. How far back the other soldiers remained, I had no idea. No one did. Scouts had once again been sent out to determine.

Draig's warriors were fierce and mobile, a good thing for those who resided in my father's domain. The people here seemed, if not ill-prepared, at least unused to battle. Others warriors had been summoned to join Draig in the fight by his mother, his and Aeron's. My grandmother, commanding battle-hardened troops. I tried to picture what she might look like, but stopped short when I visualized my Gran, my only Gran as far as I was concerned, in combatant's gear.

Fingers reached down in front of my face. "Need a hand?"

Shame-faced, I took Draig's grasp and stood.

"Are you hurt?" he asked.

I shook my head. "Not my blood." The words sickened me.

"Good. We need to get the wounded off the field and inside. Are you able?"

"Of course," I mumbled, and followed him.

I'd heard talk the six that had gone with Grace, my sister and the others had not returned. Apparently, they weren't meant to. The warriors were to keep them safely away from here and move them on, if need be. The plan as described seemed rather vague and sketchy and I wondered what part or parts Draig left out. I didn't entirely trust him. I couldn't entirely trust him. Even if we, my friends and I, hadn't been in situations where trust had either been misplaced or didn't exist, it was hard to possess a general faith in people when once upon a time you'd made your living through trickery and manipulation.

I assisted several who could walk to make their way back inside the boundary wall, then returned with the stretcher bearers to transport the rest, taking them to the room where Grace had been kept. It was full now, and other rooms besides. According to Lyric and people like her, people better equipped to judge, casualties were not as severe as they could have been and losses were minimal. I had to take their word for it. Everything looked bad to me.

As soon as I could, I wandered away. I couldn't appear hurried, because someone might question my intent. I pushed through the repaired kitchen doors and headed straight for the bunker where the children, a handful of women and most elderly had taken refuge. My mother was there with Toma. She hadn't wanted to be. She had wanted to be fighting beside her husband. Hard to believe, my mom going into battle. I'd been less than kind in my disagreement. In the end, she'd gone underground with him, her youngest son.

I spotted Toma the second I walked in. She said he looked like me, Mom did. I couldn't see it. The hair, maybe, but there the similarities stopped. He looked too much like his father—our father. Skinny now, Toma had the bone structure of someone who might bulk out, like Aeron. I had Pops' build, my mother's father. Lanky, often too thin, no hope of ever being musclebound and scary.

Sprawled across the floor, Toma and several other kids played a game I didn't recognize. It seemed to involve little glass balls and things that looked like large seeds in a chalked circle on the stone. Beyond them, packed supplies had been piled against the wall. Near the door. The door they would all take into a passage to a natural cave somewhere, and then on should things go badly.

I let out a long, slow breath, took a step forward. My foot struck something metal, causing it to zing across the floor with a whine. Toma turned at the noise, spotted me, pushed up from the floor and ran at me headlong. I stopped him midjump, to keep him from getting smeared with the still-wet blood on my clothes. I held him out at arm's length, my muscles protesting.

"Did we win?" he asked.

"Not yet."

His face sagged in disappointment. "So, we're stuck down here?"

"For now." I lowered him to his feet. "What's that you were playing?"

"Conks and Chasers. It's fun. Wanna try?"

"I'll watch," I said, stepping closer. "For a little while. I have to get back."

He took up his place once more on the floor, scooped up a glass ball and shot it into the seeds bunched center in the circle. They scattered, much to Toma's delight.

"Where's Resa?" he asked, glancing up, then back down to the game, picking up another ball. His tongue slipped out in concentration as he aimed it. The point appeared to be nothing more than to knock all the seeds from the circle.

"Didn't your—weren't you told?"

He shook his dark head, sent the glass ball scooting across the uneven floor, missing his target altogether.

"She left with Grace and the others," I said.

"I hope they're far away."

I hoped so, too. Away and safe.

"I like the way she talks," Toma went on. My respiration caught with a hitch until Toma raised his hands, moved his fingers, the arrangements resembling the figuration for hello.

"Who taught you that?" Not Grace. I couldn't imagine she'd had the time with Toma. "Carina?"

"I did."

At my mother's voice, my spine stiffened. I spun on my heel to face her.

"You're hurt!" she cried.

"I'm fine," I responded. Coldly, I knew. "You know how to sign? You didn't, when you were on Reilly last."

She folded her hands in front of her waist. "No. I learned later."

"Why?"

"In case—"

"Don't say in case you ever saw her again. You know you had no plans to see either one of us again."

I noted Toma watching and immediately regretted my words. Not because they weren't true, but because he didn't need to hear them. Taking a steadying breath, I dropped the subject. "There's been a break in the fighting. I just came down to see how Toma is doing."

"I see. He's content with his friends. I'm doing well, too," she added with a tone like a jab.

"Good," I said, jerking my head in a funny little nod. One I couldn't help, even though it made me think of the puppets I'd seen at a passing show in the casino. Looking back, it seemed odd, a show for kids in a place like that.

We stood for another minute or so in awkward silence, my eyes on Toma as he returned to his game with his friends. Someone else took a turn, since Toma had missed, and the play continued. "Toma," I said, "I'll be back."

"Promise?"

Strange word, his choosing it. Little cold feet tramped down my spine. "I promise," I said.

I left without saying anything else to my mother. I felt eyes on me, though, and turned once, expecting to see her gaze boring into my back. But she'd gone. It was Toma who watched and I heard his voice in recall in my head: *Promise?* I nodded at him, raised my hand in a quick gesture, wondered if perhaps I really had heard his voice piercing my own thoughts just then, wondered if this might be his gift. But maybe he didn't have one. Maybe, like me, he was quite ordinary.

*   *   *

The scouts returned with news. Another snowstorm was making its way into the mountains. The attacking army had retreated to set up camp at a lower elevation. I asked whose fighters they might be and although my question had been tolerated, perhaps due to my relationship to Aeron, no one possessed an answer. Draig had taken me aside, wanting to know my thoughts.

In more detail than I'd provided previously, I told him what I knew about the Lyoness and her Wildron warriors, as well as the replicants, and also about Stone Tiran. We'd discussed the creatures from Emerald since the meeting. The others— soldiers and warriors—were human, putting them into the same basic category. The beasts constituted a threat with a difference that needed to be drummed in. Fortunately, they hadn't been present among those we'd recently fought.

Walking with Draig across open ground, snow trampled and bloodied, I suddenly remembered a dream I'd had the night before. Grace had been calling my name. She hadn't sounded distraught or desperate or even particularly annoyed the way she sometimes could. It had almost been like she slept, too, and had accidentally called out. I'd woken up with the unnerving feeling she and the others had gone very far away. Determined to find out where they'd been taken, I questioned Draig.

"Kan has said—"

"Who?" I interrupted.

"One of my captains. He and five others accompanied your friends."

"So, he's come back? Without them? Where are they? Why—"

Draig cut me short. "I thought to secure them in a place where they would be kept safe until they could be moved on."

With recent experience, the word 'secure' caught my attention. To me, secure meant a cage, a cell, a sentence. "Secure? Explain that."

He tossed his head. The beads in his tangled hair clacked together. His hand fisted at his side. "I don't need to explain my decisions to you. It doesn't matter anyway. They've gone on, on their own. My warriors would not—did not go after them."

I caught his stumble and wondered at it. Perhaps Resa had done her thing and frightened them off. Whatever had happened, wherever they'd gone, I feared I wouldn't be able to find them, wouldn't see them again. Ever.

Draig studied me, lips twisted, brow furrowed. "This war isn't what you think it is," he said.

"Since I don't know all that much about it," I quipped, "that's not surprising."

His fisted hand came up and I stepped back, but he merely brushed his beaded hair over his shoulder. "There's more at work here, binding them all in a common pursuit, but not the way they see it."

"The Darkness, you mean? And I don't think I'm wrong in assuming that word carries a capital D in this case."

His shoulders jerked. His hand dropped to his

side. He stared at me without speaking, hard expression revealing nothing of his thoughts.

"A man who helped me and Mika and the other escapees from the glass mines, he told me. Everyone instigating and directing the fighting has their own separate, private reasons and believes they'll come out on top individually, no matter who else is involved, and that's never going to happen. It's not meant to ever happen. Something else is behind this. I'm afraid Kerrick couched his explanation in mysterious references, but I do know one thing. He scared the living hell out of me."

Draig turned away, staring toward the snowbound forest. "If you knew this, why didn't you mention it before?"

"What would be the point? I'm not sure anyone can do a thing about it."

"You're wrong," he whispered, harsh and low.

"And you might be lying to yourself," I said.

He moved, quickly, and was gone before I had picked myself up off the ground. A small hand clutched my soiled sleeve, pulled. I allowed myself to be helped up and stood a moment brushing snow from my hands and tentatively touching my sore jaw before looking around. When I did finally pivot to find who'd aided me, I spotted Brand, dressed as always in his hunting attire. He was definitely stronger than his size.

"Thanks. Why aren't you in the bunker with the other young ones?"

Brand shrugged. "Too old."

"How old are you?" I asked.

"Why? Does it matter?"

"Call me curious."

"Older'n you think, I'm sure. I'll reach thirteen years, soon 'nough."

Wow. Yeah, he was right. I never would have guessed that. Tiny, like my sister. Maybe some here were, in an inherited trait.

Brand lifted his chin, jutted it out away from his collar. "Do you want to find 'm?"

"Draig? Not really. I'll steer clear of him for a bit, thank you." I rubbed my jaw for emphasis. Brand shifted himself around until he stood right in front of me. He tipped his head back, scowling.

"Not 'im. Them others that were with you. The hurt girl and your sister an' the rest."

I exhaled, gaping, grasping what he'd said. "Do you know where they are?"

"Nah," he said, shaking his head and the furred hood on it. "But I can track."

I looked over my shoulder, following Draig's movements across the compound. He was met on the far side by several warriors. I turned back to Brand.

"What about the snow?" I asked him.

He glanced around, then back at me with a face crumpled in scorn. "What about it?"

"I'm not talking about what's on the ground. I'm talking about what's coming."

"The storm moves slow. We 'ave five hours. Could be six."

I frowned. "That's not what I heard. The army has hunkered down because of it."

He made another face. One my Gran would never have tolerated. "Because they don' know better," he sneered.

"And you do?"

The look he gave me now clearly said *of course, I do, you moron.* I didn't much like it, but I waited for his answer.

"Weather. Animals," he said. "Those are my gifts."

"Oh."

"What are yours?"

I didn't answer. I didn't need to. He snorted.

"Then you trust," he said. Not a question. An order. This kid was too much. I'd thought him annoying when I figured his age to be so much younger than mine. Now I knew the gap to be less, my cold cheeks heated in anger. But he did have skills I didn't and never would.

"Yeah," I said, "I trust you."

He nodded, started past me and paused a short distance away. "First, you need different clothes. You stink. Blood'll bring the beasts."

He began walking again. I caught up with him in two strides. "No, first," I said, "I need to see my mom."

Brand stopped short, turned his head, his eye-roll saved until he could be sure I saw it.

"About my brother," I clarified.

"Right. I'll come there."

I couldn't be sure if he meant to accompany me, but after a minute he turned off and trotted away. I kept going until I reached the place I'd hidden my pack, stocked and ready. Shoving my arm into the crevice between two large foundation stones, I felt around for the straps, grabbed them, yanked the pack out and fit it under my arm before hurrying back to the bunker.

I didn't know what I would say to Toma when I saw him. I really didn't want to leave him here, but I recognized the dangers were greater with me. On the surface I believed I could keep him safe, but the dark doubt deep inside had quickly advanced to the lead in my inner argument.

At the heavy, subterranean door, I paused. Collecting myself. Seeking forgiveness for my decision to walk away from the only brother I had. But he wasn't alone. As Aeron and Marcella's acknowledged offspring, he had a whole army to protect him. My friends, well, they had each other, but they also needed me. I believed that still. We were better together.

When I pushed the door open, I discovered my mom and Aeron talking only a few feet away. They turned as one, saw me, eyes then moving in unison to the pack I held secure beneath my arm. Mom shook her head, hurried forward. She snatched at my elbow, opened her mouth. For a moment I thought she might beg me to stay.

"You can't take him," she said. "You can't take Toma."

I jerked back, the air rushing from my mouth. I felt like I'd been physically tackled, yet somehow still stood. "I know," I said. "I know that."

Suddenly, she had both arms around me, her face pressed against my bloody shoulder. Her gratitude made every muscle in me tighten, made me want to push her away. Instead, I patted her spine in an awkward rhythm, trying to accept her concern for the child she'd been raising over those she had abandoned.

"Duncan," she whispered.

Don't say thank you, I thought feverishly. *Don't say thank you.*

"Duncan," she said again, "you'll come with us. Please come with us."

It took me a full five seconds to understand what she'd said. When I did, I stepped away, set her back with my hands on her upper arms, studied her with a confused expression I could feel, twisted brows, tensing jaw.

"Come with you where?"

"Gabrilon," she said.

I shook my head, lifted a shoulder, perplexed by the reference.

"Your grandmother's lands. Draig has offered some of his warriors to escort all here in the bunker to her court, and the rest will remain to fight. It's foolish to stay. He's certain we'll be overrun once the full force is sent forward. It's best to go now, before there are ships in the sky to spot us, before the snow can delay our departure."

Dropping my hands, I shook my head again. "Not my grandmother. My Gran works in a casino on Reilly. She lives in a little house about a quarter the size of this room. She raised me, took care of me, took care of Resa while she could. I hope she is safe up there on the gambling moon, that Reilly is too inconvenient for conquest. Why haven't you asked after her, your own mother? She took you in, both times you came to her. She loves your children as her own."

My mother's mouth dropped open. Her eyes glittered. Aeron stepped up to her side. "Son," he said.

Son? Had he just called me son? No. He was looking at Toma, squeezed between them, watching.

But he said the word again. To me, his eyes on mine.

"Son, what do you need? What can I give you to aid you in finding your friends? Draig told me they went on without his warriors' assistance."

"I don't need anything," I said. "Brand has offered to join me, to track them."

Aeron looked for a moment as though he might object, but he subsided without comment, only a nod.

"We could use a *conjure* to carry us," I suggested. "If one will accept me. I don't know that any will, but I can try. Are they still here or have they been freed?"

"They're here," Aeron said. "But you'd better hurry. They're not ours. They serve Draig and those who ride with him. In his present frame of mind, I don't know that he'll take kindly to you commandeering one."

I thanked him, reached out and shook his hand. When I let go, he yanked something from his finger and handed it to me. I turned the ring with its large red stone over on my palm.

"What's this?"

"It's mine," he said. "My ring of office. I'm giving it to you. It may get you through places where you might otherwise not be allowed to pass. And if not, you can always trade it in a time of need."

"I don't—"

"Take it."

I slipped it onto my finger beneath the fabric wrapped around my hands. The ring felt strange, heavy, like something I didn't really want, but I didn't return it. It meant a great deal to him, to who he was, and he had given it to me. I didn't know what to say except thank you.

"I'm sorry," he said.

"Don't," I responded. "It's…" I swallowed the words *too late* and said instead, "It really doesn't matter now. Toma?" I crouched down, yanked him into a one-armed hug. "Stay safe. We'll see each other again, okay?"

His arms tightened around my neck for a moment before he abruptly let go and stood back, squaring his narrow shoulders. I straightened, ruffled his hair, which he then smoothed down, wrinkling his nose with a crooked smile, blinking back tears. I dashed my own hand across my eyes, hardly able to breathe. It felt like someone had stuck a corer into my heart and removed a chunk. Looking away from him, I shoved the pack handles up onto my shoulder.

"Let us know—" my mom began and trailed off.

"I'll try," I said. Communication wasn't likely and I'd have no idea where to reach out to them, even if I did locate an active system somewhere. Until they returned here, I supposed. Maybe one day they would. Maybe one day I would, too.

Chapter Eighteen

I located Brand not far from the bunker, heading my way. On his back he carried a rucksack and, in his arms, what appeared to be a coat much like his own. He handed the latter to me when I reached him. I shucked my bloodied garment off and slipped into what he'd brought. It felt quite as warm as the one I'd been given by Kerrick, the inside surface also treated with some waterproofing substance, which smelled a little, but so did I.

"Leave that," Brand said, noticing my hesitance to discard the coat from Kerrick. "Some'll find use for it here."

I didn't argue, hanging the stained gear on a post nearby. "Have you already told your family you're leaving?" I asked him while I fastened the coat.

"Don't have none."

I glanced at him and away. He obviously didn't want, didn't need, my pity. "So, we're ready?"

He nodded.

I slipped my arms into the handles on my pack, shunted it up onto my back, wriggled my shoulders to distribute the weight. "Okay. We just need to claim ourselves a *conjure*, then."

"No."

"I'm kidding. I know we can't claim one. It'll have to choose us."

"No," he said again.

"What do you mean 'no'?"

"We walk. I track."

Among the companions, Ren's surliness was renowned. This kid had him beat. "I get that. I really do. But we need to get out of here fast, or we'll be stopped. A *conjure* can be faster than I ever imagined. They're great allies in a fight, too. Not only that, but they sense their own kind, which means it'll lead us in the right direction until we're far enough away, and then you can hone in on the trail."

He crossed his arms. "They'll kill you."

"Yeah, they could, without a doubt, but that hasn't been my experience yet. My head's still on my shoulders." I gave a knock on my skull with my knuckles to further the point, then replaced my face gear, pulled up my hood. "Okay?"

He grunted a sound I took to be an affirmative. I started off in the direction I remembered the paddock and shed to be. Brand fell in beside me. I soon realized I didn't need to adjust my stride to his. In the forest, when he found us, he had walked at a slower pace, still hunting as he brought us in. Not hunting now, he walked with an odd loping gait, low to the ground, making his stride an equivalent to my own.

"What're you starin' at?" he snapped.

"You," I said. I certainly wasn't going to permit him to give me a hard time. We could be together for a while. Honestly? I hadn't thought about what he would do once we found the others. He seemed a loner, and any consideration I'd given in the brief period since his offer, I pictured him making his way back here. Yet, here might not exist by then.

"Brand, do you know where Gabrilon is?"

"Why? You're surely not wantin' to go there. Are ya?"

"No, but that's where everyone else is going, I was told. Those who fight will remain, but if things go badly, they'll need to retreat. I just…wondered what your plans are."

"Oh," he said. "Y'mean after we find your friends."

"Yes," I said, reluctant to admit it.

"Dunno."

He continued walking, silent after that. Beneath his coat his shoulders dropped, almost not enough to be seen, but I'd been watching for it. I understood.

"You could join us, if you want," I said. "I can't promise it'll be easy. It won't. But I have an idea you know hard better than most."

His head bobbed in what I assumed to be agreement. When I heard his mumbled, "thanks," I understood when we were all together again, we'd be eight. And why not? He might not be a conversationalist, but he possessed excellent skills the rest of us didn't. Besides, he was alone.

"Welcome to the fold, then," I said.

Brand lifted his head, gave me a sidelong look. If he smiled, I couldn't see it, the fur on his hood blowing across his face. "Right," he said. "We gotta find 'em first."

Right. Indeed, we did.

Without the noise from fighting, I could hear winter birds in the trees surrounding the paddock. Brand named a few for me, showing off a bit, I figured. Beneath the shed roof, more than a dozen *conjure* shifted and bumped and made their peculiar growling sounds. I hoped not at us. Brand paused while still some distance away, let me go on a half dozen steps without him. I looked back.

"Coming?"

He hesitated, face impassive in his attempts not to look unsettled. I saw the fear in his eyes, though. Even so, we had little time to get underway. I said something I wouldn't have under other circumstances.

"You're not scared, are you?"

He shook back his hood, lifted his head, said, "O' course not," and tromped forward as though he would march straight into the pen. I had to stop him.

"Slowly," I said. "They need to accept us."

"Okay," Brand mumbled and allowed me to take the lead, but he stuck close on my heels.

Determined, I supposed, not to seem afraid again.

I lifted the latch to the gate with a quiet tug, slipped inside, blocking Brand behind me just in case. Great shaggy heads turned my way, long, spiraling horns pointed unthreateningly upward. Good sign. I released my held breath.

"What're they doin'?" Brand asked at my back.

"Watching me," I said.

"How d'you know when they don't want t' kill you?"

"I don't. Know, I mean. We wait, I guess. For a bit. We can't wait long."

Brand made a noise behind me, a snort through his nose.

Grace would know exactly what to do, what to expect with these creatures. She had an uncanny connection, not only with Chauncy, but with all the *conjures*. Possibly, this could be a result of her affinity with Chauncy, but I had no clue. Neither Grace nor Chauncy happened to be present, so I wondered what danger we might be in, Brand and I, standing here before all these great, hairy, volatile beasts.

I heard a sudden commotion at the rear, wondered if it might be a warrior, tending to them, perhaps spotting me in the open gateway. No one called out. I waited a few seconds longer, weighing retreat against meeting up with someone who might not let me leave. While I wavered, the *conjure* started to part from each other, moving to either side inside the paddock, making way for the gods only knew what. I put a hand behind me, preparing to shove Brand to safety, and saw it coming toward me. A *conjure,* smaller than the others—though not by much—possessing a light brown hide and eyes not much darker than my own. A female, Grace had said. I don't know how I recognized her, not really, but it appeared she recognized me, too. One of the three who had brought us to this place. She came forward until a little less than her horn's length separated us, a horn which she lowered onto my shoulder.

I waited. She lifted the horn again, tapped it on the ground. The *conjure* behind her massed together again, blocking any entrance from the paddock's other side. I turned my head, whispered to Brand.

"We're in."

"We're what?"

"We've been accepted," I said.

Blankets lay spread across several railings beneath the roof's cover. I took one down, bringing it back to the female *conjure.* Brand stood before her, staring up at the horn hovering above his head. The horn crashed onto the ground as she bowed and bent her knees, lowering her front end. Brand leaped away. I thought he might run, but he stood fast. I tossed the blanket over the female's back.

"Does it have a name?" he asked.

"Probably, but I don't know it."

"I think it might be Bell."

"It might be what?"

"Bell."

"How do you know?"

He looked at me, rolled his eyes in irritating habit. "I told you. Weather and animals."

I smoothed the blanket flat over the *conjure's* back, fastened it, jerked my head for Brand to get on. He approached eyeing Bell's large head, the long horn making sideways grooves in the trodden ice as the creature moved it back and forth. He climbed up.

"If you 'sense' animals, why were you so afraid you might get your head bitten off?" I asked, hoisting myself over the *conjure* behind him.

"Because I seen it done," he said.

I shut up. I'd heard such behavior attributed to these animals more than once. I really needed to remember it.

Outside, I reached down to push the gate closed, then straightened, looking out over my parents' home. Odd, to think about it in that way. Yet, it was true. Their home. Not ever mine, not even for these few days. I glanced at the buildings nearly hidden beneath snow, behind trees, the settlement spreading out into the forest. The paddock had been cut into the hillside, the elevation giving me a view I hadn't seen before. The main fighting had taken place at the far side. I couldn't see the bloodied clearing from here. I turned away from the scene, determined to give it no more thought.

*   *   *

Bell raced along a disturbed track in the snow, heading upward through the woods toward the mountain pass. Several times she halted, let Brand dismount, complying with a need she sensed in him

221

rather than any command. I remembered Grace had said that. The *conjures* didn't accept command, but chose to follow what they gleaned through an existing connection. Bell as easily could have taken off in another direction, had it seemed indicated. Each time Brand clambered back up on Bell, however, he said the trail remained strong. Eight laden *conjure* had gone up, six had returned. This news didn't mean the others were safe, I knew, but I kept telling myself it did.

Once again, we stopped and once again Brand slid down to the snowy ground. Hands on hips, he stared up the trail. I followed his gaze and saw what he did through the trees—the pass my friends and I had spotted from the valley days earlier, where we'd originally been heading to meet up with Draig. Bounded by craggy, unpassable terrain, the village lay cupped in the only gentle landscape. Closer now, it appeared different, the village less indistinct and featureless, naturally, but something more. I frowned, narrowed my eyes, slipped from Bell's back and took a few steps forward to stand beside Brand.

"Is that smoke? They must be camped there! Waiting where they expected I'd look for them."

Brand whipped his hand up from his side, a fist really, indicating I should stay still and quiet.

"What is it you see that I don't?" I whispered.

"Why'd they expect you t' look for them here?" Brand asked as quietly.

"Before you found us, this was our destination. Draig told us to meet him at the abandoned village in the pass."

With a hiss through his teeth, Brand pivoted and hurried back to Bell. I followed, gave him a boost onto her back with my cupped hands and climbed up behind him.

"It's a trap," he said.

"What?"

"A trap," he repeated, taking my question at face value. I'd heard him, though. I'd heard him just fine.

"What kind of trap? And for who? Us? Them?"

"For all who travel this way," Brand said. "'specially mage."

"Resa. Crap." I supposed Grace would be in danger, too, with what she carried, even lacking mage blood. I didn't say this aloud. No one else could know. Not even Brand.

"More'n your sister. All who enter."

I pointed toward the gray smoke drifting against the backdrop of mountain above. "They must be camped there, though. We need to warn them, get them out."

Brand pulled my hand down. "Smoke's not real. Look. Understand what I say."

I stared at the curling haze, doubting what I saw. In doubting, the smoke disappeared. I groaned, not only because I'd nearly been duped by the trap and, I supposed, my own desires, but because Draig had known. He had to have known. And yet he had sent us here. "Can we go around?"

"No. That's the trap 's well as anything else. Only way's through."

I chewed my mouth on the inside for a moment, gnawing and thinking. I didn't mistrust

Brand's tracking abilities, especially when confirmed by the *conjure's* insistence on this path. Grace and the others had been brought here by Draig's warriors. Draig had said they'd gone on without the escort. He'd been angry about it, I now realized. Which meant to me one thing: my friends had made it through to the other side. Draig's warriors had refused to follow.

"What lies on the other side?" I asked.

"Unknown," said Brand.

I was liking this less and less. "What direction is that?" I indicated the road twisting out from the village toward the mountaintop.

"West."

West. Into the setting sun. The way we all needed to go.

"Okay," I said, "through it is, I guess." I yanked the laser cutter from my belt, pulled out the glass blade, too, and held the latter out to Brand. He shook his head.

"Got my own knife. Don't matter anyway. 'less we run into some beastie in there, weapons won't do no good."

He had an odd, gruff way about him, Brand did, like a sour old man, but he was starting to endear himself to me, even when he said things that tended not to reassure. "So, how do we fight this trap?"

Brand shifted on Bell's back, pulling his hood closer around his face. "Pay attention," he said. "Don' think."

Easier said than done, I thought, and silently thanked Gran again for another handy expression. I had a sudden vision of her, sitting in the lamplight at the little table in the kitchen corner. Playing cards, a solitary game requiring no other players, flipping them over one by one, placing them where they belonged or discarding them. I used to watch her for hours in silence, fascinated by the pattern the cards made. I missed my Gran. Didn't do any good to think about her, not now, not when I had no idea when or if I'd ever see her again. And not when Brand had said 'don't think.' The smoke had likely manifested from my wishful thinking. I figured Gran could be next on the list.

Bell made her way without any obvious qualm into the village. I noted a peripheral shadow, a dark but nearly transparent fog encasing the area. Like a dome, maybe, but not solid. When I looked directly at the grim stain, it disappeared from my focus but remained along vision's edge.

"I see it, too," Brand said, noting my distraction. "Ignore it."

"Ignore it. Got it," I muttered.

Buildings lay tumbled all around, draped in snow and long, fierce ice needles. Bell avoided walking directly beneath the hanging ice, and for good reason. The vibration from her footsteps caused many to crash to the ground, occasionally shattering broken wood beneath. I began to hear echoes in the noise, a repeated drag and thump following a mere second behind the noise from fracturing ice and materials.

"Do you hear—"

"Yep."

Bell halted as if on command. I started to turn.

"Don' look back," Brand said.

"But—"

"Eyes front."

Now that we'd stopped, I could hear the sounds more clearly, coming closer. "Do you think—"

"Quiet."

"—they could be real?"

Bell spun, the whole huge hulk of her, so quickly she nearly threw us off. I was grateful I still clutched the cutter in my fist. An animal the likes I'd never seen before stopped about sixty feet away. A good enough distance for us to beat a retreat, except it looked fast, agile, deadly, and Bell didn't seem inclined to back down from it, anyway.

"I wasn't thinking about anything like that," I said to Brand. "Were you?"

Brand grunted a 'no'.

"Real, then?"

"Or Bell."

I shook my head, incredulous. "You're saying Bell thought about this thing?"

"Dunno. Could be."

I refused to believe he might be right. Not without preparing for him to be wrong. I took the glass blade out, too, the one Brand had refused. Now I had a weapon in each hand, the broken fingers recently reset for a fighting grip holding on so much better than they had. I couldn't be certain arming myself with two weapons requiring proximity would help. The animal rose up onto its hind legs to a height well above my head, even seated on the *conjure*. Large teeth, long teeth, sharp teeth and, when I drew a breath, a thunderous howling roar.

I felt Bell's muscles bunch beneath the blanket. "Hold on!" I cried.

Bell charged, struck the creature straight on with her horn, jerked back her head and tossed the long, dark body through the air and behind us before spinning around again, her cloven feet gouging the icy ground. She charged again, unnecessarily I thought, because the animal had clearly expired from the impalement. She trod right through it, the noise loud and sickening, and raced on. Glancing aside, I saw why.

On four long legs, looking more like gangly humans playing dog than anything else, more rushed down from the mammoth rocks, scrambled over buildings. Elongated snouts emitted roars and screeches and sounds too much like cackling laughter. Still clutching my useless cutter and blade, I squeezed my thighs together with every ounce of strength to maintain my seat. Brand yanked out his hunting weapon, loaded it with something from his pocket and set it flying, striking the nearest creature, the projectile exploding on impact in vicious sparks against the animal's skull. It went down, tripping up those who came behind. Brand repeated the action again and again, until I saw him start to slip sideways.

Shoving the cutter up against the blade in my broken hand, I grabbed him with the other, my arm around his chest, trying to pull him back, to hold onto him, to keep him upright. Bell turned again, arresting momentum, shifting gravity. Brand and I went over and down and hit the rising ground so hard the world turned black.

Chapter Nineteen

I opened my eyes, rolled over, leapt to my feet and lashed the glass blade in blind fear through the air. Beside me, barely visible, Brand ducked.

"Watch 'at!"

I spun, staring all around. Trees, rock, snow, and far below, the village, dark in the dying light. Something hung over it, black and confining, but without blocking my vision. I looked around again. "Where are we?"

"Not there," Brand stated, nodding back down the mountain.

I almost rolled my eyes Brand-style. Instead, I dropped back down onto the ground, put my head in my free hand. "What happened? I remember creatures and falling from Bell's back. Not real?"

"Nope."

"Not even those exploding projectiles? They were pretty impressive. Too bad. They could come in handy."

Brand patted his pocket. "In here. Didn't use 'em, though."

"Then how did I know?"

"I thought about 'em, I figure," Brand said.

"And I picked up on that?"

He shrugged.

"What about those animals?"

"Bell."

"Really? Did you see them?"

"Did," he said.

"So, then what—"

"Ignored them," Brand drawled. "Like I told you t' do."

Ignored them. I didn't understand how. I also didn't understand how I'd gotten through to the village's other side. Succumbing to hallucination or whatever it was had to make for a difficult passage, and yet we'd made it.

"Thank you," I said to Brand. He shrugged again. I moved, feeling tender in more places than I had from the hours of battling. "Falling off Bell. That part actually did happen, didn't it?"

"Yep, 'fraid so. You were flailin' around and off you went. Tied a rope to you and Bell dragged you out."

"Oh," I said, picturing it, understanding now the new soreness, bruising. Even imagining, seeing, the creatures, Bell and Brand had remained clear-headed. What did that say about me? Or, more importantly, what did that say about them? *Conjures* were an enigma. I couldn't really question their abilities, their strengths. But Brand? I pushed up from the ground and rose, looking at him, thirteen-soon-enough, standing barely taller than the bottom of my ribcage, and I felt somewhat diminished, somewhat in awe of him.

"Well, okay," I said, slapping my hands across my thighs. "My thanks again. Where do we go from here?"

He jerked a thumb over his shoulder. "That way."

I wondered why. What he saw. What he could tell from the area he viewed to lead him in the proper direction. I ended up asking him, once we'd both mounted up again.

"First," he said, pointing again, "there was 'at."

From a nearby tree trunk a fabric strip, neatly tied, fluttered in the wind.

"It's hers. The hurt girl's. I smelled 'er on it."

Hope surged through me. "Do we each have a distinctive smell?" I asked.

"Y' do. Everyone does, but 'specially her."

Curiosity compelled me. "What does she smell like?" I imagined quite a few things, fanciful things and no doubt far from the truth. None of us smelled too sweet, after all.

"Like she's ain't recovered yet. Like she's still sufferin'."

Brand jumbled words when he spoke, pushing them all together. I figured he talked to himself a lot and diction didn't much matter. But I had begun to understand him well enough and those two statements dashed cold water over hope, leaving it soggy and not at all palatable. Urgency once again took its place. As if sensing it, Bell took off in a jarring lope.

Similar to before our sojourn in the village, we stopped and started, stopped and started. Each time, Brand got off and examined the packed ice beneath the drifted snow, fingered broken twigs and branches, smelled them, sniffed the air, sometimes hunkered right down over the ground for a closer look at something I couldn't see. I observed the process in fascination. My staring bothered him, I could tell.

"I'm just curious how you do it," I explained after he shot a less than friendly look my way.

"You come down next time. I'll show ya."

I extended my hand and yanked him back up onto the *conjure*. "I'll do that."

"Good. 'bout time."

I laughed. I couldn't help myself. After a moment, he joined in with a sound I clearly recognized.

*　　*　　*

Brand taught me an astonishing amount in the next hour or so before darkness fell. I discovered what he looked for, what clues he sought, although I understood it would be a long time, if ever, before I spotted those things on my own. Night came suddenly on our side of the mountain, as if a light had been shut off. I looked around and it was completely dark, only a residual glow from the sky on the snow revealing tree shadow and rock. Movement, too. I experienced immense gratification when I noted it at the same moment Brand did.

"Small," he said. "No worries. Yet."

On the Emerald, many creatures hunted in the night and in the day's perpetual twilight. Grace had always been better at spotting them than I. So had Carina, for that matter. She possessed one hell of an aim when lobbing stones at them. Did some damage, more than once. I supposed it might have something to do with where they were raised with the outdoors vast all around them. Me? I'd gotten darned good at spotting marks, people I could con in the casinos and beyond. And data mining. I had a knack for that, too. But I'd always been willing to learn, anything and everything, and carried information in my head which had come in handy more than once in our various predicaments. I wasn't entirely useless.

"Y're not useless," Brand said.

"I said that out loud, did I?"

"Yep."

"Crap."

He snorted. In the next instant, he slid down from Bell's back and raced to a sapling beside the meandering track we'd been following. We'd left the road a while ago, following their trail. It had concerned me, finding they'd left the obvious roadway, but perhaps that had been dictated by a specific need. I saw Brand reach up, tug something free from the bark. He brought it to me, dropped the item onto my open hand before dragging himself back up onto Bell's blanket-covered spine.

I lifted my palm close to my face, trying to focus as Bell bounced onward. "My sister's beads," I said. "A few of them, anyway, from her hair. That's her hair, too, tying them together. She must have broken a handful off to do it."

"We go on," said Brand.

"Yes, we go on." I slipped the beads with the thin lock of my sister's hair into my pocket for safekeeping. We continued into the wee hours, having decided to ride for as long as Bell's stamina would allow in the hope we could prevent missing Grace, Resa and the others by a day and would eventually catch up. A constant wind shifted the snow, covering tracks, although Brand seemed to pick out clues despite the disturbance. As the night darkened, the animals roaming the forest grew larger. Not all, according to Brand, were predators. Whether hunter or prey, the animals appeared to be avoiding us, most likely due to Bell's presence. At one point, however, a large gray bird swept down on silent wings and snatched something from a tree branch only a few feet away. Surprisingly, Bell shied to one side, nearly unseating both Brand and me. We held on tighter after that.

When morning came, shadowed still since we'd crested the mountain and had begun traveling down the other side, Bell came to an abrupt halt and refused to budge until we climbed off. I decided she had finally reached a need for food and rest.

Quickly, I removed the blanket from her back. As soon as I did, she trotted off.

"Why'd y'do that?" Brand demanded.

"Because I've seen what *conjures* look like when they return from feeding. We don't need the blanket covered in blood."

"D'you really think she'll be back?"

I stared after her, watched her disappear into the snow-covered forest. "I hope so. If not, we'll go on without her. That's what you wanted in the first place, wasn't it?" I eyed the blanket's size before I folded it into a more manageable burden. "We'll hang onto this, at any rate. It'll come in handy in the cold."

We set about making camp in a grove of nearby trees, where we would eat and wait for the *conjure* to come back. Chauncy had only taken about an hour to complete his sustenance consumption, so we shouldn't need to wait long for Bell. Bell might have to rejuvenate with some sleep, too, although I'd seen Chauncy go long stretches without. We might possibly get underway as soon as Bell returned.

If she returned.

I let out a long breath, frosting the air, and broke open my pack, digging into it for food. Brand and I divvied up some bread, cheese, dried fruit, wolfing it down. "Do you think they're all right, my friends?" I asked, trying to sound casual, as if I had no doubt that they were fine.

"They've gotten this far," Brand answered.

I frowned. I hadn't seen him check the area. "How do you know?"

Licking crumbs from his glove, he pointed upward with the other hand. I followed with my eyes. Above us from a tree limb another cloth strip hung rippling in the air. The knot and fabric looked similar to the first Brand had found.

"I missed that," I said.

He nodded, lowered his hand, reached for a fruit scrap fallen onto his leg, popped it into his mouth. "Soon ya won't."

His short, odd sentence seemed to hold several different meanings. I didn't bother asking him to explain. My eyelids had grown heavy from the long, sleepless night, as had his. "You sleep for a short bit. I'll take first watch," I said. "Then it's your turn."

He agreed, yanking his face covering back on. Crossing his arms, he leaned his head against the tree trunk behind him. The snow we'd pushed from the ground and piled around our camp provided protection from the wind, but the chill still cut deep. I unfolded the riding blanket and tossed it over us both. He mumbled his thanks and immediately dropped off, testament, I supposed, to his faith in me to keep him safe. I positioned both weapons across my covered legs and mentally prepared myself for the task, determined not to let either of us down.

Beyond the tree branches, the morning sky brightened, clear and blue. I found it hard to believe another storm approached from behind us. With the mountain we'd traversed at our backs, that direction remained hidden to me. I heard bird song in the air, including a strange ack-ack-ack sound. I assumed the call came from a bird, yet it could have been anything. I'd only been a short time on this planet before my run-in with Stone Tiran so no surprise everything appeared new and strange to me.

Except it didn't. Not overwhelmingly. Somehow, I settled into everything we came up against, Grace, me, Mika and Carina, and now my sister and the others with us, too. Resilient, Gran called me after the last time Mom left. I remember I researched the word, not sure what it meant. I'd latched onto tough and durable, resolved to make them some sort of motto, something to live by, something to aspire to. But before my friendship with my companions from the facility, I hadn't quite possessed the means to truly accomplish the goal, to *be* that strong.

I sighed, listening to the ack-ack-ack grow softer as the creature making the noise moved away. The sun glittered on ice follicles and snow, the shadows long. I watched for animals and for the *conjure's* return. My need for sleep vanished. I grew restless, watching. Agitated. I picked up the blade made from glass and started carving things into the skim-coat of ice left on the ground. Shapes and symbols and words I didn't understand. Faster and faster.

A gloved hand dropped onto mine.

"What're ya doing?"

I glanced up at Brand, then back to the ground littered with my scrawling. They made even less sense to me now. There were no words and no actual symbols and even the shapes revealed themselves as mere scratches and meaningless slashes. "I don't know," I said.

He studied me from beneath his hood. "We keep moving, then. You sleep on Bell. I'll walk."

"Bell?" I echoed stupidly. I looked past him and discovered Bell's hulking form a dozen feet away. I hadn't heard her approach. Hadn't seen her. Brand strode past me, kicked snow over the senseless markings on the ground. Dazed, I leapt up, tossed the blanket over the *conjure's* back and secured it before sweeping my pack from the ground. I held it against my chest.

Brand tugged my sleeve. "Time to go."

I stared down at him, realized I'd somehow slipped away in my mind. "How long have I been standing here?"

"Too long," he said.

I swore.

Brand pulled me toward the waiting *conjure*. "Y're touched now. It'll pass. I hope it'll pass."

"Touched? You mean affected by what happened in the village?" Brand shoved me closer to Bell. "Have I behaved like this before? Do I not remember?"

"Climb up," he said. "An' maybe. Brief. Not like this. Get on!"

I did, straddling Bell's back. I shifted my pack into place against my shoulders. "You, too, Brand. I'm fine."

He gave me an eye-roll, long and slow and quite purposeful. "You need sleep. More'n me." He tossed a rope coil over my neck and shoulder, one he must have had stowed in his rucksack, and basically instructed me to lie face down and hug the *conjure* so he could secure me in place.

"No," I said.

"Don' be stupid. Don' need ya fallin' off again."

I growled at him, less in dispute than annoyance. Sensible Brand. Okay. As I leaned forward, I spotted something in the air, raised my hand, pointed toward the top of the nearest ridge. "Am I seeing things? More than I've been seeing?"

Brand turned toward a large shadow on the mountainside ahead. Sucking in a breath, he tossed his bag in my direction. Somehow, I managed to catch it, even when he knocked into it on the fly as he threw himself across Bell's shoulders. Gripping her fur, he righted himself.

"Not seeing things," he said. "Hold tight."

Chapter Twenty

I trusted Chauncy and Vigor, their intuitiveness, their stout determination. I had wanted to get as far away as possible from Draig and his warriors, from the ensorcelled village, from battle, but not so far Duncan couldn't find us if he managed to follow. I knew we couldn't wait forever. We had a mission, or at least I did, and the others voluntarily joined in it. I could not endanger them by waiting any longer.

Unfortunately, the *conjures* had other ideas.

"What's wrong with them?" Mika asked again. I did not allow myself annoyance at his question. We all wondered the same thing.

Our morning meal had been concluded, packs restored to their proper state, evidence from our camp swept away by an evergreen branch. The only thing to be seen in the snow now were our footprints, ours and the *conjures*. We would do our best with those, sweeping them, too, but honestly, there seemed no point except to disguise the number in our party. After all, a clear trail would be made in the snow by our leaving and we could do nothing about that.

Pointless, too, because the *conjures* refused to move.

Suddenly I heard a strange beat at a distance. Not like the drumming around the ceremonial fires at home. It sounded like a sharp, rhythmic rapping against wood. Ack-ack-ack. Ack-ack-ack. And it was getting closer.

Hannah appeared at my side. "What's that noise? Some animal?"

"Probably," I answered her, keeping my tone even, as though indifferent to the noise-maker and its possible identity.

"Sounds small," she said.

"Distance can be deceiving. So can echoes."

She wrinkled her nose and walked away. I glanced over my shoulder, called her name. She returned.

"Hannah, I keep forgetting. This is yours. You gave it to me for safekeeping. I think I should give it back." I reached into my pocket and pulled out the talisman Hannah had pressed upon me, it seemed like years ago now, even though it had only been weeks. How strange that seemed. Palm open, I held The Crone out to her. She shook her head.

"You keep it," she said. "I was never meant to

have it back."

Unwilling to argue, I replaced the tiny statue in my pocket. "Thank you."

"You're welcome." She stayed beside me then, following my gaze into the distance. "You might put it in that bag around your neck. You won't lose it."

Don't you dare! Skelly shouted in my head, annoyed more than anything else.

Ack-ack-ack.

"What *is* that?" Hannah asked again, clearly unnerved.

"I don't know." I didn't like the repetitive noise either, more because I had no idea what made it rather than anything to do with the sound itself. A moment later something large and white appeared in the sky, soaring in an updraft on enormous, membranous wings. My mouth dropped open. "There's no such thing," I whispered. Hannah clutched my hand, her fingers digging in.

"There are tales—"

"Tales I don't believe in," I cut over her.

"With all you've seen, how can you doubt one more thing?" This came from Carina, who had wandered up behind us. Resa stood at her side, ever-present without her brother nearby.

Duncan, I thought, do you see this where you are?

Not likely. We were so very far from where we had been. Perhaps, I should stop believing he would come after us.

"Believe," said Carina, reading my thoughts. "Believe in him and believe what your eyes are seeing."

My gaze followed the creature in the sky almost against my will. It dipped and rose on a wingspan which appeared to have a length far more than four times the height of the tallest men I had ever known. It just was not possible. For some hours after my experience in the village, I had been sickened, distracted, hallucinating on and off. I thought the effects had passed. Perhaps not.

"Grace," Carina said, "we see it, too."

Get her out of your head, said Skelly. *Make up your own mind.*

Enough, Skelly, I fired back at him. *She's right.*

"A wyvern," I muttered, using the ancient name for the creature, a name older than time and from a world not our own. An animal of flight and guile with a poisonous spike on its tail, or so the stories told.

"Not a wyvern," said Hannah. "Look at it. Four legs. It's a dragon, Grace. A dragon. Do you know what this means?"

"We're all insane?" I quipped in such Duncan-like fashion foolish tears sprang to my eyes.

"No! We're not far now from where we need to be. According to the tales dragons exist only in that place where all things are possible."

I didn't like where her speech headed, but if true—if true and our journey for answers would soon be at an end, I wanted to accept it. Needed to accept it. Mika and Ren now stood with us, mouths agape, eyes following the dragon in its cavorting roll through the sky. The creature possessed a beauty and grace beyond anything I could have imagined, but the tales related about them also acknowledged their ferocity and dangerous appetites. Even so, I couldn't look elsewhere. Not until Carina spoke again, pointing in a direction away from the dragon.

"Look! Is that—"

"A ship," Mika answered her unfinished question.

A dark aircraft rose by a ridge in the near distance, bucking in a wind not reaching us here. It sank down and shot up again, fighting the strong and obvious gusts we could not feel, likely strengthened by the mountain's geological dynamic. Something else appeared, darker still in the snow, moving quickly, low to the ground, heading across the flat open plain we had recently crossed. Chauncy and Vigor thundered forward, careening to a stop beside us before lifting their heads in rumbling call.

"Grace!" Mika shouted. "What is that? Can you see?"

Narrowing my eyes, I struggled to focus on the moving object, but I think I already knew. From my mouth came a keen of shock and joy and fear.

"It's Duncan!" I cried. "I'm sure of it! I don't think he's alone. Everyone, mount up. We meet them and ride on, before that ship manages to follow."

Secure again on the *conjures'* backs, we sped and slid down the steep incline to the narrow plain below. The *conjure* racing toward us I could see clearly now, no more than thirty lengths away. Vigor called again, head thrown back, horn sparkling in the clear, brittle air. He received an answering call. I could only assume the animal belonged to one of the warriors. I had no idea how Duncan had gotten it to accompany him, more surprised Draig had let him do so. As we neared, whoever rode in front on the *conjure* waved at us madly, indicating we should turn around.

We wheeled about, the *conjures* we rode slowing their pace, waiting for the other one to catch up. I glanced over my shoulder, witnessed with little relief the wind still buffeting the ship from side to side. Struggling against the air currents, the ship dropped and rose, dropped and rose, yet each time gained altitude. We had to disappear into the forest quickly.

In seconds, the three *conjures* bunched together and increased speed, barreling back up the incline and into the trees. We had no time for greetings, for speech exchanged, hunkering instead over the *conjures'* backs to prevent being swept from them. Air whistled into my hood, stinging exposed skin. My dangling leg throbbed. I willed my mind away from it, away from the pain, concentrating instead on maintaining my seat. At this pace, if one fell, those behind would be knocked off also. None would remain unscathed.

Deeper into the snowy forest the paths formed by foraging creatures became entangled with undergrowth. In their headlong stride, our mounts plowed through thorny vegetation, ripping strands of curling fur from their hides, and snagging our clothes, the packs on our backs. When enormous boulders loomed before us, the animals careened around them without slowing. I heard the occasional cry, swiftly muffled, as snapping branches struck my companions' heads and arms. I had lost all directional awareness, had no idea how far we had ridden. We could never outrun the airship, though, once it escaped the winds shearing up from the cliff. We could only hope to hide.

Ahead, a huge outcropping of rock, a black shelf, leaned out over the terrain. Skidding on icy surfaces, the *conjures* stopped abruptly beneath it, throwing everyone forward. Hannah and Ren slammed into me, squirmed back off. I sat up, raised my head to locate the ship. Instead, I found us effectively concealed by the rock from anything in the sky.

Ignoring my leg, I threw myself from Chauncy's back and half-limped, half-ran to the smaller, female *conjure* and Duncan, who had already dismounted. Propelling myself with my uninjured leg, I leaped through the air and into his startled embrace. He leaned his head against mine, both of us barely breathing. I think he might have been crying contained, silent tears. I know I was.

Finally, self-conscious, awkward, I stepped back, glanced down at his companion. "Brand!"

"He's one of us now," Duncan said.

I couldn't look Duncan in the eye, so instead concentrated on scrubbing my face with hasty swipes from one hand. Once I regained my composure, I raised my head, defying the silent urge to squeeze him a few more times, to make sure he was truly here.

"What happened?" I tipped my head sideways.

"Back there."

"Which thing?" Brand asked with clear sarcasm.

Right. I wasn't making myself very clear. We would talk later. I funneled in a deep breath, turned to the others. "Someone needs to go out and see if they can spot that ship. Then we must make a plan."

Realizing my hand had somehow made it into Duncan's, I snatched my fingers back, crossed my arms. Duncan eased past me to hug his sister, who had come forward with Carina and Mika. Carina met my eye with an amused expression. I bit my lip and turned away.

"Watch 'im."

I looked down at Brand, my eyebrows lifting. Spending my time in the infirmary, I hadn't really seen him since he'd come upon us while hunting. I had thought him young, very young, but I could see in his face now I had been incorrect in my judgment.

"'e's been touched by a warding, in Yunlen."

"The abandoned village? So was I," I said quietly.

"Not surprised. 'ave you recovered?"

"I think so."

"Not 'im. Not yet."

"I'll keep a close eye," I promised.

He nodded and went to talk to Ren and Mika. A minute or two later they left together, all three, to check for the ship's whereabouts. The *conjures* shuffled to one side beneath the overhang, rocking and making a low, booming in their throats, nearly beyond sound. I wished I knew what it meant. I had never seen them act in that way before and worried they might be afraid. I wouldn't have believed *conjures* feared anything. Something that frightened them had to be very bad, indeed.

Duncan came back to me. He jutted his chin toward the *conjures*. "What's up with them?"

"I'm not sure. Frightened, maybe?"

"The dragon?" Hannah suggested, having overheard us.

"The *what*?" said Duncan.

"The dragon," I said. "Did you not see it?"

"Yeah, maybe in a nightmare after I ate something that didn't sit right. Are you telling me you did? You saw one? That sounds like—are you hallucinating, too?"

"We all saw it," I said.

His breath rushed out. "Where?"

"In the sky, right before we saw the ship."

Duncan's head went slowly from side to side, still fighting belief. "Are they dangerous, then? I mean, if the *conjures* are afraid."

"The old stories say so, but…" I lifted and dropped a shoulder. "From all I'd heard, I would not have believed we'd ever be mounted on *conjures,* either. And they might not even be afraid right now. I could be misinterpreting what they are doing, their display. They could be communing or, I don't know, healing weary muscles." I shrugged again.

We stood silent a moment, me, Hannah and Duncan, and then Duncan spoke.

"Wow. I'm sorry I missed it. I think I'd really like to see one."

I grunted. "If what Hannah has told us turns out to be true, you will."

*　　*　　*

Brand, Mika and Ren returned a short time later sharing a tale which, given the circumstances, appeared even more unbelievable. The ship had not pursued us. Upon reaching a clearing they had been able to see it, a small dot in the distance still fighting the currents and unable to break free, like an insect caught in another's web.

"Might not be the wind at all," said Ren. "Could be a force field."

"Whose?" I asked.

"I don't know," he answered. "Maybe we should just be grateful for it."

"Maybe we shouldn't trust it," I said. "It isn't necessarily going to last." Power fields had been in use around Citadel to secure certain locations, I had heard. In the end, those fields hadn't saved the city from ruin.

Ren frowned, clearly annoyed by words he could only view as dismissive. He tossed up his hands and strode over to where Carina and Resa stood rummaging through Carina's pack. Carina yanked out a brush. Carina felt it important to maintain certain routines with Resa. The morning hair-brushing had been delayed by our recent flight. Since we were well hidden here, we had time. I suggested we take that interval of safety to regroup, plan, and to let Duncan sleep. He looked nearly dead on his feet.

I apologized to Ren, explained to him what I knew about the power fields in Citadel. He nodded, still grumpy, and found a place on the barren ground to sit. At least, the overhang had kept snow from piling up, leaving most areas scrubbed clear by the wind. Brand strolled over to me, the same wind whipping the fur from his hood around his face so I could barely see it.

"He ain't slept," he said, his head turned toward Duncan. "It'll help."

I watched Duncan, too, saw his eyelids drift down, his mouth open, and knew he had dropped off. He wore a fur garment similar to Brand's and lay on his side, his arms folded over one another and his hands tucked underneath them. It seemed odd he had discarded the coat Kerrick had given him. He'd highly regarded Kerrick, seeing in him perhaps the father he had never known.

I suddenly remembered the illusion in the tavern in the warded village, the skeleton on the floor, with its dried and deteriorated garments and pushed the memory away. Still, I couldn't help asking, "What happened to the coat Duncan was wearing?"

"Bloody mess. 'ad to leave it behind."

Although Duncan appeared tired and aching, he didn't exhibit signs of serious wounding. This could only mean the blood was not his.

"Was there fighting?"

Brand nodded before strolling over to sit near Duncan. He leaned his head against the rock wall and closed his eyes, too.

Duncan had never wanted to hurt another

person. I had known eventually he would have to, that his hand would be forced to shed another's blood. I had seen it without foresight, with only the knowledge of the inevitable. It would likely be the same with all who sheltered here, as much as we wanted to prevent it. Perhaps even Resa.

My gaze slid to where she stood, Carina at her back running the brush bristles through her dark, unbound hair. Much of this, for us anyway, had been about Resa, about saving her, about keeping her away from those who would use her, about not letting them make an unwitting infiltrator and killer from a twelve-year-old. And yet...

Yes, perhaps one day even Resa.

I turned and strode away from my friends into the trees where I crouched, hidden. Ignoring the pain in my leg, I lowered my head into my hands and wept, not this time in joy.

Chapter Twenty-One

Duncan slept soundly and unmoving for about an hour. By the time he woke up, I'd spent a while among the *conjures* trying to get a feel for what might be troubling them and had come away still ignorant as to the cause. They had settled down, though. The low booming and rocking had ceased. It remained to be seen whether they would comply with us moving forward. We might have to continue unaccompanied and leave them to return to The Wilds or to Draig. I didn't expect Chauncy would willingly abandon me, though. He hadn't yet, even negotiating a long, cramped, underground tunnel to reunite.

I stood with my hands against my lower spine, stretching backward to alleviate the stiffness from our race through the forest while holding myself in a ridiculous posture.

"That help, does it?" Duncan asked.

"Give it a try," I said.

He did, slowly, comically, grimacing.

"Here," I said, stepping up behind him, "let me help you." When I touched him, he shot away.

"Are you hurt? What happened?"

He stood a moment, head bowed. He breathed, deeply. I watched his replacement coat from Brand rise and fall.

"I'm just sore. I fell off Bell."

"Bell?"

He dipped his body sideways, toward the light brown, female *conjure*. "In order to get me out of that village, Brand had to drag me behind her. He couldn't lift me up onto her back. I—I was affected by something in there."

"I was, too, Duncan," I murmured.

He glanced back at me, bit his lip, looked forward again toward everyone gathered beneath the overhang, shirking packs into place, preparing to ride.

I moved closer. "The physical pain from being dragged, that will take time. But as far as the effects from the warding or whatever, you should feel clearer soon."

"Are you sure?"

"Yes," I said, even though I was not. He needed hope, though. We all did.

Abruptly, Resa grabbed Carina's hand and tugged her forward until they both stood before Duncan. Resa gazed off into the distance, at what I didn't know. Carina lifted her face, studying Duncan's. She raised a hand to touch him. He reeled back, away from her fingers before she could make contact. Carina lowered her hand to her side.

"You've changed," she said.

"Yeah," he said, "I have."

I knew he didn't mean what happened to him in Yunlen. I didn't think Carina meant that, either. I could see in his eyes what the blood that had made its way onto his discarded coat had cost him; also, perhaps, the hardship caused by leaving his brother behind. Yunlen just added a pall to an already heavy weight.

If not for Stone Tiran, Duncan would still be plying his trade in Citadel's streets and I, I would be home among my family and friends—as obstinate and cross as always, but home. At least for a time, until the tribes set out to fight Tiran's forces. Because we would have. The tribes were fighting now. That much I had learned. But Resa would still be secure with the Sisterhood, nurtured, guided. Despite those thoughts, I could not help recalling that without Duncan and me being on Emerald, Mika and Carina would still be there, imprisoned far from their homes for the remainder of their lives.

And I would be alive.

Yes, I admitted quietly to Skelly, *you would be alive.*

So, did you really see a dragon?

My lip quirked at Skelly's unexpected tone. *Yes*, I thought at him, *didn't you?*

I don't always have vision through your eyes. I'd like to see one, though.

He sounded so wistful. Likely a ploy, but it tugged at me nonetheless. *Maybe one day you will.*

Don't lie to me, Grace. Don't feel sorry for me and don't lie to me and we'll be okay. Got that?

Wistful Skelly had gone like a spark. I turned my mind away from him. Something shoved my shoulder. I pivoted to find Chauncy's huge head inches from my own. He pushed me again with his snout, leaving a shining trail down my coat sleeve. Bell and Vigor had approached as well, pressing close.

"I think it's time to move on," I said.

"And the *conjure*?" Ren asked.

"Willing to stay with us, I think."

Ren and Hannah mounted up on Bell, Carina, Mika and Resa on Vigor and Duncan and I took places on Chauncy. Duncan extended a hand down to Brand, helping him up to a seat between us. It made sense, Chauncy being larger than Bell, but even so, it felt odd to me having Brand there. Chauncy accepted his new passenger without complaint.

"At least the sun's shining," Mika said. "It'll be easier to follow it into the west."

"Not for long," said Brand. "Snow on the way."

I glanced back at Brand. Duncan caught my eye over Brand's head. "Weather and animals," he said. "His gift."

I nodded, pivoted front. Mage blood. Funny how it jumped over some, landed squarely on the shoulders of others; and those such as Resa more gifted than they could handle. Yet not all gifts were tribal in origin. Perhaps even Resa's resulted from a heritage far older, one which, like the dragon we'd sighted, had roots in ancient tales and times nearly forgotten. My own mother was said to possess a lineage tracing to that other world where dragons had their birth. The same blood ran through my veins. It was hard to believe. I'd never given it serious thought until this moment. Before, I counted the tales merely embellished histories. But now, I had seen a dragon with my own eyes. I had friends whose gifts were real, whose actions I had witnessed firsthand and not in words told around a fire or brought up in lessons. I felt suddenly shaken, trembling inside. I tightened my grip on my *lathesa*, afraid it would slip from my hand.

"You all right up there, Grace?"

Duncan, sounding a little more like his old self. I lied to him and told him I was. None of us were, of course, but what point in saying so? Together however, we had a fighting chance to find all right.

You really believe that, do you?

Yes, I said, angry, angrier than I usually permitted myself to get with Skelly, *I do.*

He snorted. I heard it, felt it, before he lapsed again into silence. The *conjures* followed the overhanging ridge until they no longer could, exiting into an exposed area of frigid sunshine high above the open field we had crossed below. The ship, a mere speck now, continued to bob in the wind or force field. Whichever it might be did not matter, as long as it kept the ship at bay until we could get under cover again. Mika asked Duncan and Brand if they had recognized anything about the craft, an insignia or similarities to those previously seen, but it hadn't appeared to possess any markings or a familiar shape.

"Others who have joined forces in this war," I said.

"Not necessarily," said Mika. "Could be someone fighting against."

I looked back over my shoulder at the dark spot vanishing in the distance, feeling a surge of hope. For so long the odds seemed stacked against those who had no intentions in this war, those who wanted to continue their peaceable lives. Maybe more than I had imagined and better matched to the task wanted to see its end. Even as I recognized that possibility, I realized, too, how increasingly lethal it all would become.

We rode on through the daylight following the sun, crossing rocky terrain with sporadic coverage. Although I looked for the dragon with hopes to point it out to Duncan and Brand, I didn't see it. I described the beast to them, though, wanting to fill up the time with more than thoughts of doom.

"How big was it?"

"Hard to tell," I said. "It was high in the air. Maybe the length of three *conjures* nose to tail?"

Duncan whistled in appreciation.

"It made a sound, too," I added. "Like wood

on wood. Like this." I did my best to imitate the ack-ack-ack sound Hannah and I had heard.

"I heard that," Duncan exclaimed. "I didn't know where it came from."

"Me, too," said Brand and for a while they seemed to drift off in their minds to the moment when the dragon might have been nearby. My contemplation returned to the journey ahead and the war behind.

As if picking up on my thoughts, Duncan said, "Trill was evacuated. Only the warriors remained, I think. My...my parents and Toma left with the others."

"Trill," I said. "I didn't know the name of your home, Brand. No one told me. You chose not to stay?"

"I ain't got family," he said. "No more."

"Trill?" Carina echoed. I turned to her, nearby now on Vigor's back. Mika and Resa sat behind, only their heads showing above the blanket wrapped around them all. Carina's brow lowered in a frown, below it her face barely visible behind the wrap she wore. "Back in All Dwellers, Resa connected with a place called Trill during testing. Pointed the city out in one of those images. It didn't look the same to me when we arrived and I never knew the name either, until now. Duncan, do you think she realized your parents lived there?"

Duncan's gaze slid toward his sister, her head bowed and bobbing between Mika and Carina. She might have been dozing. She might have been seeing places far away. She might have been remembering a moment with her mother. Who could know?

"Maybe," said Duncan. "She didn't seem surprised when I told her who they were. But then, she's not surprised about anything. Not that she shows, anyway."

Brand's eyes narrowed. "What's wrong with 'er, your sister?"

"Nothing," Duncan said. "She's different, sure, but nothing's wrong."

The *conjures* drifted apart. Everyone returned to their own conversations, whispered and frequently interrupted by stretches without speech. On Chauncy, we three maintained a musing silence as we traveled westward into the sun.

*   *   *

The snow caught up with us late in the day. For a time, the sky behind had been filling with pale gray clouds rolling after us on the wind. As the sun headed toward the horizon, white flakes filled the air. Gusts whipped the existing snow up to meet the ice flying from the sky. Within minutes we could barely see the way forward. Particles clung to the *conjures'* heavy fur, to their lashes, to ours, piling up on coats and trousers and blankets.

"Squall," Brand said, voice raised so we all could hear. "Could last minutes, could be hours."

"We should seek cover," said Duncan.

No one fought the suggestion. Chauncy, in the lead, slowed his pace, the *conjures* possibly having their own trouble seeing. We needed to find closely grown trees or, better still, another outcropping to shield us.

Resa started to squirm, flailing out at the stinging snow, alarmed and anxious. Carina turned to calm her, her hands within inches of Resa's, but too late. Air blasted out in all directions, knocking everyone sideways. The *conjures* staggered, we all pulled ourselves upright, and the spinning air moved beyond us, pushing back the snow into a shape like a huge, inverted bowl.

"If she could just keep that up," said Ren.

"She can't," I said. "Not for long. But it might help us find our way to shelter."

Eyes closed, face twisted, Resa waved her arms blindly. The bowl shifted from side to side, catching nearby debris and tossing it inward. No one avoided the flying branches and small stones, but no one became airborne, either. Clinging to the *conjures'* blanketed backs, we pushed slowly forward. I glanced behind at Brand, who stared at Resa, his eyes wide. He had not been present in the meeting room to witness her actions when we were all being questioned.

"It's okay," Duncan said to him.

Brand shot him a dubious look, but turned away from Resa, trying to peer through the clotted snow held back by spinning air. His hand lifted, gloved finger pointing.

"Cave!"

Chauncy had already spotted it. The *conjures* moved in that direction, picking up speed, jostling riders and the semi-controlled cyclone. Before we reached the entrance, Carina shut Resa down. Completely, I thought, until she explained through the snow's now thick curtain that Resa had collapsed in exhaustion. At the cave's entrance, everyone but Carina and Resa dismounted with weapons and lights in hand. The fact the *conjures* had brought us here likely meant we would be safe inside, but no one wanted to take any chances. Together, we moved through the large entrance into the interior. Someone gasped. It might have been me.

Our lights reflected more colors from the jagged stone walls than I could grasp. Water ran along the surfaces, frozen in places into a thin coating. The liquid returned the beams like a thousand prisms. For as far as the illumination reached, the cave floor revealed itself flat and without obstruction.

"No smell," Brand announced. "Nothing living in here unless deeper down."

Brand tended to mumble, but his message came through clearly enough. We could shelter here.

The *conjure* had followed us inside. Duncan hurried to retrieve his groggy sister and Mika helped Carina down. I removed Chauncy's blanket, shook it off and spread it on the floor for them.

After, I scoured Chauncy's hide with my fingers, pulling and tossing ice chunks back outside. The others performed the same for Vigor and Bell, adding their blankets to expand the covering on the floor. The three animals hunkered down before the entrance, rumbling deep in their chests. We had no wood to make a fire, so gathered close together for warmth and shared a cold meal. Outside the wind howled. Snow continued to fall, fast and heavy.

"How bad will it get?" I asked Brand, acknowledging his weather gift.

He looked at me, a water canister halfway to his lips. "Weren't goin' anywhere tonight, yeah?"

"No," I agreed, "we weren't."

"Rest, then."

I looked around at the others, weary all, and nodded. "When we're ready, I'll take first—"

"No," Duncan interrupted me, "I'll take first watch. There are enough of us now that we can do short stints through the night."

I met his tired, heavy stare and knew better than to argue with him. "Thank you."

"Don't thank me," he said. "You don't need to thank me. We're all together in this. We are, Grace. Don't forget that."

"I don't. Ever," I said. "I only regret the situation we're in, what I have brought you all to."

"Brought us?" Ren scoffed. "If I remember correctly, Hannah and I tried to drag you off into the unknown in the first place."

"And where would we have been if you and Duncan hadn't instigated the escape from Emerald?" Mika added. "We weren't all leading cushy lives somewhere. We were sentenced to lifelong sentences in a facility for juvenile offenders. You didn't mislead us. You didn't do anything but risk your neck again and again to keep us safe."

I shook my head slowly. "You all fought just as hard, risked everything."

"We didn't have much to lose."

"You're lives have been endangered from the very first minute," I pressed.

Beside Mika, Carina made a face, a very un-Carina face, twisting her mouth and crossing her eyes. She waved her hand at me. "Oh those. What's a life, anyway?" I couldn't prevent a small snort of laughter. Carina's face relaxed, became serious. "I'm willing to fight for what's right, Grace."

"We all are," said Duncan.

"Besides," Mika said, "this is all we know now, right? I think we're handling this crap fairly well."

As if his own words reminded him, Mika searched through his deep pockets and drew out his medication vial, removed a pill from it and popped it into his mouth. He washed the pill down with water Carina passed to him.

"He remembers every night," she said to me. "As promised."

Duncan leaned close. "Everything will be all right."

I remembered us singing a song back on Emerald, me and Duncan, one he didn't really know the words to and neither did I. We sang it to give ourselves courage in those first few minutes on Emerald's dark and frightening surface. I wanted to ask if he remembered, but I didn't say anything. The memory seemed sad rather than encouraging. We weren't the same. What we had encountered had changed us. Or maybe it had only changed me. Yet I could see the differences in my friends, too.

Carina leaned forward. "We are all different now, Grace. We're…more. Maybe better. Better than what we thought we were before all of this."

Not me, I thought. Not me.

I reached out and touched her hand, wondering as I did so if she would choose that moment to alter my perception, to lighten my mental state. She did not. She only squeezed my fingers and let go, her eyes on mine and a small smile on her face, visible since she had removed the covering in order to eat. I smiled back, feeling better anyway.

"So," Brand said, "where're we goin' from 'ere?"

I had forgotten for a moment Brand's presence among us. Even when talking he sat very still, nearly immobile, a practice he had no doubt perfected as a hunter.

"To the Cavern of Sleeping Myth," Hannah answered him. We all looked at her. "At least, that's the plan," she mumbled.

"You believe in it, then?" Brand said to her.

She lifted her chin. "Of course, I do."

Brand's gaze took us in, one at a time. "An' the rest of you, too?"

We all nodded silently, any small doubt we might have unspoken. Ours was a journey of faith, I realized.

"Ya should," Bran said, conviction evident. "It does."

I straightened. "Have you been there?"

He shook his head. "I've not. But one ya know 'as." His eyes shifted to Duncan.

"Me?" Duncan said. "I've never—"

Brand laughed, an odd little sound, cut short. "Not you," he said. "Your father."

Chapter Twenty-Two

I glanced at Duncan, wondering why he did not speak. He appeared frozen where he sat, as though the weather had finally completed its job.

Shock. I felt it, too.

"Aeron traveled there?" I managed on Duncan's behalf. "Why?"

"Answers," Brand said. "'bout his children's gifts. No one 'as supposed to know, but everyone did."

"What answers did he seek?"

Brand shrugged, shook his head in small slow movements. "Rumor? 'e went to ask to bring 'em home."

"But Toma was home," Duncan whispered beside me, not exactly as a statement but as though he tried to work something out in his brain. "Toma was home," he repeated, louder now. "You don't mean Resa and Toma, you mean Resa and me."

Brand nodded.

"What say did anyone in this Cavern of Sleeping Myth have in whether or not my sister and I could come to live in Trill?"

"Had t' do with your gifts, I guess," Brand said.

"I have no gifts," said Duncan.

Brand stared at him in silence, lifting a shoulder.

"And what would it matter anyway? What really stopped him bringing us to Trill?"

I looked hard at Brand and thought, please, whatever is about to exit your mouth, don't say it was Duncan's mother who stopped Aeron.

He didn't. "Something the Elder 's told while there. He came back not the same as when 'e left."

Duncan shifted his weight forward. "In what way? What was he told?"

"Dunno."

"When was this?" I asked. "How long ago?"

"Before I hunted. Four years, maybe a bit more?"

Right after Toma was born. What had Duncan's little brother displayed at such a tender age, no more than an infant, to send Aeron on his quest? What changes had occurred in circumstance in Aeron and Marcella's household for him to want to bring his other children to Trill? I expected Duncan to ask these questions, but instead he stood, strode over to where the *conjure* lay rumbling. With his arms crossed over his chest he stared out at the snow, the blanketing flakes darkening to gray as night fell.

"Do you know the way?" I asked Brand.

"Into the sun. 'at's all I know, same as you. But I reckon we could be within Beyond soon. The lands where the Cavern lies."

"Beyond?" I echoed.

He paused, scrunched up his face in thought. "Short for what the territory is really called."

"And what's that?" Hannah asked.

He frowned at her. "Don't you know?"

"We call it the place where all things are possible. In secret, of course. We are not permitted to discuss anything of what we are saying here in the City of All Dwellers. Such discussions were outlawed before I was born."

Brand's eyes widened. He dropped his gaze, flicking something from his pant leg before again settling into stillness. "Land Beyond Reckonin'. Beyond."

"You're all fans of long-winded names around here. What's wrong with Reilly, Citadel, Ogdo?" Mika asked, muttering place names with which we were all familiar. Carina tapped him lightly on the leg and shook her head, smiling at him. A small secret smile. The type she shared only with him.

"'ere they're called what they are," Brand explained, brows twisting in annoyance. "Trill is Trillin' in Swift Water. Obvious. We got lots o' fish in the streams."

"Obvious," Mika agreed with no small sarcasm and lapsed into silence.

I got up and walked over to where Duncan still stood watching the snow fall. "Are you all right?"

"About this?" he said without turning. "No. I don't understand it."

I leaned my head sideways, up against his shoulder. "It makes little sense."

He didn't move, either closer or away. "I want to go back. Ask them why. Ask them what was said to Aeron."

I straightened, my heart bumping hard in my chest. "Now?"

He shifted his shoulders as if shaking something off. "I'm not actually going back there. Trill has been evacuated anyway. But I just want to, you know? I want some answers. Some real answers."

"Maybe you will get them where we're going. Maybe you'll discover why Aeron had gone there with his questions. Find out whatever was said to him about Resa, about you."

"Anything I learn still won't answer why they suddenly wanted us there with them, Mom and him."

"Resa?" I suggested. "Your mother already knew something of her power. By the time Aeron made his journey, Resa was with the Sisterhood, and perhaps your mom found out more."

"That's what I'm afraid of. I don't want them to want her because of what she can do. I want them to want Resa with them because she's their daughter."

I studied his profile, his wrinkled brow and set mouth, the sad downturn at the corner of his eyes. "What about you, Duncan? What do you want for yourself?"

Turning to me, he released a lengthy sigh, wagging his head from side to side. "I have no idea." He sounded frustrated and rather wretched. A moment later, though, he was smiling at me. "But we're back together again. All of us."

"We are."

"That's something."

"That's everything."

Together we returned to where the others remained gathered on the *conjures'* blankets with their own wrapped around their bodies. I sat down again, extending my bandaged leg before me. Duncan lowered himself down at my side. His gaze went to Resa toying with the beads on her braids, and then away. Still thinking, still wondering, I felt certain.

Ren stirred, flipping his thumb in Brand's direction. "Brand here says he can lead us westward even if we can't see the sun tomorrow."

"Don't doubt him," Duncan said. "I'm sure he can."

"I'm not. I wish I had the skill. Us coming upon you in The Wilds way back when? That was mostly luck. Luck, and Hugo. He had a knack, too."

Duncan inclined his head. When he'd brought the others out from the glass mine, Hugo and Joy-Li had been among them, but they'd parted company outside All Dwellers the night Tiran's ships came down carrying cages filled with the mutants from Emerald. I hadn't known them very well, not like I knew Ren and Hannah now, but I hoped they had gotten away safely.

Speculation followed regarding what we might

find in Beyond, talk drifting in natural course to the dragon and other subjects. Before long, all speech began to swirl in my head. I yanked my own blanket from my pack and curled up on the ground in it. Duncan got up to return to the cave entrance for the first watch. The last thing I saw before slipping into slumber was Ren joining him. They had come a long way, those two.

Normally, I would have wakened automatically as the guard changed, either to take my turn or to check on the status of things. Instead, I felt someone shaking my arm, dragging me back to consciousness.

"Grace. Grace!"

I struggled upright, scrubbed my eyes with my palms, looked up at Hannah, her red hair spiking in all directions. "My turn?" I asked.

She dropped down onto her knees beside me. "We let you sleep."

"Why?"

She shot me a need-you-ask look. A look that said I was not what I used to be. I knew I wasn't. I'd been wounded. I needed time to recover. Nothing more.

Hush, Grace. Accept it. You're done.

Stop talking, Skelly. Please.

"Grace?"

I waved my hand to dismiss her concerns. "I'm fine. I'm getting up."

"Not yet. Eat." She pushed a mug filled with steaming water at me, and a peeled egg. The last, I figured, of the boiled eggs we had taken from the kitchens in Trill. I bit into it and chewed, glancing around the cave. Pale illumination filtered in from outside, the color reflecting off the walls much dimmer than from our handheld lights in the dark. The *conjure* stood by the entrance, blankets on Vigor and Chauncy, Carina beside them brushing debris off Chauncy's with an angled hand. Resa watched at her side. A slow chill crept along my flesh.

"I slept through all this."

Hannah nodded. "Mika was worried and checked on you, but then he said you were just sleeping, and we should let you be. You needed it."

Her words did nothing to make me feel any better about the fact I'd remained unconscious through them eating, packing up, conversation. I took the final bite from my egg, talking around it. "Where are the rest of them? Outside?"

Hannah jerked her chin up. "They went further into the cave. Ren spotted something carved onto the wall."

"What kind of something?"

"A symbol. And then they saw another farther on, so they decided to keep going for a bit. They'll be back shortly. They promised."

She couldn't keep the worry from her last statement, though. I wondered how long they had been gone.

Carina and Resa strolled up beside Hannah, Carina smiling when I looked in her direction. "You're awake."

"I wish someone had woken me sooner," I said. Carina and Hannah exchanged a glance. "What?"

"You haven't been yourself, Grace," Carina

said softly. "You needed to rest. Mika said so."

Mika possessed medical knowledge, learned from his father. Respecting his opinion made sense, but I had difficulty coming to terms with it. I felt oddly isolated by their caution and their care.

Get used to it.

"Why?" I demanded, out loud I realized.

"Because you lost a lot of blood," Carina responded, a little hurt by my question.

I raised my head to her, shook it in apology. "I'm sorry. I wasn't...I wasn't really talking to you."

"Who were you talking to?" Hannah asked.

"To him," Carina answered for me. "To it. I'm right, yes? We want to help you." She pointed at my sternum area. "Maybe you should let one of us carry it for a while."

Suddenly I recalled those moments in the warded village when the dream Carina or whatever she had been had suggested something similar. I knew what this meant. She had thought about it, even back then.

"I can't," I said.

"Why not?"

"I'm afraid."

"To lose the connection?" Carina's eyes widened in consternation; changed color, becoming quite black. I handed the cup back to Hannah and rose from the floor.

"No. Afraid of what he might do to any of you."

"Is it so hard, carrying that thing?" Hannah asked with a nod at my shirt.

"Harder." I spun on my heel, numb and stiff from having slept so long in one position on the blanketed floor. I asked Hannah to show me what Ren had seen.

"It's right here," Hannah said, leading the way. "When the sun came up, well, sort of came up, he spotted it."

I followed her over, frowning at the carving beneath her fingertip. It appeared almost like an arrowhead with a curl in the center and feet, or a pointed letter I did not recognize.

Hannah dropped her hand to her side. "Before the sky clouded over, a beam struck it."

"A beam from the rising sun?"

She nodded.

I thought about that a moment. "So, this could be pointing due west."

"That's what they agreed to as well, the boys. When Ren spotted the next marker, they decided to check for more."

How far had they gone in their search? Did they suspect as I suddenly did a way under this mountain like the tunnel we had gone through in The Wilds? If true, we would be free from the weather, sheltering as needed along the way, and warm, warmer at any rate than the temperature outdoors. Pivoting to look back at the *conjures* my thoughts staggered to a halt.

Chauncy had barely fit in the tunnel behind the falls. Bell had a smaller stature than he did, true, but Vigor stood a hand or two higher at the shoulder than Chauncy and possessed a longer horn. As far as my eye took me into the cave's recesses, it appeared quite large enough to allow passage, but I had no idea what might await us further on.

Getting ahead of yourself, Grace, aren't you?

No.

Skelly laughed and the sound echoed as though he stood beside me in the cavernous space.

"Are you okay, Grace?" Carina, watchful, perhaps listening in her way.

"Fine," I said. "Let's get the last of everything prepared to go."

Hannah helped me with Bell's blanket and then I packed up my bag. All else had already been put into order.

"What now?" Hannah asked.

"We wait."

"For how long?"

"I don't know," I said. "Until they're back or we have to go find them."

*   *   *

Chauncy rested his horn on my shoulder without weight. Flakes had begun falling again from the cloud-filled sky. Not heavily. Drifting for now like leaves in the wind. I had been watching the weather for a little while, counting down in my head to the moment when I would turn around and march into the hillside with Carina and Resa and Hannah to find Duncan and the others. Without any assurances they wouldn't get lodged below, we had to plan on letting the *conjures* go. Perhaps they would wait for our return. Yet with no assurances as to the latter, we had already lugged their blankets back off again, folded them up for carrying. The animals could do without something that would only weigh them down once snow solidified in the weave. We, on the other hand, should find the heavy blankets useful.

The way he stood by me, it appeared Chauncy was saying goodbye. Our pending parting hurt in a ridiculous fashion, not like losing home or my friends might feel to me, but real nevertheless, as though I anticipated a physical separation from something that had become part of me.

I reached over, patted his maw with its huge incisors, stroked his face, the place around his eyes where he often blinked in what seemed to be pleasure. I turned and pressed my cheek against his curly, reeking fur. They had oily hides, *conjure* did, as protection against the elements. No wonder they possessed no cares about the snow. Not reveling in it, but at least unaffected by something that often felt like it intended to do us in.

"I have no idea what we'll find, but we will try to come back." I expressed myself in words although uncertain Chauncy would understand, but he sensed things, sensed what I needed, what I felt. He rumbled a rather mournful sound, soon echoed by the others. As one, they folded their legs and lowered themselves onto the cold stone.

Don't wait too long, I thought at them all.

"I don't understand why they haven't come back," Hannah grumbled when I approached. She had been pacing back and forth from the main chamber to where the tunnel angled downward and calling their names until I had asked her to stop. It didn't make sense to alert anything they might have run into to our existence. Not that I believed they had. I told myself explorations were taking more time than expected. I had no desire to take any chances, though. And the longer they were gone, the more I worried I might be ignoring the obvious.

Laden as if we did not expect to return to the surface this way, we also carried what the boys had left behind. To make it easier, I had placed their packs into Bell's blanket, which I folded and tied to form its own container, and this I dragged behind me by a length cut from Brand's rope. Hannah produced a heatless fireball, split it in two and placed one on each shoulder for light before she gripped the rope, too.

We had no problem dragging the thick blanket behind us. The cave floor had been cleared and in places lay as smooth as barely rippling water. Most caves, I had been taught, formed over millennia from water; rushing water, dripping water, relentless water. I believed this cave's creation to have been aided by men. Rocks looked to have been cut away by some unknown means, leaving barely raised remnants, flat smooth surfaces. Once we had cleared the main entrance, the channel traveled down into the mountain with little deviation in size and no obstruction.

Although we attempted to walk quietly, our steps echoed in front and behind, along with the slithering noise from the blanket. Every so often we stopped, listening, making certain the reverberations ceased, too. Hannah didn't call out for our friends, clearly unnerved now we had left the exit into the world outside behind us. I was relieved. We did not know why they hadn't returned and if nothing else, experience had proven shouting into the unknown could be hazardous.

When we spoke, Carina, Hannah, and I, we uttered our exchanges in whispers. We kept the topics light, avoiding the serious. I think we all knew if we gave voice to our concerns, they might get the better of us.

Resa walked in silence, her hands moving as though conversing with someone, her eyes fixed on another place in a way we had become used to. Carina maintained a grip on her coat to prevent her tripping over the rare protrusion on the floor. I doubted she would. Even when like this, something in her continued to perceive her surroundings.

"How are you holding up, Grace?" Hannah asked, voice pitched low. I appreciated her asking, but I didn't like it. I thought my limp barely noticeable.

"Fine," I said.

On Hannah's other side, Carina made a noise in her throat. Pretending I hadn't heard, I focused on the darkness not yet penetrated by the glow from Hannah's shouldered flames. Like when in the tunnel we had traversed below the Perimeter in The Wilds, I felt confined, burdened, unhappy. Born to the open air, enclosed spaces altered my mental state, my outlook. The prison had been bad enough, although then I had possessed hope. Foolish hope, but hope, nonetheless. A hope that had proved warranted. My capacity for hope hadn't left me. Far from it. I still had hope, but somehow it had become twisted up with the crystal bearing the entity I still thought of as Skelly.

At my thoughts, Skelly began a tuneless humming in my head. Self-satisfied. Taunting. I pushed him down, hard, wondering if we might not pass some place with a long, long drop into nothingness. He laughed.

I increased my pace, longing for the air, even the snow-filled air. Hannah matched her stride to mine, tugging her end of the tied rope. Carina and Resa fell a little behind. Not by much, yet far enough. I slowed again. I would never leave them alone in the dark. I needed to get myself under control.

Abruptly, I halted, my feet sliding on the stone's smooth surface. The bag slammed against my ankles. "Wait," I hissed. Everyone jerked to a stop, even Resa, compelled by Carina's grasp on her garment. Her eyes shot in my direction. Her arms lifted.

"No," I said, signing the word. Resa giving freedom to her power here in this shaft would endanger us all. Aided by Carina's touch, Resa calmed, turned to follow my gaze.

"What is it?" Hannah whispered. "What do you see?"

"I don't see anything," I said. "I hear it."

I dropped the rope, my *lathesa* clutched in my fist, and started running as if the wound in my leg did not exist. Racing toward a voice, a voice I hardly recognized.

Ren crying out for help.

Chapter Twenty-Three

"Shut it, Ren!"

Yelling wasn't helping. Not at all. Ren's shrieking only served to aggravate the beast further. In fact, his hollering might be the only thing provoking the animal. Prior to Ren's falling into the crevice below, the thing had been asleep and seemed content to be so. I'd wondered when we passed above it the first time if the creature were in hibernation. Maybe it had been. Right until Ren dropped down within ten feet of its shaggy back end.

"There has to be another entrance," Mika said beside me. "There's no way it got down there the same way Ren did."

I'd noticed the same thing. Ren's misstep over the narrow fissure on the way back had sent him plummeting through a space so narrow I didn't think the animal's head could fit through, let alone it's rotund body.

I yanked the laser cutter from my belt. "I'm going down there."

"Don' kill it," Brand said. "No reason if it's no good for eatin'."

I shot him a look. "What about Ren?"

"Stupid sod. Should've watched his step."

"It doesn't work like that, Brand. We're in this together. That includes you, too, now."

"Still, don' kill it. There're proper ways 'n wrong ways."

I hadn't time to listen to hunter's code or whatever he was banging on about. Ren needed our help. Now.

The drop wasn't a big one. The creature easily could have reached up and snagged a passing leg if it had a mind to and dragged one of us down. I landed beside Ren, who'd finally calmed himself enough to take out his weapon, too. We both turned to face the animal. It stood on its hind legs, back curved against the stone ceiling above. Each paw possessed claws as long as my fingers. When the beast drew back its lips in a snarl, I received a clear view of sharp incisors and huge flat-edged teeth.

"Brand," I risked shouting up to him. "Flat, wide teeth, not a meat-eater, yeah?"

His face appeared above. "Usually."

"Do you think it'll harm us, then?"

"Probably."

Crap.

Okay.

I permitted myself a quick look around for a place to squeeze in beyond reach of those claws. A space too narrow existed behind us. The only way out appeared to be beyond the creature, likely the way it had crawled in. Zero chance we'd both be able to get past it. One might if the other distracted the creature. I wondered if we could make enough noise to frighten the beast, maybe cause it to retreat down the dark shaft, give me enough time to boost Ren up the wall, and then Mika and Brand could pull him free. It'd be a little tougher on me, attempting to scale the rocks, but I might be able to. Brand's rope would have been helpful, but we'd left it behind with the supplies.

The thing took a swipe at us, missing Ren by a handspan. On impulse, I started waving my arms and yelling. Picking up the cue, Ren did the same. Brand's exhortations not to kill the beast may have influenced my actions, but I believed it more my hesitation to put myself close enough to use the weapon that won the immediate battle. The animal reared and struck its head on the ceiling. Perhaps confusing the noise with the injury, it backed away.

"You go around and I'll—"

"No," Ren argued. "Together or not at all."

I glared at him and started yelling again, his voice joining with mine. The animal sidled sideways, a glint in its eye as if its bravery were returning. Suddenly the light from the kinetic torches above dimmed out. Something fell with a vivid squelch to the rock floor beside us. I pushed Ren away as the creature dove for it, slavering and gulping the matter down. Grabbing Ren's arm, I shoved him toward the open shaft and followed. He cried out as his shoulder struck stone but kept on going. Finding ourselves swiftly in total darkness, I yanked the torch from my pocket and lit it. Ren's was gone. I'd stepped on the shattered tool when we fled.

"Which way?" Ren whispered. We'd reached a point where the shaft split in two. I smelled fresh air in a strong gust from the left and headed in that direction, Ren on my heels. From behind us I heard noises, but not as though the animal gave chase. I hoped it had decided pursuit not worth the trouble.

Coming out in a side shaft, I saw the main tunnel in the near distance, as well as Mika and Brand, their lights, and others. I frowned, trying to focus on whoever else was with them.

"It's the girls," Ren whispered. "See? Hannah's lit up."

Yes, I saw that now. Using the light in my hand, I swept the passageway as we proceeded, hoping to avoid a fall. When we finally reached them, Hannah spun on us both.

"Why didn't you come back? We waited, you know, for as long as we could."

"We were on our way," Ren answered defensively. "I fell."

"Yeah," she said. "Down there. You should watch where you put those big feet of yours."

Behind her, Brand snorted.

I lowered my voice, hoping those two would lower theirs. "What did you throw down to the beast?"

"My breakfast," said Brand. "I didn' finish. 'ad it in my pocket."

"Good thinking," I said. "Thanks."

Only then did I note the girls all carried their packs and a *conjure's* blanket lay by their feet, lumpy with whatever they'd secured inside. Grace stood tall behind the other three, her weapon touching the floor lightly, her face twitching as though avoiding a grimace as she shifted her weight off her injured leg.

"What's the plan?" she asked. "The *conjures* may still be waiting for us back at the entrance. I don't know, though."

I pointed at the blanket. "Is all our stuff in there?"

She nodded. "We weren't stopping until we found you all. It might have been too far to go back for it."

Mika stepped forward, smoothed Carina's ruffled white hair. I looked away. "We can continue on underground, I think," he said. "This tunnel is manmade. It's leveled out and keeps running on, straight as a girder."

"Due west," I said at the exact instant Grace uttered the same. She met my eyes and smiled. I frowned at the stupid thumping in my chest. "There's plenty of room for the *conjures*. Should we—"

"No need," Grace said. "They're coming."

I skipped asking how she knew because I could hear them. I remembered the tapping, the scraping from the tunnel in The Wilds. I heard the slight music, too, almost like distant, half heard melodies as they rubbed their horns together. They appeared a few minutes later, having scented or sensed us through the long, dark trek. Chauncy went straight to Grace, laid his horn on her shoulder. She looked down and away, but not before I saw her face.

After we secured the blankets across the *conjures'* backs to avoid having to carry the heavy weight, we all shouldered our own packs and moved off. I stepped carefully over the fracture, spying the creature asleep once more in the darkness below. We'd survived in one piece, Ren and I. Something could be said for Brand's quick thinking. No harm had come to anyone or anything. I liked that.

I ambled up beside Grace. She still insisted on taking the lead, despite the strain it put on her now. And as long as she insisted, then I'd be there beside her. We strode in silence for a while, the quiet conversation from behind drifting past us like whispers along the stone walls. If I hadn't been looking, I mightn't have noticed her slight limp. She was doing her best to hide it.

"What do you think it's going to be like, this Sleeping Myth place?" I finally asked.

Grace shook her head, concentrating on the shadows beyond our lights, on placing one foot in front of the other. "I don't know."

"I imagine something a little crazy," I said, "given what everyone is saying."

Her mouth twisted, fighting amusement. "Crazier than where we've been?"

I grunted. "Let's hope not."

She reached out, circled her hand around my broken one, gave it a small squeeze.

"Seriously," I said, "do you expect to come face to face with some long-lost tribal ancestry? You know, mage that might be a bit scarier than we've met so far?"

"Could be. Could be there's nothing there. Could be these are all stories without truth, even your dad's quest. Maybe what he found wasn't an answer to his questions, but a discovery there were no answers."

I sucked in a breath. "Crap, Grace, do you really believe that? What are we relying on here? Nothing but hope? Kerrick talked about the place, too. Something must be there. It has to be."

She hung her head for a moment, watching the ground. Her dark hair bobbed with each step she took, the streak of dark blue dye long since faded, the last traces cut away back in All Dwellers.

"Grace?" I prompted. "You're not yourself, not the Grace I know is in there still. You were hurt badly. That's no reflection on you. On who you are, on what you can do."

"It's not… It's more than that, Duncan."

I lowered my voice. "Tell me. Maybe I can help you."

"Nothing can help me."

"What?" Loud. Louder than I intended. My voice shot back at me.

She lifted her chin, stared into the shadows ahead. I witnessed the struggle in her expression. The concentration. The anger. The defiance. A satisfied and rather frightening smile. "Sorry," she said. "It's *him* telling me nothing can help me. I just need to remind myself not to believe him."

"Skelly."

She nodded.

"Or whatever that thing is."

Again, she nodded. Still fighting. I could see it.

"Let me carry that stupid bag for a while," I said.

"You can't."

"Can't? Or you won't let me?"

"Both, Duncan. I don't know what would happen to any of you. I have no understanding how I called him down into the crystal or how I called him back again when he was temporarily freed. I don't know why this responsibility fell to me. I'm just a warrior. A warrior. Not mage. But it is my responsibility until such time as I can relinquish it. Maybe…maybe I'll find out I never can."

Her anguish pierced me like a million tiny needles. I could hardly breathe for it. I imagined wrestling the crystal in its sack from her, tearing it off her neck, placing it over my mine. Such nonsense was short-lived. Even in her weakened state, I knew she'd never let me. I'd be sprawled across the cave floor before I could even blink.

"We'll get answers," I said. "If not here, then somewhere else. But I hope we find them soon. I'm really tired of all this running around."

She laughed, as I'd known she would. I put my arm around her shoulder, yanked her close for a second. Well, I meant it to be a second. Five or six turned into twenty. She eased away from my grasp, pretending a need to readjust the straps to her pack, its position behind her. I glanced back. Ren watched us. Hannah, too. Ren's face I couldn't read but Hannah's expression was clear. It possessed nothing as bitter as anger. Nope. She looked hurt, plain and simple.

I let out a long breath and walked on. Didn't we all have enough to deal with?

In the next moment guilt made me wince, because we all did have enough to deal with. Even Hannah.

I looked back again and slowed my pace, grasping Grace's elbow until she slowed down, too. Not that we were walking quickly. We'd all spread out, though, me and Grace, Ren and Hannah, Mika, Carina and Resa, the *conjures* behind them, as though we were separate factions. I figured a little camaraderie might be in order.

Wait. We were down one. Where had Brand gotten himself to?

"Brand!" I called. Not too loudly. I didn't like the echoes and I didn't like the idea I could alert another hibernating creature. We might not be as fortunate next time as Ren and I had been with Brand's intervention.

Spotting short legs in fur walking between Chauncy and Bell, I called out again. Brand scurried forward, a scowl on his face.

"What?"

"I thought you didn't like *conjures*," I said. "Didn't trust them not to eat you."

His eyes widened, started to roll and stopped.

"Weather. Animals. Me. Got it?" With that, he slipped back to his place between the two beasts.

"Strange kid," I whispered for Grace's ear alone. "Great in an emergency."

She snorted. "But you like him."

"Yeah. More importantly," I said, "I trust him."

She nodded. We strode on, all a little closer together. Without the sun, or at least the light glimpsed through snow falling from the sky, it became more difficult to judge time's passage. We stopped and ate when the majority got hungry. It could have been midday. It could have not. As Grace pointed out, you couldn't tell by me. I was always hungry.

Fortunately for us, the tunnel's dimensions varied very little. We encountered an occasional outcropping of rock or stone hump in the floor too difficult, I supposed, to cut through. Otherwise, the wide shaft ran on in a smooth, half ellipse. No chance, then, for the *conjures* to get trapped.

"If it's almost night when we get to the other side," Ren suddenly said, "I vote we stay in here until the morning."

Everyone turned and stared at him, because up until that moment we'd been walking for some time in silence. His comment had come without context. I could only imagine what thoughts had led him to his statement. It made sense, though. Had he actually waited until we reached an outside view, we all would have been saying the same thing. Still, for fellowship's sake, I stuck my hand in the air and said, "Seconded."

Grace shot me a glance from the corner of her eye. "You two seem to be getting along," she said in an undertone.

"Well, yeah. He's not so bad."

"I heard that," Ren grumbled.

I laughed. Suddenly we all were. Except Resa, for obvious reasons, and Brand, who'd missed the exchange, his ears shielded by the muffling contours formed by a beast to either side. It felt good to laugh, I mean to truly laugh, hard and because something struck us all as funny, rather than a way to stave off misery for a minute or two. Yet, as the laughter faded, Grace's eyes immediately reflected something other than amusement.

I wanted to help her. I wanted so badly to help her.

"You can't," Carina whispered from behind. Talking to me, I knew. *Please, Carina*, I thought back at her, hoping she would hear it or sense it or whatever she did to read what went on in our heads, *stop listening in. Give me some privacy.*

Focusing my eyes on the shadows beyond the glow from our lamps and the flaring lights still balanced on Hannah's shoulders, I tried to steer my mind from Grace. Instead, I thought about those small balls of flame. I'd noticed the more practice Hannah had with them, the better she handled the ability. She needed less concentration to keep them lit. Before, it had been a hidden art, revealed only in secret, but now she understood none of us would ever condemn her for her gift, she used it openly. Not for the first time, I wondered what else she might be able to manifest in her freedom and spun on my heel, walking backward, opening my mouth to ask.

I didn't get the chance.

Chapter Twenty-Four

I wished I hadn't yelped. Yelping is so much less dignified than an actual shouted warning. "Back there," I managed to direct, raising a hand to point into the shadows behind. Yet, even as those words passed my lips, I realized the *conjure* plodded along unruffled, the beasts who were first to sense anything extraordinary.

Beside me, Grace raised her weapon and peered into the darkness. "What did you see?"

The others stopped, turned around, frowned toward the shadows.

"You're going to think this is crazy," I said. "I saw eyes."

"Eyes?" Grace echoed. Not as if she didn't believe me. More like I'd puzzled her. I couldn't blame her. I saw nothing back there now.

"How far back?" Brand, moving away from the

conjure. He lifted his head and sniffed the air, darted a look at Vigor, who was nearest and whose scent no doubt carried straight into his nose, and moved several feet to the right.

"That's the crazy thing," I said. I pointed again. "Right there. Right there where the light fades away into darkness."

Brand took a step, glanced back at me. "You coming?"

I nodded and started after him. Ren fell in beside me. Mika began to follow, too, but I asked him to stay put. I hoped he might discourage Grace from coming with us. Sometimes she respected his opinion more than mine.

"If anything gets past you, we'll be here and ready. Right Grace?" he said, picking up on my glance in Grace's direction. Good old Mika. To think I hadn't known what to make of him back on Emerald. He'd seemed… I don't know. Breakable. But weren't we all.

"What did the eyes look like?" Ren asked as we made our way into the shadows. The lights we carried pushed the darkness back with every step, revealing nothing in their glow.

"I only saw our lights reflecting in them. They faced forward though, both of them."

"What color?" Brand again.

"The reflection? I don't know. Does it matter?"

"It could," Brand said.

"What?" Ren piped up. "Do different animals' eyes reflect light in distinctive colors?"

Good question. I wished I'd thought of it.

"Yep," said Brand.

"So," I said, "they seemed kind of red. That mean something?"

"It could," Brand repeated. Ren and I exchanged a look, eyebrows lifting, but said nothing further, following Brand. Suddenly, he stopped at about the same time a pungent odor wafted into my nostrils. A low whistle escaped his lips. "Look here."

He pointed his torch toward the cave floor and a huge, stinking mound.

"What's that?" Ren asked.

"Really?" I drawled. Brand's expression reflected my sarcastic response.

"Oh," said Ren.

"Can you tell what made that?" I questioned Brand. "Specifically, what it eats?" As I spoke, I raised the kinetic torch for a look further down the tunnel. Considering the smell and the heat coming from the steaming waste, the creature couldn't have gone far.

Brand bent closer, removed a knife from a sheath on his boot and poked at the mass. He straightened. "No."

"No, what?"

"Can't tell. Smell's not familiar. Could be like us. Eats everything."

I muttered a particularly strong profanity.

"Well, now you know you weren't seeing things," Ren said to me. "We should get back to the others and keep going, perhaps a little faster."

I concurred without hesitation. We didn't need to identify the creature. It had apparently retreated. Despite the size indicated by what it had left behind, perhaps the animal possessed a timid streak. We could only hope.

Running lightly on our toes and with ears straining for any noise behind, we hustled back to Mika and the girls. Hannah darted up to me.

"Did you find anything?"

"We found signs of something," I said. "Excrement."

Hannah wrinkled her nose.

"Whatever it is, it followed us in here," I added.

"How do you figure that?" Ren asked.

"We didn't find any of that before, did we? A pile that big isn't something we would have missed. I'm not saying it followed us deliberately, but I'm saying it entered the cave after we did."

Brand agreed with a curt nod. Grace slipped past me, striding up to Chauncy. She placed a hand on his neck, stood a moment gazing down the long tunnel. "How big?" she asked.

"We didn't see it," Ren said.

I stepped around Hannah, who had placed herself in my way, and up to Grace. "You mean based on the droppings."

Grace nodded.

"Well, I'm no expert, but about three times the length of a *conjure*." I held her gaze, attempting to remind her what she'd mentioned earlier when describing the mythical beast she and the others had seen in the sky. Grace inclined her head, let it bob once or twice, clearly thinking. She released a long, weighted breath.

"I don't detect the slightest tremor on

Chauncy's hide," she said. "But I think…I think we should all ride now."

She wasn't getting any argument from me.

We mounted up in the same order as before. This time, however, Brand took the rear place on Chauncy, facing backward to keep a lookout behind. Brand possessed a practiced eye. I trusted him to alert us the second something came into view.

We maintained near silence now, the fact a large animal had crept up on us noiselessly or at least undetected not far from anyone's mind. Weapons remained sheathed, but handy. No one relaxed, no one dozed propping themselves up on the *conjure's* backs. I had no idea how many hours had passed since we'd first set out. I'd be more than happy to see the sky again, even filled with clouds and icy flakes.

Before me, Grace kept her gaze dead ahead. Despite her clothing's bulk, I could see how stiffly she held herself. Her spine seemed like it had turned to steel. Normally, Grace was what my Gran liked to call loose-limbed, a term she'd reserved for certain women in the casino and their locomotion across the floor. For Grace, the word meant something else entirely, to me anyway, having to do with her natural posture, her long stride, her warrior's training. Right now, though, she looked like a board bolt upright on Chauncy's back. I wondered if she might be in pain. I leaned forward so I wouldn't have to raise my voice.

"You feel okay?"

"What? Yes. Fine." Her tone said otherwise.

"You look like you're hurting."

She snorted out a breath, a short laugh. "I am."

Enough said. I couldn't do anything about it but at least now I knew. Still, I asked anyway. Shockingly, she took me up on my offer.

"Help me roll this blanket up so I can put it under my leg. I think I'll feel better if my knee's bent."

I lowered myself sideways, stretched my hand out to the blanket's edge and paused. Abruptly I sat back up, chin lifted. "Feel that?"

She glanced back at me.

"It's a breeze," I said. "Not much of one, but it smells fresh. Smells like outside air." I knew how much Grace disliked being underground, being confined. The possibility we could be near the outer world might lift her spirits.

"Hope so," said Brand from behind me. "I 'ear somethin' coming."

Grace pivoted from the waist, as did I, looking back into the darkness. "I don't see anything," I said, "and the *conjures* aren't reacting."

"Didn't before, either," Brand reminded me.

"If they're not recognizing any danger, maybe there isn't one," said Grace. She didn't sound certain and as we all knew, a *conjure* responded in its own time, when it sensed a need, either its own or one of ours. I started thinking really hard about the many possibilities we could be facing if they didn't pick up their pace, but the beasts continued to plod along.

"Do you see anything yet?" Grace asked.

Neither Brand or I did. The others turned to

study the shadows over their shoulders. In the glow from the dual fireballs, Hannah's eyes widened. She began vibrating in her coat, her whole body shaking. My gaze shot past her to the darkness, finding nothing visible. Had she spotted something or had she just started to panic?

Panic. That was obvious a moment later, when Ren tried to calm her down. Fighting him off, she slid off Vigor, landing on her hands and knees on stone. The flames on her shoulders vanished. A unified growl rose into the air from the *conjures*. As one, they lunged forward into a gallop, leaving Hannah behind. I launched myself from Chauncy's back, hit the ground and rolled. "Go!" I cried, not that anything could stop the *conjures'* forward momentum. "I'll get her!"

Sure, I would. By the time I'd scrambled to my feet any light had vanished with my companions. I had stowed my torch away in my pocket and unsteadily wrestled it free in near-total blackness, hoping it hadn't broken when I struck the solid cave floor. Not far away I heard Hannah's whimper of pain. In the distance I heard something else, a sound like something wet sliding across the ground. I hurried back in Hannah's direction, bent low, skipping the light. I almost fell over her.

Crouching, I patted around until I felt her shoulder and gripped her coat, pulled her up. She cried out, bit it back.

"How badly are you hurt?" I whispered.

"I'm okay. Do you hear that?"

I nodded, realized she couldn't see me, and told her yes in an undertone. "You need to get up quietly. Now." I helped her upright and gripped her elbow. "This way."

"I can't see anything."

"I'm not lighting the torch. We'll go slow. Try not to shuffle."

The thundering from the *conjures'* cloven feet had all but disappeared into fading echoes. Behind us the slithering continued, along with an occasional click. The noises to our rear had gotten no closer. Not yet. I had a sinking, gut suspicion whatever followed us merely bided its time. If the *conjures'* presence had been any deterrent, it no longer existed. They were gone.

"Duncan—" Hannah began.

"It'll be all right. Just stay calm."

"I'm sorry I—"

"Stop talking."

We crept silently on. I kept one hand to the wall, marking our course, the other wrapped around Hannah's, leading her forward. It felt odd, Hannah's hand clutching mine. Not like Grace's. I'd gotten used to hers. So very used to hers.

As if following my thoughts, Hannah asked, "Are you and Grace—"

Once again, I interrupted her. "Shut up, Hannah. We're trying not to be heard."

She sniffled behind me. Crying because I'd cut her off? Or crying because she was that scared?

"It'll be alright," I whispered again. "Just…no talking, okay?"

"Okay."

She pressed up close to me. I could smell the fear on her. Could feel it, too, her violent shaking working its way up my arm. She wasn't always so afraid. She'd been pretty brave, actually. I figured the darkness, the unknown, must have been working on her. The fact a large, unseen beast trailed us couldn't help, the lifting hair on my nape proof of that.

Click, click, slither. The noises repeated themselves over and over, no closer, no farther away. Perhaps the creature's eyesight in the absolute blackness happened to be as bad as mine. I doubted it. We couldn't be so lucky. Within minutes after these thoughts crossed my mind, our luck ran out altogether.

I noticed it first on the walls, a dull dark gray mixing in with the black. Next, I spotted the bit of light seeping across my boots as I put each foot forward. Not good. I still hadn't located the tunnel's exit. I didn't know how far we had to go. Weak, still almost non-existent, daylight had begun seeping into the cave.

"Duncan," Hannah whispered, "I see you."

"I know," I said. "Run."

*   *   *

Bad move, I supposed. Not something I would recommend under normal circumstances. But I couldn't remember the last time I'd enjoyed normal circumstances.

Still gripping Hannah's hand, I took off at a lope, literally dragging her until she got her feet under her and scurried behind. Her stride was never going to equal mine. Heart pumping, a thousand swearwords bouncing inside my skull, I urged her onto a faster pace. Behind us, silence descended. I imagined a dragon, the dragon Grace had described, readying itself for a lunging kill. It didn't have to be the dragon. It could have been any darned thing. Anything intent on its next meal.

Abruptly, so abrupt I stumbled, the tunnel floor started to rise. Regaining my feet, I kept on, Hannah clinging with her free hand to my borrowed coat, the other still wrapped in mine. Breath rasped from her throat. Illumination shot into the cave in greater volume, coating the walls with the gold of a setting sun in a clear sky, nearly blinding me. A setting sun. A clear sky. I didn't think we'd survive to see either one, yet I wouldn't give in, wouldn't succumb to that doubt. The thing in the dark was coming now, picking up speed. I glanced back once, glimpsed those eyes, reflective red, and didn't look back again.

Not until Hannah fell.

She dragged me down with her. I spun on the ground to face the coming danger, slapping around on the stone for my fallen laser cutter. Snatching it up, I switched it on, its dull orange glow barely visible in the light pouring in from beyond the rise. My shadow ran before me, shielding Hannah in blackness. It didn't matter. The creature already had one clawed foot on her ankle, its cream-colored, scaled and feathered hide gilded by the sun. I opened my mouth, prepared to yell as Ren and I had before, vainly hoping I might frighten this creature off as we had the slumbering animal earlier. Before a sound left my mouth, I heard something snap.

Hannah screamed.

Shadow fell over everything. I threw myself across Hannah, the cutter raised. A long, high whistle pierced the air. From behind us footsteps pounded, echoed, preceded a body dropping beside mine.

"Stay down," a voice hissed. Ren's voice. I looked past him to a silhouette in the dying sun, casting its shadow down through the tunnel. Light glinted off the crystals at each end of Grace's weapon. She whistled again.

The dragon—because I had no reason to believe it might be anything else—lifted its clawed pad from Hannah's leg and charged up the slope. A folded wing's barbed segment slapped my face, drew blood.

"Grace, no!" I shouted.

"Shut it!" Ren yelled into my ear.

In horror I watched the animal approach Grace at speed. *You won't win*, I thought. *You can't.* But she had no intention to win or lose. She merely stepped back, plastered herself against the rockface, turned her head away and let the beast pass her by. The moment it disappeared from sight, she hurried down to where we lay on the ground. Rubbing her thigh, she asked if we were all right.

"I'm pretty sure Hannah's ankle is broken," I said.

Hannah pulled herself up into a sitting position. "It's not. That snap? It was this." She held out a huge claw, longer than her hand. One end showed a jagged circumference where it had broken, the other end cone-shaped, curved and sharp. I took it from her, turned it in the fading light. The dragon's claw possessed a colorful iridescence.

"Can you stand?" Grace asked her.

"Sure," Hannah answered. "If Duncan helps me."

I couldn't look at Grace. Couldn't look at either of them, truthfully, but Ren caught my eye. His lips twitched.

"You get one arm," he said. "I'll grab the other."

Shoving the claw in my pocket, I fitted my other arm beneath Hannah's and together Ren and I helped her up. I could have done it alone but was glad for the joint effort. Took the focus off me.

Grace started up the incline. "Let's get back to the others."

"Yes, m'am," I said. Hannah snorted. I regretted my taunt. It had been meant for Grace alone, a touch at humor. I had a feeling that things were going to get tricky now I'd gone and done something gallant. I wouldn't change my actions, but I suspected Hannah viewed them as more than what they were. Heck, if Ren had hit the ground with a creature tracking us, I would have been just as quick to try to save him. I doubted an explanation would make a difference to Hannah. She'd already made up her mind. I could tell by the way she leaned into me as we walked, as if she needed my support when I could tell she didn't require any such thing.

When we topped the rise, I released Hannah's arm and went to stand beside Grace, who waited with feet apart where the cave opened up about thirty strides away, one point of her *lathesa* balanced on her boot. Below, a valley spread into the distance strangely free from snow, maybe due to the geography of the mountain we'd just passed through. On the other side another mountain range ran from north to south. Like arrows shooting skyward, the orange light from the setting sun lit fire to the white peaks. Grace raised her hand and pointed. I followed her finger's direction and spotted the dragon floating aloft, wings spread, a wind not felt by us keeping the animal elevated as it spiraled in daylight's last.

"Poor thing only wanted to get out of there," Grace said.

"It really is a dragon," I whispered.

"Seems so," she answered.

"This is a beautiful place."

"Seems so," Grace repeated, her inflection flawed.

I frowned. "Do you think we'll find danger here?"

"I hope not. I'm tired."

My belly quivered at Grace's words. Grace, the girl who always envisioned a happy ending for us all, who from the very beginning determined to find it. Grace, the tenacious. Grace the resolute. Not so much right now. Her flagging strength, her weary outlook, shouldn't have surprised me. And yet it did.

My fault, that. I'd come to expect more from her incredible nature than she could provide.

The others ambled back up to the cave mouth from below, the *conjures* following. "We'll camp here for the night," I said. "Inside. Make a fire. We could all use some warm food."

I heard a few grunted assents. Everyone seemed tired. When I passed Hannah, her eyes trailed me, her mouth set in a rather grim line. Feeling betrayed most likely. I mentally shrugged her off. One of Gran's many sayings popped into my head. *Bigger fish to fry.*

Yes. Bigger fish. Fish would have been nice. I'd had the first in my life with Kerrick and his people, from a fresh catch cleaned and broiled. No chance on finding a stream before dark. We'd make do with what we carried. Followed by sleep. Once again, we wouldn't wake Grace for her turn at watch. I'd take doubles if I had to.

As I stood contemplating the best place for us all to settle down, Resa came up to me, tapped my hand. I smiled down at her. Resa looked the most rested, but what did I know, really? She didn't complain. I remembered how hard it had been to read her when we were both younger. Even Gran struggled.

I signed, asking her if she was okay. She signed back one word. Outside.

I looked to Carina. "Outside? Does she want me to go outside, or is there something outside she wants me to know about?" Reliance on Carina to explain to me my own sister's meaning shamed me. Yet, Carina's abilities helped her connection, abilities I would never possess. I had to accept it.

"Don't be so hard on yourself," Carina said in response to my guilt, I knew.

"Carina, please, stop doing that."

She lifted a hand. "I apologize. Your guilt was slapping me in the face, though. I couldn't help but sense it."

I grimaced at her in understanding. "Do you know what Resa means by 'outside'?"

"I don't think she's saying 'outside'. I think she's saying 'beyond'."

"Beyond?" Grace echoed, having come quietly up beside us. "As in the place Beyond?"

Carina moved her head in an affirmative. "She knows it. She's seen it. Where or when, I couldn't tell you."

"Her usual way," I said. A way that defied us all. I'd tried imagining it, many times, her near-constant bombardment by visions and conversations, words she could hear in her head when she couldn't hear anything outside of the bizarre functioning in her brain.

"Have we come to Beyond, then?" Grace asked. She nodded across her shoulder, toward the valley. "Out there? Have we reached Land Beyond Reckoning?"

Carina pressed her wrapped fingers lightly on Resa's shoulder. "I think so. It's what she saw."

Grace closed her eyes, shoulders dropping beneath her coat. "Beyond is real."

"So real, Grace," I said.

Her lids lifted. She smiled at me. Behind her, I spotted the dragon in a sky turning dark blue. With two flaps of its wings, the beast sailed toward the mountains across the valley. It seemed a sudden definite we'd locate the Cavern of Sleeping Myth there. Returning my gaze to Grace, I saw she believed it, too.

"I'm going to find some wood," I said. Brand and Ren volunteered to help. Together we trooped back outside to gather dry branches and twigs lying in abundance on the hillside. With the valley below us, the sharp peaks in the distance, the lowering night, I experienced an odd sense of peace. I said as much to Ren, who nodded, admitted he felt the same. Before returning to the cavemouth, we spent a minute watching the last glimmer of sunlight disappear behind the long, spiked range. At the exact instant it did, something huge and brilliant flared deep in the mountains in its stead, and was gone.

My mouth dropped. I exchanged a glance with my wood-gathering companions. Serenity fled.

Chapter Twenty-Five

"Say nothing until morning," I said. "But we keep a close eye out there."

"Carina'll know,' Brand muttered. He contorted his fingers into a gesture I recognized, nearly hidden beneath the fur hanging across his wrist. It irked me that even gifted people viewed Carina and my sister with superstitious anxiety. I mean, Hannah fashioned flame balls from thin air. I'd seen her lob them around like stones. Did anyone react in fearful prejudice toward her?

Well, yeah. They did. Back in All Dwellers they did. Hannah and others like her had been persecuted, locked up when discovered. Released by Grace, most had fled rather than remain with her and Carina and Resa, though. The warrior, the witch, and the thrice-gifted child, feared by so many. After finally hearing the truth about the escape, I could understand why and yet, they weren't only that, not only scarily powerful. Not by any means.

I piled the wood into a mound and had a fire going in short order, using the indispensable instrument from Kerrick to ignite the dry tinder. As before, the *conjures* took up protective positions, Bell and Chauncy by the opening, Vigor hunkering down behind us, guarding the way we had come. I had been guilty of prejudgment myself, basing an aversion to Chauncy on his fearsome reputation and appearance. Part of my apprehension was Grace's fault, although I couldn't blame her. She'd made sure we all knew the dangers first, and rightfully so. I don't think she had any notion about a *conjure's* capabilities, especially since she'd never met one before that moment in the desert outside Ogdo. Now, we'd all bonded with them in ways I didn't think I'd ever understand.

There was Ren, too. My urge to smack him had greatly decreased. In the beginning…well, in the beginning I hadn't believed he held any value at all. He'd been arrogant, rude, way too interested in Grace and his looks rubbed me the wrong way. His recent run back into the tunnel, flinging himself over Hannah and me despite the dragon standing three feet from him, had moved him up a few more notches on the approval stick. I'd definitely call him friend, even without that. We were, all of us, companions by choice, and that made a difference.

With food prepared, we ate, including several small creatures Brand had managed to snag and clean while Ren and I lugged in the wood. I thought about what we had seen outside on the far mountain. It couldn't have been a reflection. The sun set behind the mountain, not in front.

Several times I caught Ren and Brand watching me or exchanging glances, no doubt dwelling on the distant flare, too. It hadn't been small, not like light catching on a glass surface. More like an explosion. An explosion noiseless and powerful and then gone without trace. I hadn't seen any beam in the sky. I hadn't heard any ship nearby either. We would have to proceed with caution in the morning, but for now I felt it best to let everyone who had not witnessed the phenomenon sleep without this particular worry. We possessed enough. No need to add it to all the other concerns we carried around in our heads.

Brand had other ideas. I could tell when he turned to address Grace. He leaned toward her following a quick glance at me. His mouth opened. I slammed a hefty branch into the fire, sending sparks flying. Jumping, angry, he pivoted in my direction.

"Who leads this group?" he asked.

I didn't answer, while everyone else said, "Grace."

Grace shifted where she sat, easing her leg a bit as she sucked marrow from a narrow bone the way Brand had showed her. He had insisted the fatty substance would help her heal. "What's going on?" she asked me.

I glowered at Brand before answering, my brows bunching together. He stared back, unperturbed.

"We saw something outside when we were

grabbing the wood," I said, reluctantly. I couldn't not speak now, though. And maybe Brand was right. Tomorrow could be too late to prepare. We should be discussing what might be out there before we trekked back into the open.

From the corner of my eye, I spotted Carina studying me with a small frown.

"What?" I said to her.

"Stop doubting yourself," she said.

I scowled at her in a way that made her laugh and turn to Mika with a look that said, *see*? I spun back to Grace.

"A light appeared—"

"Like a white sun on the mountainside," Ren interrupted.

"Yeah," I said, "and disappeared right away. I don't know what it could have been. Before you ask, not a reflection. The sun went down behind the mountain."

Grace tossed the hollowed-out bone into the fire. "All right. Then we must be careful."

I watched yellow and orange flames lick along the discarded object. "I thought most of us might be able to sleep better, not knowing."

"Appreciated," Hannah said, sending me a beaming smile. I looked away. Not quickly, not without a little nod, trying to keep her pacified. Maybe that was the wrong tactic. I had no idea.

"Actually," said Ren, "the sun went down directly behind the part of the mountain where we saw the anomaly." He looked proud of himself, a set to his shoulders, a lifted chin, a toss of his yellow hair. Perhaps because he had noticed what I hadn't. Perhaps because he'd used the word 'anomaly' in a sentence. My lips curved despite my inner sarcasm.

"Could the sun have been shining through the mountain somehow?" Mika asked.

"I hadn't considered that," I said. "I don't know."

"Perhaps that's the Cavern of Sleeping Myth?" Hannah suggested, eyeing me for confirmation.

"Since we're headed that way, into the sun, I suppose we'll find out," Grace answered before I could.

I agreed. "We'll continue to stay undercover as much as we can. In case it is something we need to be worried about."

The day had been a long one, much like they all were anymore. Everyone settled down after cleaning up. I added more wood to the flames and bundled up for first watch. I figured it best not to sit too near the fire, where the warmth would make me drowsy. I headed outside first for another look across the valley, easing past Chauncy and Bell. A few seconds later light footsteps sounded behind me. In the past, I might not have heard Grace's approach at all but her healing wound continued to alter her gait.

"Hey," I said, "you should be resting."

"Hey, yourself," she answered. "I don't care. I wanted to talk to you."

"About what?"

"Hannah."

I groaned. Inwardly, I hoped. I was trying my best to keep an unemotional demeanor. In a second, my false calm cracked. "You're not my Gran, Grace. She used to try to talk to me about this sort of thing, too. Really, though? Not appropriate. Not at all. I'll handle it."

Grace had taken a step away when my rant began. I found her eyeballing me now with one dark brow arched and a twitch in her tattooed cheek. I thought she might laugh at me. She didn't though. She sobered.

"I just wanted to thank you for going after her," she said.

"Oh." I shifted my weight from one foot to the other. "Nothing else you wanted to talk about?"

"Like what?"

"Like…you know."

Grace stayed silent.

"She likes me," I said.

"We all do," said Grace.

"Not like this. You told me to be kind. Is this why?"

Lips compressing, she nodded.

I lifted my head to the distant mountains. Cloudy streaks were working their way into the night sky from behind us, maybe bringing the bottled-up snow. "I like *you*, Grace," I said quietly.

"And I love you, Duncan. You have become the friend I never thought to have."

Is that all I am? I thought and hoped I hadn't said it out loud. I could do that when stressed. Grace spoke and I recognized my mouth had betrayed me.

"Not all," she said. "But all for now."

Yeah, I understood. I didn't know how Mika and Carina managed it. If Grace and I got closer and something happened to her, I'd—well, I didn't even want to think about that. Best not to. Things were difficult enough. My feelings already existed. And now I had gone and let them loose, too, into the wide world. I couldn't suck those words back in, secret them away again.

Grace extended her hand to my arm, wrapped her fingers around my sleeve and squeezed. "Make sure somebody wakes me for watch this time."

"Will do," I said in an outright lie.

She made her way to the fire, to warmth, hopefully to sleep. I had already picked out a place to hunker down and watch both those around the fire and the approach from outside. As I turned, I caught movement near Bell's far flank. Silver-blue eyes reflected the meager light. Without a word, Hannah pivoted on her heel and marched back inside.

I couldn't say I experienced any remorse she'd overheard, but I did curse my own cowardice for that revelation.

*   *   *

We started out as soon as light touched the valley. Grace groused at being left to sleep the night through again. She looked better, though, clearer, stronger, so I took her grumbling in stride. We mounted the *conjures*, divided up as we had been before and headed down the mountainside into the morning. The sky had gone pale gray with clouds. Brand announced with confidence snow would begin within the hour. He was, of course, correct.

315

Flakes fell gently onto ground still free from ice. Compared to former conditions, I think we enjoyed it. I did, anyway, especially watching my sister catch flakes on her tongue, animated in a way I could understand. She had changed. Not that she had to, not for me or for anyone else, but I could relate a little more to this Resa, could see, I suppose, a bit of myself in her. Although we shared a blood connection, she had always seemed so different, not only from me but from everyone I knew.

My friends had made the difference, Carina, Grace, and Mika. They shared a closeness with my sister I did not. Not like they did.

Carina's head turned. Her eyes sought out mine. I pretended I didn't see.

Give me this, Carina, I thought. *If I want to recognize I failed her, even if only in the past, let me.*

I kept my gaze on Grace, on the back of her head, her hood pulled up against the cold. She carried her *lathesa* across her lap. After several minutes the crystal at the nearer end caught the light, glinted. I resisted the urge to shift my seat and look around, reminding myself the glow came from daylight and nothing more. We had traveled far from All Dwellers. Too far, too fast for those creatures from Emerald to track us, not without transport by Tiran and his airships, and we'd seen none of those. Still, the glowing crystals would always be our first defense, an early alert to the proximity of the genetically manipulated creatures. We who had been on Emerald knew by the time mind-shift began, it would be too late. If not for Grace back there on the prison moon… Yes, if not for Grace. Always.

"What's got you so antsy?" Brand asked from behind me.

"What? Nothing. Just thinking about things."

A lot of things. Too many things. I realized no one was talking, which didn't help. We had been journeying in silence.

"How did you end up a hunter?" I asked Brand, to start a conversation going. We were passing through an open area and could see in all directions. I knew that meant we could be seen as well, but being able to spot something coming eased my mind a bit, enough to figure some talking wouldn't hurt.

"Lost my folks. 'ad to do somethin'. I know animals, 'ear 'em, sense 'em, talk to 'em, understand their ways. Feel bad every time I kill, an' they know it. They get it. They all have t' eat, too. One day might be me."

I didn't think I'd ever heard him string more than two sentences together at one time. A reticent guy, was Brand. His last statement sent a shiver down my spine, however. "I won't let that happen," I said.

"You might 'ave to," he answered in a flat voice. I could tell by his tone the discussion had ended. Ren and Hannah had drawn alongside us, hearing everything. Ren glanced at me with a horrified expression he barely suppressed. Hannah didn't look at me at all. Fine.

Grace always said when people responded to a

situation with 'fine' they seldom meant it. But I did. I couldn't help Hannah's hurt feelings. Anytime I tried, the effort only dug a deeper hole. She would have to get herself back in line with reality. Not my job.

Having thought those things, did I feel a twinge of guilt? Of course, I did. I turned my head slightly to glance at her, to gauge her emotions, and caught her staring. She wrinkled her nose in a scowl and looked away. I released a long, slow breath over my lips.

Fine.

Without warning, Chauncy lurched into a gallop beneath us, the other two *conjure* following his lead. Suddenly, we were all clinging with fingers shoved into the blankets' weave to keep from being thrown off. I looked back, saw something in the air, drawing closer. Dark hull, clearly damaged, a ship moved through the snow still some distance away, bobbing like a limping animal.

"Is that the same—"

"Looks it," Brand said.

Somehow, the ship had managed to break free from the forcefield or whatever had been holding it back. Not unscathed. The ship's pilot must have been fighting to push through for some time. From its appearance, the ship had crashed before the pilot tried again. That would explain the passing time between when we'd seen it and this minute.

I spun back around, bending low as we approached the trees. Branches swept over us, snagged clothing, skin. The animals finally stopped in a grove so closely grown it presented as a solid wall all around, except the way we'd crashed in. I leaped down, returned to the opening, cast my hand above my eyes to shield them from the frozen precipitation. I raised my other when footsteps crunched fallen evergreen needles behind me.

"There!" I said. "Does anyone recognize the shape? I don't see an emblem."

"There isn't one," Mika said on my right.

"Is it going to crash?" Hannah asked, gasping dramatically when she realized how close she stood to me on the left and then scurrying a foot or so to her left. Grace came and took her place, peering up at the sky.

"I'm not sure it's after us," she said. "Are you?"

"Why do you say that?"

"Look," said Grace, pointing as I had done. "We'd wandered a little off the straight line crossing the valley, but the ship seems to be trying to maintain it, maybe heading to the mountains."

"I think you're right," I said. At our backs, Hannah huffed. She shuffled quickly away. I didn't look to see where she'd gone. She needed to grow up. We didn't have the time for tantrums. Returning my attention to the ship, I saw it continued to bob and weave in the sky, losing altitude. "It's coming down."

"Not intentionally," Mika said.

"No," I agreed, "not intentionally."

A second later, beyond a small incline, the ship plummeted. A shock wave reached us, driving snow into the grove, followed by a delayed boom. Smoke swirled up into the sky to mingle with the ice coming down. Grace swore.

"Let's go," she said.

"What, out there?" Ren asked in disbelief. "What if soldiers—"

"The ship isn't carrying troops," Grace cut across him. "It's way too small. Someone could be hurt in there."

"Or dead," I muttered, starting after her.

I don't think she meant for everyone to go but in the end, we did, even the *conjures*. Despite her healing injury she outpaced us all. Grace, fueled by adrenaline. One day, that little gland's secretions wouldn't be enough.

When we arrived, a body lay outside the damaged ship on the snowy ground. Mika, prodded by an instinct he didn't fully realize he had, got to whoever lay there before Grace did. "Not dead!" he shouted out.

I dropped down at Mika's side. Grace lowered herself more slowly to the ground. Carina and Resa stood close by but the other three waited at a short distance. The *conjures* behind them rocked from side to side making their low, rumbling noises. I wished I understood what passed between them. Brand would probably know.

Mika turned the body over. He pushed dark hair away from the face for a better look. She— because it was a she, or resembled a female at any rate—possessed skin much like Grace's. Lightly bronzed, possibly mixed blood, and tattooed. Two small wings flared out from the bridge of her nose like an extra pair of eye brows. The wings looked silver in the falling snow. She would probably stand close to Grace's height when upright. Dark eyes stared back into ours, lucid and aware.

"Is there anyone else inside?" Grace asked.

The female, possibly my age, continued to stare without answering. I wondered if she didn't understand the language. Grace rose and made her way over to the busted ship. She pushed her way inside. I followed with my cutter drawn. Grace had been right about the ship being too small for troops. Its interior dimensions were far smaller, even, than the cargo ship commandeered by us for our flight from the Emerald to Talia.

"Hello?" Grace called, not loudly. We quickly searched the tiny hold, several cubicles, found no evidence anyone else remained in the ship. A satchel lay on the floor behind a swivel chair in front of the control panel. Grace snatched it up, tossed the bag over one shoulder. The vessel hadn't been outfitted for off-world travel. I wondered where it had originated and said as much out loud.

"Let's find out," Grace said.

Upon exiting the ship, we found Mika, the pilot and everyone else had relocated to a discreet distance from the smoking vessel. Grace walked straight up to the stranger and held the bag just out of her reach. The female watched it, watched Grace, and when Grace went to hand the bag to me, spoke.

"That's mine."

"So, you do understand us," Grace said.

"I know many languages," said the girl.

"What's your name? What are you called?"

She didn't answer.

"Who do you fear, that you flee with nothing but this?" Grace waggled the satchel.

"I fear no one, and I wasn't fleeing."

"Did you steal the ship?" I butted in. "Don't worry. You'll get no grief from us. We had to do the same."

The girl turned her gaze my way, studying me. Her lip curled at one side. "I know."

Grace lurched forward, stopped herself. "Do you know who we are?"

The pilot's gaze trailed over me and my companions one at a time. "Some of you. You," she said to me. "You," to Grace. "Those three," indicating Mika, Carina and Resa. "The rest?" She shrugged her shoulders, wincing after.

I opened my mouth to speak but Grace dropped a hand onto my wrist, silencing me.

"Were you looking for us?" she asked.

The girl shrugged again. "Maybe. Good thing I did not find you. You would have had to leave them behind." She tossed her head toward Ren, Hannah, Brand and the *conjures*.

"You act as though we'd have had no choice about accompanying you," Grace said in a quiet, even voice I recognized so well. Keeping her annoyance under control, or trying to.

The girl didn't answer Grace's statement directly, but said instead, "They knew you were coming, said it was only a matter of time before something or someone prevented you. We decided not to wait, not leave things to chance." Her mouth wrinkled in disdain, reminding me of Ren when first we'd met. "Some of us decided we had to get to you first."

"Who is this we?" Grace asked.

The girl met Grace's gaze, silent.

"Carina," Grace said, her voice cold, flat. To be honest, her whole demeanor alarmed me a little. Carina stepped forward.

The girl's eyes widened as she looked Carina up and down. She didn't seem to notice Resa at Carina's side. "Don't you dare let her touch me!"

"She actually doesn't need to," I said, "to know what you're thinking. Believe me."

The girl swiped melting snow from her forehead and stared around at each one of us. Finally, she huffed out a breath. "My name is Valeah. I come from—" She raised her hand and pointed to the mountains. "There."

"The Cavern of Sleeping Myth?" Hannah ventured, having drawn nearer.

"No," said Valeah. "The city around it."

"What city?" I asked, squinting at the gray, green, and partially white wrinkles making up the mountain's sides.

"Landing is well hidden. It has needed to be," Valeah said, frowning. "I thought—well, it does not matter what I thought. Or what I think. I am not like you. I am a naught. I have no gifts. For anything, apparently. I cannot even fly a Dante ship through a simple forcefield. The field was down when I left. That is no excuse, I know. I should have expected it to be repaired upon my return."

"And why were you looking for us?" Grace asked, her voice suddenly gentle.

"Like I said, I was tired of waiting," Valeah

said.

"Not quite what you said," Grace murmured. I stepped forward.

"Doesn't the ship have some kind of control to enable you to obtain passage through your own forcefield?" I asked.

"I am a naught," Valeah said again. "Do you not understand? Besides, the forcefield is not ours. It was put in place by the Lady of Gabrilon."

I had been bending toward her while she spoke. Abruptly I straightened and shook my head.

"Oh yes, Duncan Oaks," Valeah drawled, "your grandmother."

Chapter Twenty-Six

If not for the serious situation facing us, I might have laughed at Duncan's expression. But I never would. Recent discoveries about his family remained fresh in his mind, discoveries with which he had yet to come to terms. I stepped in, extended my hand, helped Valeah up from the ground. Upright, she stood less than half a head shorter than I, yet as narrow as a sapling tree. Except for Brand, we were all quite thin due to deprivation, but her form seemed natural, like she'd never known another. Whip-strong was a term that came to mind. I sensed tensile strength in her grip on my hand, in the way she held herself despite being shaken by the crash in what I suspected was a stolen ship. I shrugged her satchel off my shoulder once again and held it out to her.

"Thank you," she said.

"Are you still planning on heading home despite the ship?" I asked, tipping my head toward the wreckage.

"Where else would I go? I'll pay the price for that, nonetheless. Not monetary," she added. "I have no credit, no funds of my own. No, I expect I will be made to serve a sentence."

Beside me, Duncan gasped and pointed toward the sky. "Not on—"

"The Emerald? No. Nothing like that." She opened her bag, rummaged through it quickly then, apparently satisfied nothing had gone missing because of us or otherwise, slung it over her back. "I assume you are all coming with me?"

Right. She knew where we had been headed. She had said her people were awaiting our arrival in the due course of time. I had no plan to ask how they had known. I had gotten quite used to mysterious truths surfacing from what once had been tales. Yet I could not help wondering how many others knew through the same means or different ones. Such a possibility would certainly explain how we had been repeatedly found out, located, hunted down. It could not all be coincidence. Perhaps none of it was.

All but Carina and Resa walked instead of rode with our heads covered against the lightly falling snow. As I knew nothing about Valeah, I did not want her riding with anyone. I could not help a caution that had become second nature. Even without the necessity for vigilance, she had been eyeing the *conjure* with nervousness anyway. Since she wore sturdy boots on her feet, there seemed no reason to take the risk of her being mounted.

"Does the Lady of Gabrilon's forcefield separate your lands here from hers?" I asked as we strode. Although Duncan pretended to have no interest in my question, I could tell by his head's slight turn, his carefully controlled expression, he'd begun listening quite carefully.

"Yes," said Valeah. "She hoped to keep us in."

"Has it worked?"

"Of course not."

Somehow, based on what I had seen in Trill, I hadn't expected Aeron's mother to possess the technology for such things as forcefields. She had been called formidable by him, though. Duncan told me. This could be why.

"And the warding in the abandoned village on the northwest road up from Trill?" Valeah didn't reply, her eyes on the mountains ahead. Enough distance existed between that place and this that she possibly knew nothing about it. I persisted anyway. "Do you know which one I mean?"

After a moment, she nodded.

"Is that her doing?"

"No." She made a sign against enchantment with the fingers on her far side. I still caught it and realized it had been meant to be seen. "Not without help, anyway," Valeah went on. "The Lady, too, seeks power. He's gotten to so many of the high leaders in this world, and those who aspired to rise."

"To the Lady of Gabrilon?" Duncan asked.

"Who knows? I haven't all the answers," Valeah said.

This development would surely explain the unidentifiable soldiers dogging us. Because despite their vast numbers and our few, it seemed many involved in the war had come to fear us, while being desirous of what we had at the same time. Having witnessed Resa unleashed and knowing what I carried in the pouch around my neck, I could understand both the fear and the greed, but not from so many. Conceivably, however, and based on Valeah's reference to *he,* the fear and greed might not be the product of many, but fostered by the influence of one.

"Who is 'he'?" I asked, a cold dread creeping along my skin beneath my clothes.

She glanced at me and away. "You know."

"No," I said. "I don't."

She inclined her head further, twisting her neck in order to stare at Duncan beside me. "Then he does," she said. "Duncan does."

I scoffed, huffing a single, scornful breath from my open mouth. Valeah faced front again.

"You do, Duncan," she insisted. "He styles himself The Darkness. Sound familiar now?"

Duncan's eyes closed, opened slowly. My step faltered. I nearly tripped. "Duncan?"

"Kerrick spoke of the darkness when I was with him," he said. "I don't know if he understood it was one man. I certainly didn't. Not until recently."

My jaw tightened. "And yet you said nothing."

"I said nothing," he agreed. "I couldn't. What would we have done? What could we have done? We had enough to worry about."

"We might have benefited from being forewarned," I said.

"In what way? We were battling the immediate, not something vague and perhaps not even real."

"But you know it's real now."

He nodded. "Draig. Draig was aware. We spoke. Briefly."

I swallowed, slipped my tongue behind my front teeth, thinking, wrapping my mind around what had been revealed. "All right," I said. "I understand why you did not speak. At least we know now."

"And knowing means what?" he asked.

"Knowing means everything makes more sense to me."

"In what way?" he asked again.

"I never understood how Stone Tiran managed to make himself so powerful, so quickly. Or why the Lyoness, who had her own agenda, also appeared to ally herself with him, or where these other, unknown forces had come from. It made no sense to me that people who wanted supremacy would share their strength with others who wanted the same thing. They're all being manipulated by whoever this one man is. He is the driving force."

On my left, Valeah nodded.

"You still have not answered me," I said to her. "Who, exactly, is he?"

"I have not heard his true name. His magic is old. You know about old magic, Grace, don't you?"

I made no response. What I truly knew about old magic could fit in the palm of my hand. Words, they were. Only words.

"Well, if you don't, you'll learn," Valeah said. "Soon enough."

I slowed my stride, wondering if we should be trusting Valeah or anyone but each other, at all.

Chapter Twenty-Seven

The sun went down through clouds and snow. We all witnessed what Duncan, Ren and Brand had seen, although from much closer than the mountainside outside the cave where we had been camped. The disc of light flared, forcing prisms into the precipitation, and died. Valeah and I walked in front, Duncan right beside me.

"What is that?" I asked Valeah. "A beacon?" I had seen one in Citadel, years ago with my parents. A beacon light atop the Quadrate to alert ships to the landing pad on the high building. A building that barely existed anymore. Stone Tiran had set himself up in the damaged skeleton. As Revered, this would have been his place had he not brought it to ruin. Rather than light and green growth within its stone boundaries, only shadows and terror existed there now. I had discovered that when housed in a dank cell before my trial. For the first time in many days, I wondered about all the others who had been brought to the Quadrate with me, a single offspring from every desert family held to ensure the tribes did not join the battle. The dessert warriors were fighting now. Had Tiran killed the hostages as he had threatened?

"Grace? Are you ill?"

I glanced aside at Valeah, realized I probably looked quite sick. "I'm not ill," I said and repeated my question. "Is that a beacon?"

She turned slowly away, speculation in her expression. "It is more than a beacon, but you can call it that, if you like. It stands in the Cavern mouth. It is part of the Sleeping Myth. For time out of mind it has also signaled the last of daylight each day. This is the only time the light is seen across the land. We call it then The Last Breath."

Frowning in the direction we had seen the flare, I considered what Valeah said. I had not expected to see visible evidence of the Sleeping Myth. I anticipated…something else. Nothing physical, in any case.

"These fanciful names are going to kill me," Mika muttered. "How many words in the name of your city?"

Valeah's eyes narrowed. "Only one. Landing."

"And that's not shortened from anything else?" he persisted.

Valeah's made a dismissive movement with her hand. "Could be. I suppose no one would remember anyway. These mountains were settled longer ago than history recounts."

"Really?" I said, gazing up. How did I not know this? As a people we considered ourselves versed in factual history as well as lore and legend. I had spent many hours at lessons in addition to warrior training. If Landing or the Cavern of Sleeping Myth had ever been mentioned, I would not have forgotten.

"The climate seems a bit off-putting for settlement," Ren drawled.

Valeah glared at him. "It suits us fine."

She wasn't lying. I had already noted her clothing didn't provide the same protection ours did, and yet she appeared not to suffer from the cold or the precipitation. "Some would say that about the desert," I said to Ren, attempting to calm any acrimony. "One becomes accustomed, especially through generation after generation."

"Exactly," Valeah agreed, rather smugly. They were somewhat alike, she and Ren. I wondered if they realized that or would go on rubbing each other the wrong way without any idea why.

"Grace!" said Duncan sharply. He raised his hand, pointed. The crystal on my *lathesa* glowed with blue fire in the dark. Duncan yanked the cutter free from his belt. Behind him, I heard a whisper of leather as Mika and Ren did the same. Swearing, I pivoted full circle, peering into the deep shadow. No one had lit a torch yet. The light had only just left the sky. The *conjures* paused as we did, their rumblings still quiet.

"Wait." I spun the *lathesa* in my fist, brought the other point around to view. "This is the one from the orb."

The orb shard glinted, but did not flare into life as it would if the creatures from Emerald were near. I glanced at the opposite end where the crystal broken from Duncan's dagger had been attached. It showed only a faint gleam, too. I spun my weapon back around to its former position. The crystal from the glass mine glimmered again, altering as I moved the staff.

"It's reflecting something," I said.

Duncan cast his gaze in all directions. "From where?"

"I can't—" My voice faltered, breath rushing out. I whipped around. "There," I said. I had caught it from the corner of my eye, but now I could see certain things head on. The mountainside directly before us glowed from one side to the other with scattered illumination shining through trees and snow.

"Landing," Valeah said. And yes, with smug satisfaction again. I had not mistaken her attitude.

"How was it hidden from us?" Mika asked.

"Mage craft."

Ren shoved his cutter back into his belt. "So, you decided to spring it on us just now?"

"Not me," Valeah said. "You were not listening. I am a naught. I have no power."

I turned to her with a frown. "What happened then?"

"Not what. Who." She gave me a long, level look, her gaze shining in the dark. "One of you unsealed the screening for our eyes."

"None of us possess the gift." As I spoke, I checked myself mentally. Duncan and I turned on a heel in the exact same instant, seeking Resa in the dark. We located her beside Carina, immobile, staring up at the glowing mountainside.

Smiling.

Duncan swore, only one word, and hurried to her side. He dropped onto his knees in the snow, caught her attention and began signing too quickly for me to understand, although I suspected I knew what he asked. She responded, two short words. *We go.* When he clambered to his feet again, I could tell by his expression her reply had not given him the information he sought.

"It must have been Resa," Duncan whispered upon his return to my side. "It must have been."

Unless Valeah was lying, he had to be right. The alternative, that Valeah wasn't being truthful and possessed powers she had not disclosed, made me determined to stay right by her.

A wide path or road had been cut into the mountain in what Valeah referred to as a switchback, designed, she said, to keep the way from becoming too steep. She led us forward a different way, however, avoiding the easily climbed stone thoroughfare. I assumed she did not want us to be seen.

Before long, buildings became apparent between rocky outcroppings and trees, gray in color, almost invisible in the night. They spread as far as I could see in either direction, probably much further when seen by daylight. Even then, I expected they would be difficult to spot, mage craft or no mage craft. The dwellings appeared to blend into the surroundings as All Dwellers had tried to do, but without that city's concrete and glass walls.

"This way," Valeah said when we reached a tricky spot, overgrown but with a narrow path circumventing the impediment. When the *conjures* came up behind, they crashed right through the tangled growth.

"Sorry," I murmured. Valeah did not acknowledge the apology but strode on.

Duncan kept a careful eye on Resa. She and Carina had dismounted once we reached the mountain track. It had to be difficult enough for Duncan to deal with and accept his sister's fearsome powers without more being mysteriously added to them. I maintained doubts it had been she who unsealed the shield for our view, yet Resa saw many things beyond her immediate surroundings. I supposed it could be possible she had learned it in the special way she dealt with the world. Valeah had denied any mage gifts, a claim I also distrusted. If not either one of them, though, this left Brand or Hannah as the only two possessing any capabilities. Still, I had never detected anything which might enable them to orchestrate the recent event. Hannah admitted to the fireball and knowing nothing more, Brand understood rather than controlled anything with his gifts. I wondered if our nearness to this place had merely enhanced Resa's own.

Lights began to blink out among the trees as the hour grew later. By the time we reached a point far above the valley, the city had gone nearly dark. Valeah paused where two mammoth stones met and pivoted to face everyone.

"There is no place for your beasts. They will

have to stay here."

"Just so you know," said Duncan, "nothing will keep them out if they sense a danger to Grace or anyone else in our party."

Valeah eyed the *conjure* with wonder. "Truly?"

"Truly," Duncan said.

Chauncy tapped me lightly on the shoulder with his long horn, running it along the bone and down my arm. Afterward, emitting low growls, the three *conjures* departed into the woods.

"Follow me," Valeah instructed. She stepped up to the two huge rocks and disappeared. No one moved. "Come on," I heard her say, muffled now. She reappeared and indicated a space where the stones met and crossed, invisible to us until she pointed it out . I peered past her at a narrow pathway, open at the top. It seemed to go back into the hill, vanishing into blackness.

"Where does this lead?"

"Into the city," she said. "Not far from my home. We will be unseen."

I exchanged a glance with the others. They looked as unconvinced as I, but I could not perceive any other option besides following Valeah. I nodded. Duncan removed his glass dagger from its sheath, a noiseless weapon compared with the cutter's low hum. We proceeded single file into the dark.

*　　*　　*

The passage underground was not a long one. Hannah produced the flame-ball and held it high, illuminating the tunnel. She walked between Carina and Brand, her light throwing our shadows into wavering confusion before us. Valeah's hand shot into the air.

"Douse it," she said, having not looked behind to see what, exactly, presented the illumination. "We are here."

As soon as Hannah shut down the circular flame in her hand, I could see dull light filtering in. The light cast a very dim shadow across the stone floor. A gate, I thought, made from finely wrought metal. When we drew closer, I realized the barrier was formed from living boughs. Upon our approach, it twisted and pulled back of its own accord.

"Did you do that?" Duncan hissed at Valeah.

She spun toward him. "I told you—"

"A naught. Yeah, got it," he said. "So, who opened it?"

"No one. It opens on its own when someone nears. The living tree has been designed to do so. By mage craft."

I maintained silence, but her response astounded me. Tales and histories I had heard aplenty, and we had as a group already witnessed astounding truths and appalling lies. If the residents here had maintained mage bloodlines less diluted than All Dwellers, anything could be possible. Including dangers from which we would have no protection.

There's always me, Skelly murmured.

It won't come to that I pushed back at him.

He laughed. I struggled to keep my mouth

closed, my facial features composed.

"Grace?"

I eyed Duncan askance, compressed my lips and shook my head.

"Maybe, just for a time, you should let me—"

"No," I said. "I need everyone to stop offering. Especially here."

He released a long, blown-out breath like a winded animal.

One by one, we exited into a small clearing. At the opposite side, a staircase cut from the stony ground extended upward. We climbed after Valeah to the top. By the time we reached the upper level, I was cursing my sore leg soundlessly. My lips were moving, though. Duncan caught me at it, said nothing, resigned to ignoring me.

"Thank you," I whispered. He understood.

We waited on a cobblestone square a few minutes as we all gathered back together. Hannah circled around behind me and Duncan, her eyes on him. I experienced a twinge of pity for her, and a certain unease.

"Not much further," Valeah said, voice low. Her eyes darted around nervously. "We'll have to be quiet. Once hidden, I—"

I heard them before I saw them, footsteps racing through a sudden, swirling, snow-filled mist. Warriors appeared armed as was I, with *lathesas* minus the deadly, crystal points. Realizing I could shortly be disarmed, I snapped the orb crystal from the one end, unbalancing my weapon, and slipped the large shard into my pocket, cutting myself in the process. The crystal was our only warning against the creatures from Emerald and we might yet need it. I snapped the other end away, too, restoring balance. I did not require the crystals to fight.

Valeah threw her arms straight into the air over her head. "Wait! Don't!"

We all mimicked her, holding hands up in a non-threatening position, I with the stripped weapon in my right.

"Whoever you are," a man in front directed us, "do not move. And you, Valeah Preis, are under arrest."

"Arrest?" she cried. I couldn't see how she expected otherwise, stealing an airship. We remained still, watching and waiting. I glanced at Mika, who twitched a little, no doubt recalling the reason for his incarceration on the Emerald. But Valeah had said she had no worries about receiving such extreme punishment. I lacked her confidence in that regard. I had received a lifetime sentence on the whim of a tyrant. Duncan, too. Mika, Carina, Skelly, all would have remained on Emerald until death, if not for the circumstance none of us could have foreseen.

"Yes, arrest." The man ground his *lathesa's* blunt end into the snow beside his boot. "You stole a costly vessel."

"From my parents! You cannot tell me they have pressed charges."

"They do not need to."

I felt something touch my waist and looked down to find Resa at my side. My heart jumped into my throat.

I dropped a hand, signed to her to be calm, then

slipped my bloodied fingers around her own, hoping she understood, hoping we were not all about to become airborne. I needed help. Everyone did. If Resa let loose on these warriors, we might escape, yes, but our chance to find answers would be gone.

Two more people arrived from the path ahead, a man and a woman, the woman appearing oddly familiar to me in a manner I could not quite figure out. She flicked a look at us and away.

"Dahl," the woman said, addressing the warrior who had been speaking, "let her go. Let them all go. My daughter did not steal the ship. I allowed her to take it. My husband did not know. I had not told him her plans."

Lies, hissed Skelly. He needn't have bothered. I'd already recognized the same.

Dahl, however, did not, or if he did, he didn't own the conviction to question the woman. He took a step back, ordered those with him to stand down. He inclined his head. "As you say, madam."

She nodded at him in response before raising her hand and, with a swift, finger-curling wave, signaled us all to move up the pathway she and the man had descended. I exchanged a quick look with Duncan and followed, the rest hurrying behind. Valeah scampered sideways alongside her mother.

"Mom. Mom!"

"We will speak later," the woman said sharply. Valeah subsided, head bowed as she continued at her mother's side at a sedate pace. I wondered about the man. Valeah had not given him a glance. Perhaps he was not her father, merely someone who accompanied her mother. I wondered then what

Valeah's mother's position might be, warranting an escort.

While we strode in their wake, I examined our surroundings. Dwellings had been built directly into the mountainside, stone-faced, which explained them blending into the landscape. Due to the late hour and, perhaps, the weather, few people populated the pathway. Those who did turned and stared as we passed. Whispers trailed after us.

"Why are they gawking? Do you think they've known what we actually look like?" Duncan asked.

"Why wouldn't they? Valeah did. But perhaps it's only because they don't see many strangers here. Let alone strangers being marched through the city by whoever Valeah's mother is."

He snorted and moved closer, bumping his elbow against mine. A noise came from behind us. Not from Mika and Carina or even Brand, but a huff from Hannah, who brought up the rear with Ren. It might have been in response to anything, maybe something Ren had quietly said, but I had not heard a single word. Duncan's quick eyeroll made me think he associated the same reason I did to her obvious displeasure.

"I'll talk to her," Duncan whispered. "I'll straighten this all out."

I declined to respond. Any comment on my part was unnecessary. This was not my battle to wage.

Before long we reached another staircase. I hesitated at the bottom before putting my foot to the first step with a grunt. Duncan held his crooked elbow out for me. I pretended I did not see it. By the time we reached the top and a shut door there, a prickling sweat stood out along my brow beneath my coat's hood.

"You okay?" Duncan asked. I shushed him, trying to hear what Valeah and her mother were saying. I took several steps closer, blatantly eavesdropping. Valeah's mother turned at my approach.

"Thank you," I said, as if this had been my only purpose. "How should we address you?"

"Coness Preis," she said. "Or perhaps, Grace, you should call me by my given name: Avant."

I bowed my head. "Avant," I repeated, having been given permission to use it. "So, you know who I am."

"I know who all of you are. Well, most of you. You seem to have other followers."

"They are not followers," I said. "They are friends. We are all friends."

She stared at me through narrowed lids, assessing me, perhaps. "Let us get inside. It is chilly out here."

The man with her threw open one side of a double door. Dazzling light flooded the snowy walkway. I squinted and angled my head, wanting to see what awaited us before following them in. I saw only a room. A very spacious, high-ceilinged room with furniture along the sides. Avant and her escort paused several steps across the floor, Valeah on the threshold. Otherwise, the room held no other persons. We all hurried inside. The door was closed behind us. I spoke before Avant could turn away.

"Why would you think I possessed followers? What is it you believe I am?"

"The warrior." She looked at Carina and Resa in turn. "The witch, the thrice-gifted child. He is Duncan, and he is—" She cocked her head to one side, viewing Mika.

I made no effort to enlighten her. I would not give her my friends' names. Valeah knew them, of course. She would probably pass on the information at some point, but it would not come from me.

Avant's gaze tracked me from head to foot and back again. "I meant no offense."

"None taken," I said. I took a deep breath and moved further into the interior, my companions trailing after as I checked again for any trap or trick.

"Nothing to fear here," Avant said, as if reading my emotions. Perhaps she could. I had no idea what gifts the residents in Landing possessed. Yet obviously gifted they were. The shielding, the gate, the warrior's appearance through some cloud created from the snow and air and dust, all told the story.

As I crossed the floor behind our host, I wondered if our coming here might not have been a mistake. I caught the same misgiving on Duncan's face.

Chapter Twenty-Eight

I sensed Grace's nerves, and that made me nervous. I kept Resa at my side and my hand hovering near the glass blade I had once again sheathed. Always aware, Carina pulled Mika up right behind me, where Brand joined them. Hannah and Ren followed closely on their heels. The closeness made for clumsy strides, trying to avoid the feet in front.

Avant paused before another door about halfway along the righthand wall. She made a sweeping gesture toward it. Reminded me a bit of the presenters in the casinos, welcoming suckers by the droves. I really hoped I was reading this wrong.

"Eat first and then, after a few questions, rest. You all look like you need food and sleep."

Her lack of real questions was setting off alarm bells inside my head. Yeah, I could assume she knew what her daughter had been up to, or at least had drawn conclusions, but that didn't explain why we were with her, why we were heading here in the first place, or what we expected now we'd arrived. If nothing else, she ought to be taking her daughter aside, demanding an explanation as to the stolen ship and its present whereabouts. Clearly, we hadn't arrived in it and I didn't for a minute believe she'd allowed Valeah to take that expensive bit of machinery no matter what she'd said to those goons outside. I was grateful, though, that she had. I didn't care to imagine where we'd be right now if she hadn't.

We passed into a surprisingly cozy-sized room, considering the enormous one we'd just left. It possessed a rectangular table with chairs to either side for dining purposes. A bright red, oval rug sat beneath the setup, but the walls were strangely barren and made of some material that muffled our voices. I heard an exchange between Valeah and her mother, though, in a hissed undertone before she followed us in. I only caught one statement clearly, uttered by Avant.

"You should have stayed away."

The conversation ended when the woman shoved Valeah into the room behind us. Valeah pushed the door closed, activated the lock. Her hands clenched into fists at her sides as she turned to face us.

"We have to go."

We gaped at her mutely. Mika blew out a short breath.

"You just brought us all here," he said.

"I thought we were eating," Ren added.

"That was a lie, told for Holden's benefit."

"Holden?" I echoed.

"My mother's bodyguard." Valeah hurried across the room, started slapping her hands against the wall. "I'm sorry," she said in a breathless rush.

"Sorry?" echoed Grace. "What's happened?"

"And what are you doing?" I added, frowning at her antics.

"The guards know now there are strangers among us. Word will get back to those who wanted you dead before you ever reached Landing."

Ren uttered an expletive I'd never heard him use before. Under different circumstances I might have patted him on the back for it. My eyes, my thoughts, however, were focused on Grace. Her posture and overly calm expression indicated one thing. High alert.

"Why, then, did you bring us in?" Grace questioned. "You knew the danger."

"We don't have time for discussion," Valeah snapped in response. "Help me!"

I ran to her side. "Help you what?"

"There's a hidden panel here, somewhere. We need to open it."

I started poking and prodding, seeking a place that gave, that might indicate a door fitted seamlessly into the wall's rough surface. Valeah paused, pointing at Ren.

"When the panel opens, someone must unlock that other door. Those who will come need to believe we exited the room the way we came in."

He nodded, rushed over to the entrance, and

stood with his hand poised above the mechanical lock in preparation. The rest of us attended to the search for the panel. Even Resa seemed to have picked up on the need, or else she thought it a game, like throwing snowballs. Something everyone did together.

Carina made a small cry and stepped back. A panel shot to her left, leaving us looking into a dark, subterranean space leading into the mountainside. Behind me, the main door lock clicked, followed by Ren's racing footsteps.

"I hear voices," he said, herding us all forward like a flapping granny. "Move it!"

We crammed inside. Valeah located a more obvious control for shutting the panel and sealed us in. For a moment we stood in total darkness, listening. The door from the main room opened, hardly heard through the dampening quality in the walls. Voices came next in muted manner. I recognized one thing in them. They were many and they were angry.

"Who else knows about this passageway?" Grace whispered.

"Me, my sister, my mom, my dad. No one else since the last Elder family lived here. Each Elder and his or her offspring is sworn to secrecy. It is an escape route in case of…" Her voice trailed off.

"In case of what?" I asked.

"Something like this," she said. "Something that endangers us."

"And does that happen often?" Ren drawled quietly.

"No," Valeah said, "not in a hundred years."

"But you've been down here."

"Yes. But not through this door."

"Why do you come here?"

"I like solitude," she said.

Those words rang false, but I couldn't worry about it right then. Someone had moved closer to the wall and we could now hear their words.

"Avant, it's been made clear. They must die."

"Dad!" Valeah breathed, like a sigh rather than a cry. She brushed past me, moving toward the panel. I put my arm out, held her back.

"Since he knows about the passage, he must realize we're in here," I hissed. "Where do we go now?"

Before she could answer, Valeah's father spoke again. "Search the grounds and the hillside above. They must have slipped out before your arrival."

He hadn't given us away. Valeah collapsed against me in relief.

"Show us how to get out," Grace whispered nearby. "Duncan, light your torch but keep it shielded until we are far enough away."

Hannah made a noise somewhere off to my right. Light pierced the darkness as the flaming, heatless ball appeared on her palm. Grunting, Ren threw himself in front of her, blocking the light.

"What is wrong with you?" he growled.

"Easy, Ren," I said. "Hannah, shine it behind you. Let's see what's there."

Immediately, I knew I had said the wrong thing. Hannah's look, which had been mostly angry all day, took on an aspect between satisfaction and... I didn't dare give voice to it, even in my own head. Yet, I did, because who can stop a thing like that? Adoration. Yeah, adoration. I sighed.

"There are stairs here," said Ren.

"Where do they go?"

"Up."

We turned almost as one and followed the steps in single file, each foot carefully placed to avoid any undue noise. Hannah took the lead, with Grace right behind her. Ren and Brand dropped to the rear. Brand lit his own light and held it close to his chest.

I stopped counting at seventy-two steps. When we reached the top at last, a long tunnel ran straight and narrow before us. I vowed to myself that once all of this was over, I would never go underground again. Since our entry into The Wilds, we had spent way too much time under the planet's surface, fleeing, hiding.

Grace turned her head, softly asked Valeah where the tunnel led. To anyone paying close attention, the climb had tired Grace out, caused her to favor her wounded leg. The only one who seemed to notice besides me happened to be Hannah, who glanced back at her with an expression I couldn't quite figure out.

"A private grove," Valeah said. "It is unknown, unvisited by the citizens of Landing."

Mika looked up at her response. "Okay, that's good, but where do we head from there?"

"We hide," she said.

Grace shook her head. "I am so heartily sick of hiding. Part of the legend, the prophecy, states we must go to the Cavern of Sleeping Myth. Isn't that right, Hannah?" Hannah didn't respond. Ren answered for her with an affirmative. "It is why we have come this far," Grace went on. "If we do not hurry, if we do not make it there before anyone who wishes to stop us, it will be too late."

Valeah paused, grabbed Grace's arm. We all stopped except Hannah, who went on for several more steps before realizing we had halted. Valeah moved around to stand before Grace. The two lights hid half her face in shadow, but her glittering eyes remained visible. I wondered if she had been crying.

"And then, Grace," she said, "will you save my family, my people?"

I heard Grace's startled gasp even where I stood. She pulled her arm from Valeah's grasp and declared in hushed tones, "I don't have the ability to save anyone."

"You saved us," I said.

Grace's head whipped in my direction. "That was different. We all saved each other."

"Not true—" I began. She cut me off.

"We are a small group. What Valeah is talking about is not the same. She…they seek to use us the same way Tiran and the Lyoness and who knows how many others wished to utilize Resa. The prophecy calls on all three of us. As weapons. I will not be part of that."

"No, Grace," I interrupted. "That doesn't make sense. We weren't wanted here. Right, Valeah? Not by all your people, only the select few you mentioned. Why is that?"

Valeah tossed her head, pushed her hair back from her face. "Many have been made to believe it was your desire to attack us here, to bring harm. I never believed so. Neither did my mother and the others."

Grace spoke, still quiet, still calm despite the fire I witnessed in her gaze. "Attack a city? How many do you see standing before you?"

"I told you this has not been my belief," said Valeah. "But word of your power together has been used to instill fear."

Grace's lids lowered, lifted slowly. "This is utter nonsense. We do not possess the power you suggest."

I flinched at her statement. Not quite true, Grace, I thought. Who knew how far Resa's gift could extend? As for the thing Grace called Skelly still, trapped in the crystal around her neck? She had pretty much told us it could destroy everything in its path.

"We have no desire to hurt anyone," Grace continued. "Any time we have had to fight it is because attacks have been made against us. I am a warrior, not a mercenary. Not a…not a bully."

Valeah stayed silent.

"The guard?" Grace pressed. "Is this the truth for them? That the warrior, the witch and the thrice-gifted child come seeking—what exactly? War?"

Valeah stared. She appeared frightened, unsure of Grace and the anger she must see growing despite Grace's composed conduct. I saw it, plainly. So did Carina, who took a few steps closer.

"The others appeared among us some weeks ago in Landing," Valeah explained. "They sowed dissent. People listened because they are foolish, because they want change. But this is not change."

"Who are 'they'?" Carina asked, continuing to watch Grace closely.

"Messengers from The Darkness."

"And yet you thought it would be okay to bring us into Landing?" I growled. Mika muttered a few words under his breath.

"Who is this Darkness?" Grace asked. "Surely, he has another name. His real name."

Valeah shook her head helplessly. "I don't know. We have never learned it."

I touched Grace's elbow. "Grace, we can't just stand here discussing this." I turned to Valeah. "How far? How far to the Cavern?"

"When we reach the sacred grove outside, it is exactly one thousand el-strides to the Cavern."

I hadn't heard the term el-stride since we were incarcerated. Hearing it now sent invisible fingers wisping across my nape. "Okay," I said. "Lead the way."

Although the space was cramped, I walked side by side with Grace. She gripped my hand several times, releasing it right away. I think, even now, she wanted to hold on. For comfort, for assurance. Maybe for other reasons, too. Reasons I determined to ask about later, much later, when we were all safe again.

At one point, I felt her prod the cold-weather wrappings on my fingers. "What's that hard thing?" she whispered. "On your finger here?"

"What? Oh." I had forgotten. Who could blame me with all that had occurred since leaving my mother and Aeron, my brother behind? "My father's ring of office. He said it might aid me along the way. I guess due to recognition or something. He said I could sell it, too, if necessary."

Grace smiled, acknowledging perhaps his unexpected kindness, or what she thought it meant to me. I lifted my hand, pulled away the wrap to show her the ring with its gleaming red stone, pushed onto my middle finger because it was too large for any other. Her gaze went from the ring to my face, her head jerking back, her mouth opening.

"I know," I whispered. "It was generous of him."

She bit her lip and nodded, looking away. I re-wrapped my fingers. She didn't attempt to hold my hand again after that. I wondered if she'd been less moved than offended on my behalf, somehow. I couldn't imagine why Aeron giving me the ring should trouble her and quickly dismissed the thought as a metal gate came into view. I'd ask her later. That's what I told myself anyway. Again, with the best laid plans.

*　　*　　*

"That gate looks ancient," Mika said.

"It is." Valeah unlatched it. Dark growth clung to the sides and she detached each evergreen branch with care. "This is a private sanctuary for the Elder families," Valeah said as she pushed the gate wide. I followed her, holding back the greenery for everyone's exit.

In the grove, trees closely grown had protected the ground from falling snow, as well as a statue centered on the grass. The sculpture had a shape and size nearly identical to the one in the grove among Kerrick's people. This one, however, had been constructed from stone rather than living trees. The figure also resembled the small talisman I knew Grace still carried in her pocket. The one Hannah had given her.

I looked back at Hannah. Her pale eyes glowed in the dim light. She, too, studied the statue. For a moment, she looked frightened. When she blinked, the expression vanished.

Valeah turned to Grace. "Are you sure you want to go on? We could stay here. We could hide in the memorial for a time, devise an escape from Landing."

Grace's gaze followed hers, as did mine. A stone building like a very small house stood against the rock face. "No hiding," Grace answered, determined. "Not for me."

"Me either," I said. "Mika, Carina, I will take my chances with Resa if you wish to stay here."

Mika shook his head. "We go with you."

"Me, too," said Brand. Neither Ren nor Hannah said a word, but I knew they'd never stay behind, alone.

Valeah pointed. "Then we go this way."

The path we followed had long been overgrown, forcing us to push our way through. In five minutes or so, I distinguished a change in the atmosphere. I couldn't have described it if asked. No one else appeared to be reacting to it, so I chalked it up to nerves. Soon, though, a low thrumming seemed to find its way into my bones like the percussive impact of silent drumbeats.

"Grace," I said, "do you feel that?"

She held up her pointer finger to silence me and nodded.

Valeah stopped as though we'd reached some boundary. My skin felt like insects crawled over every square inch. Veleah looked back at us. Her whole body visibly vibrated. Mine did, too.

Beside me, Grace stood quiet and unmoving despite the energy assaulting us all. That said something. That said something important. I could feel the knowledge of it buzzing at the edges of thought. I had to hold onto what I sensed from her. Hold tight to it. Ignore the battering my body experienced. In that, I was not alone. The pinprick buffeting affected everyone. Even Grace, in small ways. The skin on her face twitched. Her fingers, too, jumping lightly along the *lathesa's* shaft. But her expression betrayed none of this.

"We are close now, aren't we?" she said to Valeah.

"Along this ledge to the entrance," Valeah answered, pointing. "I have been there before. We are all taken there, once."

"Why only once?" Mika asked.

"Can you not feel it? The sensation will only get worse. A second attempt gains nothing but pain."

"What is the purpose of going at all, then?" I asked.

"To obtain knowledge. I am a naught. I received no knowledge I did not already have."

"We're wasting time," said Grace and strode out onto the ledge. Obediently, wordlessly, we all followed. I lifted Resa into my arms, just to be on the safe side. I feared she felt the same disconcerting battering we all did, despite showing no reaction. At any moment, she could lash out. Carina came next in line, right behind me, ready for anything, I knew.

The snow had stopped, the sky had cleared. Starlight lit the wind-scrubbed stone enough to see, but the way was narrow. We continued slowly forward once again in single file. To our left, the cliff face rose sheer and high. To the right, rock tumbled away into a gully running like a black, liquid strip far below. When the ledge abruptly opened into something far wider before the gigantic cavern mouth, we were nearly staggering from the forces pounding into us. Like osmosis, the energy seemed to be leaching in beneath the flesh into bone, into brain matter. The cavern's interior caught my attention like a blow.

"What the hell are we looking at?"

"The Sleeping Myth," Valeah answered.

"That's the Sleeping Myth?"

Valeah glanced at me sideways. "Yes," she said, "and it is called such because certain mythoi are better left unawakened."

Well, crap, this didn't sound good at all.

A huge disc filled the opening some twelve feet back, appearing flat at first glance but revealing itself to be almost concave and moving, circling like a wheel. It possessed a dull illumination of its own, invisible beyond the cave's walls and the stone where we stood. At intervals it seemed solid and at others gaseous, like you could walk right through it.

Not that I wanted to. Not that I believed any of us should.

"So, this is what flares at day's end?" I asked.

Valeah nodded. "You wouldn't want to be standing here when the Last Breath takes place. You would be blinded. If you survived."

Okay, liking this even less now. Fortunately, it would be many hours before the day passed into night again. We wouldn't still be standing before the Cavern at that time. We couldn't be. We had to get the answers and move on. When we weren't found in Valeah's home, it would likely be assumed we had come here.

"Are there other ways up to this place? Other paths besides the one we took?"

"Yes," Valeah answered, "and all as narrow."

"Then easily defended for a time, I suppose." I didn't quite believe this to be the case, but it made me feel better to say it. I took out the cutter, activated it. Mika and Ren did likewise. A shockwave shot through my body, sending the cutter flying to the ground.

"No weapons!" Valeah shouted, revealing panic. "No weapons are allowed here."

Quickly, we deactivated them, returned them to our belts and took out the less effective blades made from glass. "So, if the guard came, they wouldn't be allowed mechanized arms either?"

"No."

Well, that was something at least. I glanced around for other articles to be used in defense. Stones littered the ground in large numbers. I hoisted one into my fizzing fingers for good measure. Seeing me do so, tiny, graceful, Carina-of-the-amazing-aim did the same.

Grace stepped toward the cave's opening, where she stood silhouetted in the dull light. She still held the *lathesa* in her right hand.

"What precisely is this?" she asked. "Who made it? Where did it come from?"

"It is said to hold all knowledge," Veleah answered her.

"Like the planet's most extensive library," I said.

"Yes," said Valeah in an aside to me before returning her attention to Grace, "and no. As to who made it, the ancients is all I know. They brought it with them from beyond and landed with it here. Hence, the city's name."

I glanced up at the sky in the direction I thought Riley might be, or the Emerald. I couldn't see them from where we stood. I did not believe it could have come from either moon at any rate. Yet to what star or planet in the sky did she refer? I decided to ask her outright. "Brought it with them from where?"

Grace rather than Valeah replied to my question. "From the world of my mother's forebears." She sounded dazed, yet moved by conviction. "So long ago there is no written history, only tales passed down from generation to generation. Am I right, Valeah?"

"Yes."

"A place where mage craft and magic and so many wondrous things were cast out and the people so gifted sought another place to live."

"Yes."

"So, not just tales, then," I said.

"Not just tales," Grace agreed.

"And what," I asked, "is the name of this other world? Do the tales say?"

"They do. That world was called Terra. But it had another name, too." Grace's brows lowered in thought trying, I supposed, to recall.

Mika spoke suddenly in the fizzing night. "I hear something. Someone's coming."

I turned, looked down. On a trail invisible to the eye, I saw lights moving, heard the booted footsteps now, too. Still some distance away, but we were out of time.

"How do we do this?" Grace prompted Valeah. "Do we just speak and wait for a response?"

"You do not speak," Valeah told her. "You ask through your thoughts. Hopefully it is nothing private, because all with you here will see and hear it in their minds."

"It's not private," Grace answered. "Not anymore."

She turned to face the disc. Suddenly, a sensation like fire coursed along my skin beneath my heavy garments. I ground my teeth to keep from crying out. Grace's head dropped back. Her arms spread wide. Within seconds, her thoughts splashed across mine like oil thrown onto water. Droplets and squiggles, glowing, expanding. I couldn't breathe. I couldn't think. I could only see.

Memories filtered in, spinning through mine, mixing, coalescing. Currents of moments until she regained control and focused on an event almost beyond bearing. I witnessed her view from inside the glass box. Saw myself testifying, bound, trying so very hard not to break. Saw the blood from her knuckles running down the glass, and then her thoughts moved on. I glimpsed instances on Emerald, filled with despair, hope, laughter. Saw myself sprawled across the mat during training. Saw Carina and Mika and…Skelly. Yes, so focused now. Saw her punch him in her cell, felt her guilt and her anger. Relived again his remains sliding down the cargo ship's glass. Her awareness of the entity. The exact instant she called him down into the crystal in Stone Tiran's compound. The battle to keep him contained, to keep herself sane. The magnitude of violent intent when he had been freed back in All Dwellers.

Abruptly, the visions, the shared knowledge stopped. I almost fell over backward.

Opening eyes I hadn't realized were shut, I saw them, the three, standing hand in hand before the disc's growing glow. Inches from it, Resa, Carina, Grace. The thrice-gifted child, the witch, the warrior. And Hannah. Close, reaching out toward Grace but not touching her. Her mouth moved. I forced myself forward to hear her words.

"I am as good as you, Grace. I can carry it. Give it to me now."

"No one ever said you weren't, Hannah," Grace shouted. "And no."

"Then I have no choice." Hannah rushed them as if she would push them into the swirling disc.

"Hannah," I yelled, "what are you doing?"

For a brief second, she turned.

"Giving up," she said, "as I should have long ago. We must face what is to come without hope. It'll be so much easier." Shoving her hand into Grace's pocket, she pulled out the little talisman, pressed it into Grace's fingers. "Goodbye, Grace."

"Hannah, no!" Ren pushed past me, reached for her.

I launched myself at Grace, grabbed her arm to pull her back from that frightening maw of dull light and swirling gas. Mika and Brand reacted with similar intent, snatching at Carina and my sister. A connection surged through us all like flame incarnate, burning flesh and bone.

And then we were gone.

Grace

Chapter Twenty-Nine

I did not know where we were. I did not know when we were. Not really. I sensed time had passed but could not tell how much.

Well, you have your answers now, Skelly snarled. Halfheartedly. I think he had expected something else.

I did have answers, and subsequently more questions. Like accessing a library all at once, those things I needed to know had filled my head, pressed information into every cell, reminding me so much existed I did not know. And to be honest, I had expected something different, too. A human touch. Someone to perhaps take me by the hand and show me the truths I wanted to learn. But what I wanted and needed were two different things.

I continued to listen to the soft breathing all around me, my friends asleep, unharmed, perhaps dreaming. While I listened and waited for them to come back to me from their enforced slumber, I stared at the ball of light in my hands. A light not unlike Hannah's, but still so very dissimilar. Where hers had been spiky within its shape, fierce and tumbling and determined, mine was soft and tranquil and…pink. As Duncan would say, I wasn't a pink sort of girl. Never had been, never would be. Yet the mage blood in me chose pink. *Pink.*

Maybe one day I would find myself able to change it. For now, though, it calmed me, comforted me somehow. And I needed calming, comforting, because all I had discovered in the disc and all I still did not know frightened me to no end. Afraid in this moment and in every moment hereafter. But that was all right. Fear, when managed, allowed for smart decisions. I believed it. I had to.

My gift—*gifts*, I had to remind myself—came not only from my tribal blood but from my mother's ancient line, going back and back to before history. I would not have believed it. I supposed no one had understood the duality, the unlooked-for symmetry, except the legend makers, those with the power to recognize portents and see into future events. For the legend of the warrior, the witch and the thrice-gifted child had not only been the story of three, but also the story of one. Of me.

My hands shook. The light ball wobbled on my palms.

Certain mythoi are better left unawakened, Skelly said, mimicking Valeah's voice.

It would remain to be seen how true were those words.

I suddenly recalled throwing Duncan against the wall back in Emerald the first time we met face-to-face. I had convinced myself instinct made it seem I had not touched him at all when, in fact, physical contact had never been made. So many other events before and since had been explained away by my unwillingness to believe. How had I not seen the truth?

I wondered now at the damage Skelly had caused when free, marauding through All Dwellers on my way to rescue Carina and Duncan's sister and the others in their cells. How much had been him and how much me?

Oh, Grace, don't give yourself too much credit.

Ignoring Skelly's sarcastic tones, I looked over my shoulder, having heard a noise. Duncan shifted on the cold stone floor.

"Duncan?" I called softly. He slept on. I turned back to studying the strange light that came from me, contemplating those minutes before we had all vanished from outside. Poor Hannah. She so badly wanted to believe in hope, had traversed The Wilds with just a handful of friends to prove it. At what point had she become so totally disillusioned? I supposed her commitment to hope had finally ended with the sting of Duncan's rejection.

Not true, Skelly whispered, so softly I almost didn't hear him. I wondered if he hadn't wanted me to hear. Yet at his words, I thought back to the moment when Hannah had given me the talisman. It had been before we ever reached All Dwellers, long before she had been imprisoned there. There had been purpose to it, even then, when we were still free and she and Ren were hoping to lead us straightaway to the west. She has seemed sincere, maybe possessed some foreknowledge beyond the instruction by the Far-Seer, an oracle whose identity I'd never uncovered. I only knew one thing. Without the talisman, we would not have survived our transport through the disc. By forcing it into my hand, Hannah had ensured our survival. I clung to that single fact more than the mystery of Hannah's behavior.

"Grace?"

"I'm here, Duncan," I said. "Right here."

"Grace, where'd you get that?"

My lips turned down at his unnerved tones. I lifted the light-ball in my hand a little higher. "I made it."

He stayed silent for too long. Afraid. I didn't want him to be afraid.

"Maybe you should activate your torch," I suggested.

He fumbled in his pocket, taking out and energizing the kinetic beam. Bold light surrounded us, disappearing into darkness. The cavern walls glimmered in reflection. I extinguished my own light, dropped my hands to my lap.

"Everyone else okay?" he asked, shining the torch along the floor, highlighting the still unconscious forms of Mika, Carina, Brand and Resa. "Where's Ren?"

"No Ren," I said. "He…he's been left behind." Loyal to us, in the end. To Duncan, despite their enmity. I would remember that. "The others are only sleeping. They'll be all right."

After checking each one to make sure they were merely sleeping, not hurt, Duncan came closer, studying me for a minute. Finally, he sat at my side, hip to hip, knees drawn up to his chest. He shone the torch around. "Where are we? Inside the cavern?"

I nodded.

He bumped my shoulder with his and pointed at my empty hands lying slack against my legs. "Something you want to tell me?"

I did, communicating to him certain aspects of what I had discovered regarding my heritage. Obviously, Duncan hadn't picked up on it the way I thought he had when our thoughts were shared. I would have to repeat the story again when the rest woke up but I hoped it could be delayed. For now, Duncan's knowing was enough.

"Wow," was all he said when I finished.

"Eloquent as usual."

"Shut up."

I released a short breath through my nose. My shoulders relaxed.

"If we hadn't grabbed you all," he said, "if we hadn't all been connected, what would have happened?"

I shot him a sidelong glance. He already knew the answer. I could tell by the small quaver in his voice.

"Without this little talisman, this key

connecting us all through touch," I said, picking the small icon up from the floor and turning it in my fingers, "you would have died."

His breath rushed out.

I reached out, gripped his wrist. "I would never let that happen."

Glancing down at the place where the ring lay hidden beneath the wrap on his hand, I pictured again the vision in the warding, the skeleton on the floor in desiccated fur and wearing a ruby ring on its finger.

No, I would never let that happen.

"Got it," he said. He jerked in a convulsive shiver, thoughts no doubt on how badly wrong it could have gone.

"It's all right," I said.

"Is it?" he drawled, pulling his arm away. "It is really? Where are we? What are we going to do now? What was Hannah thinking?"

"I figured she meant to get rid of us," I said, answering the last question first. "Not you, not Mika and Brand, just your sister, Carina and me. Now I'm not so certain. No matter her reasons, she knew whoever passes into the Cavern never returns to the outside world. Carina read Hannah's thoughts clearly on that. At some point, I suppose Hannah might have been influenced in these decisions. By means I don't even want to consider."

"When?"

"Back at All Dwellers during her imprisonment? I have no idea. She might even have planned to save us by forcing us in here. Clearly, she knew things we did not and never suspected."

"Why did she want…that thing?" Duncan nodded at my throat. "I heard her, Grace. I heard what she said."

"A bargaining chip? Power of her own?"

"That's just too confusing." Duncan shifted where he sat, brow creased. "Do you think Ren was part of it?"

I lifted and dropped my shoulders, bones and tendons popping. Duncan's next words surprised me into a sad smile.

"I wish he was here, then, instead of out there."

"Me, too."

"As for not being able to return to the outside world, I'm hoping you know differently."

"I think so."

"How?"

"Resa. She has seen this place."

He lowered his forehead onto his knees, words muffled. "I really thought we'd find something to make sense of her condition. Maybe protect her better. Will we ever help her?"

My mouth twisted. "I think we already have. She's surely not the same girl we rescued from Stone Tiran, don't you think?"

We said nothing for a while afterward, sitting, breathing, understanding we still lived. How many times had the odds of survival been against us? Brand awoke next, followed by Carina, then Mika and Resa. I explained to them where we were, what had happened outside. Carina filled in where necessary.

"Have you found your answers?" Mika asked at the conclusion.

"Not all," Carina said, before my mouth opened. She was right. The answer to Skelly had not been given to me. Of all the revelations swirling in my head, the one I'd come seeking remained sorely absent.

Mika nodded. "What's next, then? Can you use that thing in your hand to get us back out?"

I twirled the talisman in my fingers and shook my head. "Not from here. Not the way we came in."

"Then where do we go?"

They were oh so willing to follow me, my companions, my dear friends. Pride and guilt and shame and love filled me nearly to overflowing. Home. I wanted to go home. Take them all with me. But I couldn't.

I stood, gathered my bag from the floor. Everyone else already had theirs, having been awkwardly unconscious against the packs strapped to their backs. When I spoke, it was with Resa's unique vision in my head. Because there was that, too. Another link I didn't understand. "We go through the mountain and out the other side, then south and east."

Mika snorted. "One big circle, eh?"

I smiled at him. Mika, the first honestly friendly face I'd met on Emerald. "Exactly. When we're back outside, I'll understand if you want to leave, make your way to some other place."

"Like where?"

"Wherever you want to go. You don't have to make this journey with me. I have led you into danger for long enough."

"Incorrect," said Carina. "It's not long enough

until it's over. And it isn't over, is it?"

"No," I said. "No, it's not."

"So, what's the plan?" Brand asked.

"I haven't got one," I said. "Stone Tiran, the Lyoness, who know how many others still seek us. But I know this. I'm tired of running."

"Then we don't run," Duncan said. "Not anymore. We face the danger head on. Am I wrong?"

A chill danced down my spine. I inhaled a short breath, released it, spoke. "No. You're not wrong."

Brand raised a finger, like a student asking permission to speak during lessons. "Just us, here? Alone?"

A good question. Because how ridiculous the notion we could. Yet, Duncan was so very right. I looked at Brand, looked at all of them, one by one. "Not if I can help it," I said, "but if we must, if we really must, it is because we are enough."

Duncan bent and snatched his torch from the floor. Mika and Brand lit theirs. Together we turned away from the darkened disc, the source of transport, the storage of knowledge from this world and another, and headed deeper into the cave. Carina and Mika walked arm in arm, Resa beside her brother. Duncan reached out, ruffled her hair. She kept her gaze straight ahead with that unseeing look. I understood she saw more than I could ever conceive, though I, too, had become part of it. Brand strode at her other side, taking up a defensive position. I snatched Duncan's hand into mine. Duncan turned his head, winked at me. I blushed. Like an idiot.

"Grace," he said.

"Duncan." I held on tight to his fingers, not letting go the way I normally would. Yes, held on tight to the boy who had betrayed me, to the boy I never wanted to leave my side. To the boy whose powers were yet unrealized. I had witnessed that as well in the fluttering, flying knowledge. Duncan Oaks, the con-artist with a heart designed to put mine to shame, would someday be more than he had ever imagined.

I only hoped I would be there to see it.

Skelly

Chapter Thirty

I wouldn't count on it, Grace.

AUTHOR'S NOTE

Book three in the Shadow Journey series might have been the hardest yet to write. It is the longest so far, but length was not the issue. The characters (are they really characters?—to me, they are living, breathing people) meet challenges in The Sleeping Myth beyond any they have yet had to confront. Emotions run deeper, dangers are more intense, and extremely difficult decisions must be made.

For those who have stuck with me and the series thus far, you have, of course my gratitude.

Coming January 2024

The final book in the critically-acclaimed
Shadow Journey Series

BOOK FOUR – IN DARKNESS WE BREAK

More by Jo Allen Ash

The Shadow Journey Series

THE SHADOWS WE MAKE, BOOK ONE

THE THRICE-GIFTED CHILD, BOOK TWO

Where to find out more about the author, her works
and her interests:

www.joallenash.com
Facebook.com/JoAllenAsh